Praise for
City of the Dreamers

"*City of the Dreamers* has a wide appeal. For all of us, it is a sparkling reminder that whatever you can dream is possible, now."

Candace Apple, Owner
Phoenix & Dragon Bookstore, Atlanta

"…genuine appeal…scenes resonate…a distinctive voice."

Scott Meredith
Scott Meredith Literary Agency, Inc.

"*City of the Dreamers* enveloped me in a feeling of eternal summer full of infinite possibilities, and affirmed my belief in the magic of human existence."

Sue Leland, Policy Analyst
The World Bank, Washington, D.C.

"The novel is strong in action and character development…a splendid job of telling a story."

Dan Liss, *Aquarius* Newsletter

"I found the book superbly written and richly detailed, which brought the book to life for me. The book has helped me understand how success is a frame of mind, and once you clear out the destructive thinking, it's magic!"

Tom Chapin, Ph.D., Polymer Chemistry
AT&T Bell Laboratories

"Jordon Avery is a masterful storyteller. I was a captive from the first page. What a delightful book!"

Cathi Barlow, Principal
Ridgeview Middle School, Atlanta

"An inspirational book—funny, wise, compelling. *City of the Dreamers* takes a close look at the dark side of human nature and offers a convincing vision of planetary transformation and healing. Its characters are dynamic, vividly drawn personalities whose creative growth is the central focus of the book. Powerful evocation of the ocean as spiritually nourishing and perilously threatened by ignorance and greed. The book deserves to be widely read."

Katherine Legan, Ph.D., Creative Writing
Faculty, Georgia State University

City of the Dreamers

Jordon Avery

STARSTREAM
PRESS
P.O. Box 11668 • Atlanta, Georgia 30355

CITY OF THE DREAMERS

For information, address:
StarStream Press
P.O. Box 11668
Atlanta, GA 30355
404/842-0060 • 800/673-0240

First Edition

Cover art by Dori Hale, Margie Deeb and Margaret Fortson

Graphic design and calligraphy by Margie Deeb

Chapter illustrations by Phillip Jay Cox

Cover painting and chapter illustrations Copyright © 1993 by StarStream Press

ISBN 0-9636355-0-6

DEDICATION

*This book is lovingly dedicated to
Peny, Michaell, Jach and Lazaris,
who are, for so many,
keepers of the dream.*

ACKNOWLEDGEMENTS

I have drawn inspiration from many others in the creation of this book. I would like to acknowledge those who played important roles in the birth of "City of the Dreamers."

First, my deepest appreciation to Lazaris and Concept:Synergy in Palm Beach, Florida, for the Lemuria material, and other contributions too numerous to mention.

And to Auriga, my fellow travellers. It is so much fun being on this journey with you!

Special thanks to Ginny Deal and Sylvia Thorne for their professional guidance and insights in the psychological development of the characters. And to a group of friends, without whose inspiration and help this book would not have been possible. They include Karen S. Adler, Bob Edwards, Betty Fortson, Ed Gibson, Eileen Kupersmith, Jan Nance, Sylvia Neese, Marie Sutton, Arlene Witte, and Lindsay Wyatt.

There were several who made special contributions to the research and development of this book. They include Pat Harris, Phillip Cox, Leanne Mitchell, David Fisher, Margaret Fortson and Brandybuck.

I am very grateful to the presenters of the First Annual Cold Fusion Conference in Salt Lake City, Utah, in March 1990, and to F. David Peat, author of *Cold Fusion*, upon whose work I relied extensively.

I would also like to acknowledge my weekly support group, with love and light, for their total honesty, help when I needed it most, and unqualified love in abundance.

Although I realize I cannot list everyone who has influenced this book, there are some others I want to mention. They are as follows: Dolores; Tony, Jake, and John; Ellen Edwards; Tom, Peter, Ed, Ray and Seymour;

Phil and Jesse Bridgewater, Midnight and Diamond; Maurine, Izzie Crow and Coxie Davis; Nina Young; Dick; Sam LaBudde; Lloyd Borgess of Dolphins Plus; Gail Fore, Margie Sullivan, Linda Howard, Dori Hale, Nioshii, Judy Perdue, Cathy Barton, Katherine Bever, Michaell Bever, Becky Vashon, Sarah Hayes, Marcia Partin, Debra LeGere, Nadia Giordani, Margie Deeb, Glenda Giles and Spencer Tunnell. Many thanks to all of you.

Sincerely,

Jordon Avery

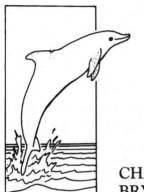

PART I

CHAPTER ONE
BRYSON BEACH, FLORIDA

Iris drifted, weightless, through the cool darkness. There was no sound except that of her own exhalation, the soft burbling of air escaping in a rhythm matched by the languid movements of her legs. She had no need to be purposeful, or to concern herself about things to be done. She was content simply to be, to experience the sensations of her private world.

The darkness was tangible, fluid. She could feel it slip along the skin of her forehead and neck, insinuating itself under her wet suit to create a delicious chill that ran from neck to ankles. She imagined herself a bird, soaring high over snow-capped mountain peaks, in air that was crisp and cool and exhilarating. She felt caressed, every movement bringing a rush of coolness, an inexhaustible, tingling freshness.

She was flying, set free from the pull of gravity by the darkness surrounding her, by turns gliding, body still, letting the currents determine her direction, then doing slow-motion somersaults, reveling in the feeling of weightlessness.

Now she descended, to drift just above the ghostly forms that rose before her. Surrounded by the blackness, each form seemed to spring suddenly into being when struck by the beam of her light. What in the light of day seemed ordinary, even comical, in the darkness took on a magical eeriness that coaxed the mind to fanciful speculation.

Through the frame of her face mask, Iris saw a staggered row of shapes littering the sandy bottom at fifty-five feet. In the daylight, she knew, this area looked like a junkyard, with rusted old car bodies, scattered worn tires and a wrecked motorcycle. Someone had even dumped an old record player. But at night this "artificial reef," as they euphemistically called it, became a scene of magic.

Iris moved in close to the shell of an old Ford and shined her light through the glassless passenger-side window. Weaving in and out through the spokes of the steering wheel was a cluster of tiny fish, glowing purple and neon yellow in the flashlight beam as if lit from within. Iris watched them for long minutes, enjoying their soundless ballet and glittering colors. The colors seemed brighter at night. Was it because of the flashlight, or because the surrounding blackness made it easier to focus on detail without distraction? Iris wasn't sure, but one of the special pleasures of night diving was enjoying the miniature sea creatures, surprised in their nocturnal wanderings by the beam of light directed at them.

The movement of a dark, amorphous shape inside the car body resolved itself into Iris's own shadow, and she turned to see Ray, her diving companion, approaching her. Seeing that he had her attention, he turned his light so it wouldn't blind her, and floated over to her side. Iris motioned toward the school of tiny neon fish, and just as they both turned to peer once again into the car, a pale shape the size of a small tennis shoe darted up from under the dashboard and out the driver's side of the car. Iris and Ray both followed the little octopus with their flashlights until it was out of sight, then nodded at each other in shared enjoyment.

Ray motioned her to follow, and together they swam over to a cluster of small rocks. Nearby was the record player and an old motorcycle, in pieces scattered across a small area of sand. Iris could see nothing of interest as they approached the rocks, although from the direction of Ray's light, the rocks were clearly their destination. When the two divers were literally on top of them, Ray pointed to an object partially obscured by shadow.

Moving her flashlight to eliminate the shadow, Iris was entranced by the sight of a nudibranch, a sea snail so brilliantly colored it looked dressed up to go to a clown convention. The ruffle-like ridges that ran down the six-inch length of the bizarre creature were tipped in fiery red, a color repeated in irregular spots sprinkled over its lemon-yellow skin. Iris turned to Ray, her eyes crinkling in amused appreciation. She might have laughed aloud at the comical sight, if it weren't for the constraints of her mouthpiece.

Iris turned back, lying almost flat on the sandy bottom to keep her face within inches of the rock on which the nudibranch sat. She quickly became absorbed in watching it move in minute increments, ripples running along its length as it inched forward. She projected herself into the tiny, creeping body of the creature, trying to conceptualize time as it might be experienced in such a life. *If it took a day to move twelve inches, would I have any concept of "hurry" or "urgency"?* she wondered. Then she let her mind drift into the peace she assumed must accompany a life spent in such slow motion.

It took an effort of will to pull herself back into her own body. She realized that time did exist for her and she needed to pay attention to it. The gauge on her console showed that her air pressure was down to seven hundred and fifty pounds, so it was time to think about heading back to the boat. She looked around and spotted Ray exploring a group of old tires about fifteen yards away. She swam over to him, pointed to her gauge, then motioned with thumb raised, her meaning clear. Ray nodded in acknowledgment, and together they began their slow ascent.

Iris reached the surface first. She rotated her body in the water, looking for the lights of their boat. Without warning, she was struck from behind by a six-foot swell. When she surfaced again, she saw Ray break the surface about ten feet away. She tried to yell a warning before he got broadsided, but she was too late. He disappeared under the wash of sea and foam.

Iris saw the cabin lights of the boat bobbing about a hundred yards away. She looked around her and up at the pitch-black sky. A storm was almost upon them. It had come from nowhere. When they had gone down forty-five minutes earlier, the sky had been clear and star-filled, the water calm and quiet. Now, the wind was whipping the waves and pushing the boat hard against the anchor.

Ray swam to where Iris was treading water.

"The wind's blowing out of the northeast and the tide's running out," he yelled. "The bottom must have dropped out of the barometer. We've got to get to the boat, quick."

"I know," Iris shouted back, nodding vigorously. "Let's take a reading on the lights and go back down and swim for it. Watch out for the anchor line."

"Okay," Ray responded, "but we've got to come back up and sight again every few minutes."

Iris rode the crest of the next wave, looking for the boat lights. Finally she saw them, and quickly took a reading on the compass strapped to her right wrist.

"A hundred ninety-two degrees, almost due south," she shouted.

"The wind's going to be pushing it westward. Let's start out at two hundred degrees and check again in two minutes."

"Roger," Iris called.

They submerged and began swimming at a steady but moderate pace, knowing they had to conserve their energy and strength as much as possible. Iris was well aware of the now-critical importance of the anchor line staying intact.

When they came up for their second sighting, the rain had begun. The storm was now in full force. Wind whipped the tops of the waves into froth. Lightning splintered the ebony sky, and thunder reverberated like a thousand timpani.

It took them twenty minutes to reach the boat. They struggled to climb into it, as it pitched and fell in the turbulence. She tried to start the two hundred and fifty horsepower Evinrude, but it only sputtered.

Too late, Iris turned to tell Ray to leave the anchor in the water. As he hauled the anchor in, the boat was released to the mercy of the storm-wracked Gulf waters. It turned broadside as the next wave crashed into it, catapulting Iris, Ray and most of their gear overboard.

Iris thrashed her way to the surface, choking and gasping for air. The rain pelted down upon her as she frantically looked for the boat in the inky darkness. She heard Ray coughing and swam in the direction of the sound. Her arm came down on one of the boat cushions and she grabbed it. Still gasping for breath, she let the cushion stabilize her long enough to find her regulator, so she could breathe without worrying about taking in lungs full of water.

"Ray," she called. There was no reply. She called

again.

With growing urgency, Iris again looked around for some sign of Ray or the boat. The salt water burned her eyes. Then, in a lightning flash, she saw a streak of neon yellow standing out against the dark water. That had to be Ray's wet suit.

Iris kicked her long legs as hard as she could to propel her in Ray's direction. When she got to him, his head was bleeding and he was barely conscious. His buoyancy vest was still inflated, which probably accounted for his being alive at all.

Ray did not respond to Iris's voice. She circled around behind him and supported his head on her chest so he wouldn't swallow more water.

"Damn!" Iris cursed out loud. She saw no sign of the boat. She had no idea how far they were from shore or in which direction to go. Her compass had been torn off in the commotion. She was tired and starting to get cold. It was still six hours until the earliest light, and probably eight hours until someone would miss them and start a search.

All too aware of the danger they were in, Iris took several deep breaths. She needed to use the adrenaline rushing through her body, not succumb to it, or neither one of them would make it.

Something bumped up against her in the water. She froze. *Sharks!* Panic seized her—she could scarcely breathe. She felt as though anchors were tied to her legs. Then it bumped her again.

In angry desperation, she ducked under the water and yelled as loud as she could, hoping to scare the attacking shark away. She came back up, her chest heaving with fear, and struggled to regain control of Ray's unconscious body. The crest of a wave rose over her. A strobe of lightning flashed and, in the freeze-frame second of illumination, Iris saw the elegant arc of a dolphin poised in mid-air.

It seemed to Iris that time stood still, and she felt the dolphin looking at her. The grip of panic released her. Then the wave crashed, almost tearing Ray from her grasp. Seconds later she felt another bump against her legs—the dolphin, not the shark she had feared. She could breathe again.

The dolphin's head rose from the water in front of her. It clicked and cried and wiggled its head back and forth. Then it dived under Iris, came up behind her and gently nudged her on the buttocks.

The dolphin seemed to be trying to communicate, trying to help her. It circled back around and, as it came by again, Iris reached out and grasped its dorsal fin. The dolphin gently began towing Iris and Ray, but Ray was too heavy for Iris to pull for long.

Iris let go of the dolphin and reached down to Ray's waist. She fumbled at the buckle on his weight belt, her hands numb from the cold water. Finally she loosed it, dropped the weights and fashioned the belt into a loop. Its bristly nylon fibers bit into her fingers, drawing blood. She grabbed the salvage line coiled at Ray's side, ripping the Velcro strap in her haste. Silently she cursed her clumsiness and the effort it was taking. Finally, she was able to force the clip of the line into the end of the belt, and thread the other end through the straps of the boat cushion. She positioned the cushion under Ray's head, then wrapped the line around their waists, securing it with a bowline knot.

When the dolphin came by again, Iris looped the belt carefully over its beak. She maneuvered her body under Ray's to support him. Then she felt the line tighten as the dolphin began towing the two humans. Iris noticed the line was pulled over the dolphin's fin, but after several feeble attempts to free it, she gave up and concentrated on keeping a firm grip on Ray and the cushion.

She had no idea if they were headed in the right direction as she surrendered their fates to this creature. Her arms ached and her hands throbbed. The adrenaline reaction and the cold Gulf water began to numb every muscle in her body. She soon ceased to feel the intense pain that wracked her body from the dead weight of her friend and the awkward position she was forced to maintain.

After what seemed like hours, on the edge of surrendering to the oblivion of her exhaustion, Iris was jolted awake. As she came to her senses again, she realized she was standing in the surf only yards from the shore. The storm had subsided, and with it the wind and waves. It was as if all evidence of danger had disappeared into the smooth breeze of the night except for the excruciating pain that shot through her body as she changed position. With supreme effort, she struggled to unharness the dolphin, untie herself, and hold on to Ray at the same time. Once free, Iris, on hands and knees, pushed Ray toward shore. She felt the cushion beach itself. With her last remaining strength, she rolled Ray's unconscious form onto the beach and collapsed next to him. He didn't move. She reached up and held her fingers against the side of his neck and felt for signs of life, a pulse. When she found it, faint but present, she wept with relief.

Recovering from the initial waves of exhaustion, panic and relief, Iris slowly opened her eyes. They rested on Ray's salvage line, still connected to the cushion and the looped weight belt. The gray belt was now spotted with blood. The dolphin! She struggled to her feet and looked out over the now-calm Gulf. A few stars and a half-moon peeked through the receding clouds.

A scant twenty feet off shore, Iris saw the elegant body of the luminous, silver-gray dolphin arc out of the water. Once again, it seemed to be looking directly at her. Iris whispered a soft "Thank you."

She watched the dolphin turn and swim out to sea. In the moonlight Iris saw a large tear at the front of its dorsal fin where the belt had rubbed it raw. She began to sob as she turned and clambered up the dune, toward lights and help.

On the evening of the fourth day after the storm, Iris stood on her porch, gazing out at the water. She had told no one about the dolphin. Ray remembered none of it, and everyone else just kept saying how lucky they were to be alive. She had chosen to keep it secret, though she scarcely thought of anything else. Her strength and composure were returning and she longed to be on the beach. She slowly descended the steps and stood on the beckoning sand.

She moved quietly through the soft, rolling dunes above the beach, elegantly working her way through the tall, prickly sea grass. Absorbed in the moment, her body was flexible, lithe, intuitively responding as if by sonar to the ever-changing obstacles on the pathway. The soles of her feet felt the warm sand reshape to the pressure of her weight, then subtly adjust again as the heel lifted and the toe pushed off. She knew all record of her trip eventually would be obliterated, blown away by the current of air which continually swept the dunes, just inches above the surface. It was this current which, in one action, erased evidence of invasion yet created a living surface, ever-changing, highlighted by the evening sun's colors and shadows. She felt a part of this place, undergoing constant change yet following a dependable rhythm within.

At the end of the winding path, she bent to sit where she could gaze at the unbroken line of wind-constructed dunes. Clear skies this evening allowed the stars to burn, sputter and glow, their light reflected against the black water. The water took the moonbeams and playfully broke them apart, reconstructing them after each crest of wave. A very few clouds, far against the horizon, hovered at earth's edge, as if waiting for permission to dispose of their watery contents in some other time. The moon's light sparkled against the crushed crystal sand, snow-like in its whiteness. The relatively quiet surface was only a facade for the life which teemed beneath it, life connected to the water and all it brought in at evening and carried out at dawn.

She pushed her toes down through the surface and into the coolness below. Closing her eyes, she breathed in the salt air, cool, pungent, reminding her that the earth took back into itself what it discarded, breaking it down by the beating waves, waterlogging it to pieces, then sending it against some surface, producing a filmy overlay until further natural action returned it to its essential elements. She knew she, too, was connected in some primal way to this place. The very rhythm of the ocean waves seemed a part of her. Her pulse slowed, taking on the tempo of her surroundings. Her breathing deepened, refreshing her from the inside out, bringing stillness and relaxation. The night wrapped around her protectively.

Here on the nighttime beach her body quieted, allowing her mind's voice to be heard. It was a voice she knew well, her most trusted friend, the reliable one who waited until the static subsided, then quietly asked a simple question or made a simple statement which reached the core of the issue at hand. Iris understood that her solitude was essential.

When she opened her eyes, she gazed seaward across the glistening path blazed by the moonlight on the dark water. She rose and walked down to the water to stand just inside the line of the surf. The water washed over the tops of her feet, and she could feel its coolness adjusting the temperature of the blood that flowed past her ankles and rose to her heart. Stepping in further, wanting to follow the path of the moon, she felt the water playing around her calves and knees, swirling sand over the tops of her feet as each wave made its outward sweep.

The water pulled at her, gentle, insistent. She closed her eyes and imagined letting it take her out, beyond the waves, into the deeper water of the Gulf. Its movement around her legs made it easy to imagine the journey, to feel herself sinking deeper and deeper into the cool blueness of a private, underwater world.

As she drifted into the image, she called to the dolphin in her mind. *I wonder where you are, my friend.*

The ocean washed against her, filling her ears with its sound, leaving its fertile tang on her lips. Iris waited, her mind falling with each movement of the night's breeze farther from her own awareness into the world her friend inhabited. Inwardly she matched her movements to the dolphin's, arms held close to her sides, feet together as if fused, body pulsing and rippling to create forward motion. *How cool it is here, warmer near the top, even at night. The bubbles cling as I dip below the surface, leaving a trail of the otherworld. Over, under, around, the water glides over me, almost as if it were still and I alone were moving. Here below*

I move wherever I please, water separating as I head into it, closing quickly behind me, mild current remaining. No resistance, only support.

Yet past the water's surface, such chaos! Its smooth skin splits open and rolls on top of itself! Dragged from below, the water hangs on until I'm clear, then falls back to the sea, laughing before me. The air is thin, quick, savory. Below, all is thick, slowed, silent. And I am part of both.

The smooth, blue-black sea rose and fell calmly. *Dear friend, come swim with me. Let me be part of your world. Dear one, come.*

Slowly, Iris let her mind focus back on the night air and opened her eyes. She knew this dolphin. Would it know her?

No answers came to her across the waves. She turned back toward the dunes, toward home. Behind her, the dark water occasionally splashed, the breezes continued their work. Far out, past the channel buoy, a dark fin cut across the moon's beckoning path as a lone dolphin turned toward the shore.

CHAPTER TWO

Early risers at the beach were usually amused and intrigued when they first glimpsed the two uncommon silhouettes etched by the morning's first rays of sun, as Jaid and Miss Natasha made their way along the shore. Soon, however, tourists and local residents alike were greeting them as they took their daily walk along the beach.

As the flamboyant creator and proprietor of the Indigo Moon Gallery and Studio complex of Bryson Beach, Florida, Jaid had long ago discovered that an early morning walk with Miss Natasha—Natty for short—was the most joyous way to begin her day. It cleared the cobwebs and gave her some thinking time.

Jaid enjoyed discussing new ideas or mulling over solutions to problems as they walked their usual two-and-a-half mile route. Characteristically, Jaid provided a nonstop monologue, so it was quite acceptable that her people-loving, intelligent companion rarely made any comment other than an occasional grunt or two. Miss Natty did, however, listen with great intensity. Her loud, enthusiastic squeals were reserved for the end of their walk, when they reached the lagoon and fed the gulls, pelicans, sandpipers, cranes, and terns who regularly awaited their arrival.

Nearing her sixty-first birthday, Jaid made an imposing, handsome appearance. Just under six feet tall, she carried her ample figure with the grace and pride of the athlete she'd been as a girl. She had moved to the beach twenty-two years ago, after a decision to establish an art studio, and as her reputation as an artist grew nationally.

Jaid wore her thick, wavy white hair in a single braid that reached the middle of her back. Miss Natasha had short white coarse hair, tipped the scales right at three hundred pounds, and stood two-feet-six, the perfect figure for a five-year-old Poland China pig.

The fourth of Jaid's beloved pet pigs to carry the same name, Miss Natty had brown eyes rimmed with pink and large, erect ears lined with sensitive light hair. Her face was dominated by a round, pink snout. She turned her ears like miniature radar dishes to whatever caught her interest and she, too, moved with dignity and grace, on her cloven-hoofed legs of sinew and muscle. She did not tolerate the heat and blaze of the midday summer sun, but preferred to conserve her energies by resting in the shade of her pen on the studio grounds or cooling off in the shallow pool Jaid had built for her. But early mornings were very comfortable, particularly at dawn. Jaid's companion led the way on their walks, carrying her corkscrew tail like a banner.

Jaid regularly rose each morning around five. She would shower and prepare for the day, preferring to dress in long, flowing skirts of printed cotton, topped by a loose, hip-length Egyptian cotton tunic, usually long-sleeved and loosely belted. She wore large, ornate earrings, several bracelets, at least two over-sized rings, and always a faceted quartz crystal on a chain around her neck. She had a collection of big, floppy-brimmed straw hats, and each day she would select one and tie it on with a coordinating scarf for their walk. In contrast, Miss Natasha wore only her customized halter and a bright bandanna.

Due to a late start and numerous delays, the day was in full swing when the two beach-walkers finally made their colorful way along the shore. Jaid was grumbling under her breath as they rounded the dune, "My gracious, I certainly hope our fine feathered friends haven't given up on us. If it wasn't one thing, it was another." Jaid stopped. For over twenty years now she had made this identical walk, but the simple beauty of the place always fascinated her.

The large brackish pool, referred to as the lagoon, was a favorite spot for early morning beachcombers. The white sand beaches were ideal for sunning, and high tides cut a channel to fill the pool. At low tide the beach separated the Gulf and the lagoon. The pool was perfect for swimming regardless of the conditions in the Gulf. Numerous houses and shops had recently been built on the shores of the lagoon, and a road now dead-ended into the dunes. The main part of the Bryson Beach community was several streets over, closer to the bay side.

Other morning walkers had begun to gather at the lagoon when the twosome arrived. The air was filled with dozens of squawking birds soaring above Jaid's head, each competing for their share of the treats she artfully tossed into the air. On the ground Miss Natty squealed with pleasure as she sat upright, her front legs planted wide apart and her back legs tucked under her for support as she swayed back and forth in time to the swooping of the birds.

Jaid and her portly companion completed their morning ritual and turned back toward town. Friends and neighbors greeted them as they strolled by.

Iris's house sat on the far end of the beach, near the point where the bay joined the lagoon and the Gulf. It nestled among running oaks, pink and white oleander bushes, elegant clumps of tall pampas grass and large Spanish bayonet plants. Jaid stopped to study the weathered wood frame house just beyond the grass-fringed dunes. The house sat back away from the road and a tiny sleeping porch faced the beach.

Iris stood on the adjacent deck, watering her hardy tropical philodendrons. When she spotted the twosome making their way homeward, she waved for them to join her.

A smile crossed Jaid's face as she headed over the dunes to Iris. It had been several days since they had talked, and Jaid genuinely enjoyed the opportunity to spend some time with the thoughtful and private woman she had called her friend for over six years.

"Morning, Jaid, Miss Natasha. You two look like you could use a little breakfast," Iris greeted them, reaching down to rub Miss Natty's ears.

"As a matter of fact, Iris, I think a cup of coffee for me and a little water for Miss Natty here would be a perfect complement to our morning walk," Jaid said, as Iris led the way to the deck.

"Looks like a good start to my week," Jaid noted. "First a glorious sunrise, and now I get to catch up on what's happening with you. Have you fully recuperated?"

"Oh, yes," Iris nodded. "I've taken my new boat out several times this week and now I'd like to dive. I was going to check with you to see if you'd like to come along. We can spend the day."

"It's a shame Ray had to go back to New York. I'm not much of a diving buddy for you, but yes, I'd love to go. I'll bring my sketchbook. I'm working on a series now that explores the play of light, like sparks, and spending time out there would be most helpful."

As long as she lived, Iris thought, she would never lose that feeling of surprise upon first entering the water, surprise that she could breathe in this alien world.

Of course, it was something of a nuisance getting up to that moment. Lugging the equipment to the boat was a major chore, since what was weightless under water was anything but weightless on land.

Today, loading the new boat for her first dive trip since the storm, Iris was freshly aware of details that had become automatic until her experience with the storm three weeks ago. Taking extra care with everything, she checked off the gear she would need for her dives. The two yellow-painted tanks, each charged with thirty-five hundred pounds of air, were tied down securely with strong elastic cords under one of the seats at the back of the boat. They were the heaviest part of the load, so she always loaded them first.

The rest of her gear fit efficiently into her dive bag: buoyancy compensator vest—BC for short—regulator with hoses, mouthpiece, depth and air pressure gauges, mask and snorkel, gloves, dive boots, knife, underwater flashlight, compass, fins and weight belt. Her small zippered satchel of odds and ends—silicon grease, anti-fog drops for her mask, and extra batteries for the flashlight—was in the side pocket.

Last into the bag, and first out when the time came to suit up, was Iris's one-piece wet suit. She liked to wear a full suit to protect herself from chance encounters with jellyfish or sharp edges of sunken ships. The lightweight neoprene suit provided ample insulation in the warm Gulf waters without stifling her at the height of summer. It was Iris's one concession to dive fashion, featuring diagonal stripes in vivid Day-Glo colors of pink and neon yellow bordered in black.

It was not yet eight-thirty in the morning when Iris looked up from her careful assessment of dive gear and saw Jaid striding majestically down the dock to the boat. As always, Jaid looked regal and decidedly over-dressed for a simple morning boat trip. Not one to diminish her imposing height, Jaid wore a brightly-colored caftan with bold vertical stripes, topped with a white straw sun hat. Under one arm was a flat two-by-three-foot vinyl portfolio that Iris knew contained her drawing materials, and in the opposite hand she carried a large red thermos and a net bag of food. The bag bulged, so Iris knew Jaid had been indulging in one of her "cooking frenzies," as she called them.

"Good morning!" Iris called out as Jaid approached the boat. "Hope you're set for a long day. The weather is perfect, and I know I'll want to stay out for a while."

"Good morning to you, too," Jaid replied. "Look, Iris," she said, thrusting a printed notice toward her friend as she readjusted her various bundles. "I found this stuck on my front door this morning. It's a flyer announcing public hearings to stop oil lease sales off the Panhandle. You know, there's something to the idea of 'No Drill, No Spill.' "

Scanning the notice, Iris folded it in half and slipped it into her satchel. She shook her head slowly. "If people knew the wonderful gifts the ocean gives us, they'd think differently."

Jaid relieved herself of her parcels. "It's a big problem, and I'm not sure what it will take to solve it." She opened both arms to the sea and sun, stretching and shrugging as if to drop the subject. "A gorgeous day, my friend. This brilliant calm sea is a real inspiration. I brought my sketchbook along, and I think some time out there will refresh both of us. You know, dear, I never tire of the way light plays on the water."

Iris cast off, and as the boat cleared the marina she picked up speed, letting the fresh breeze wash over her skin. She steered the boat out from shore about three-quarters of a mile before turning parallel to the coastline, and then stayed on that course for nearly forty minutes. During the trip, the two women shared a companionable silence made comfortable by their close friendship.

It was nearly nine-thirty when Iris cut the engine and lowered the anchor. They could see the shoreline off in the far distance, the modest beach houses forming indistinct shadows on the dunes. One house sported a tall pole with a brightly colored windsock, positioned at the side of a cedar deck that dominated the dune on which the house stood. This was Iris's landmark. When it was a certain size, and positioned just so off her port bow, she knew she was in position.

"Do you want some breakfast before you go in?" Jaid asked, as Iris finished setting the anchor. "I have some spanokopita left over from last night, and some fresh rolls with brie," Jaid smiled. "There's even some baklava and a few other pastries, but we can save those for later."

"Looks delicious!" Iris said, as she took a small portion of spanokopita. "Jaid, you're a woman of many talents," she said appreciatively, chasing the food with a swig of hot strong coffee from the thermos.

Jaid smiled in acknowledgment, "Sometimes I work off my creative energies with cooking instead of painting." Jaid ate heartily, liberally spreading a roll with cheese and consuming several pieces of spanokopita. Iris indulged only in coffee and spanokopita, restraining herself from overeating before going into the water, and ignoring Jaid's urgings to have more.

When Jaid finished, she put the remaining food in the cooler out of the sun and leaned back in the seat. "I love your new boat," she said. "It's so much roomier than your old one."

"Thanks," Iris smiled. "I splurged, and got all the features I'd always wanted to put on the old one but never got around to adding, especially the extended dive platform at the back. And the engine's more powerful, too. I'll have to watch myself, or I'll be flying in this thing." She looked around the shiny, new boat. "I miss the old one, though."

Jaid nodded. "She was like a friend to you. I'm just so grateful that Elmore found you and Ray that morning."

"I know I was out of it, but it felt like the ambulance came immediately."

Jaid studied her friend. "Are you looking forward to diving again?"

Iris was quiet for a moment. "Jaid, I desperately want to go back down there again." She looked up. "There's something I haven't told you. Something that happened during the storm. Even Ray doesn't know, since he was unconscious most of the time. It's a little... strange..."

"Strange? How do you mean?"

Iris's forehead wrinkled in thought, then she laughed and shook her head. "To be honest, I've hesitated to tell anyone. Afraid they'd think I've lost my mind."

"Except me," Jaid said, smiling encouragingly.

"True. Well, I told you about being thrown overboard, when Ray was knocked unconscious. I had grabbed hold of him, and was going to start towing him, but I was disoriented, wasn't sure which direction was the right one. Then

I felt something bump my legs. It was almost like someone was prodding me."

"Oh, good lord, that must have been frightening!"

"Yes," Iris agreed. "All I could think about was sharks, and getting out of the water. But of course, there was nowhere to go."

"What happened?"

"There was a flash of lightning, and I saw the most amazing thing…" Her voice trailed off as she remembered. Jaid said nothing, letting her relive the memories at her own pace.

"It was a dolphin, Jaid. And I swear it looked at me, eye to eye, in the instant the lightning flashed. The next thing I knew, it was nudging me from behind. I got the feeling it was trying to show me which way to go, so I headed in that direction. Then it came up beside me, and I took hold of its fin. It even waited for me when I got tired and had to stop for a minute, then it let me loop a belt around its beak to make it easier to hang on. It towed us, for what must have been over an hour, all the way back to shore."

Jaid's eyes were wide, trying to visualize the magical scene Iris was describing. "That's incredible," she said. "I've never heard of a wild dolphin behaving like that."

"I know," Iris said, excited. "I hadn't either, but since the storm I've been doing some reading. Did you know there are all sorts of—I guess you'd have to call them legends because they're undocumented—of dolphins helping people lost at sea? And there are documented cases, like a recent one of dolphins saving a diver in Australia from a shark attack." Her eyes were shining. "There are all kinds of stories about dolphins interacting with people. It's hard to believe it happened to me."

"You're very lucky, and yet…" It was Jaid's turn to pause.

"And yet?" Iris prompted her.

"Well, I guess it doesn't really surprise me that you, of all people, would have an experience like this. You're such a part of this place, it's as if you have a special relationship with the water and everything in it."

"Then you don't think it was a hallucination?" Iris asked, smiling now.

"Of course not!" Jaid laughed, hugging her.

"That's why I'm so excited about diving again. Jaid, I want to look for the dolphin. I want to find it again. I feel such a connection."

Jaid smiled, "Well, there's no time like the present."

Iris pulled up the Bimini top over the rear deck, providing a shady place for Jaid to sit. She worked her long, bushy hair into a French braid, fastening the end with a rubber band she retrieved from the dive bag. Then she began to suit up for her dive.

She stripped off the oversized striped tee shirt and white canvas shorts, revealing a black tank suit devoid of decoration. With her smoothly tanned skin and tall, slim frame, the simple black suit made Iris look more elegant than plain. Over her bathing suit she pulled the neoprene wet suit, straining to get the tight sleeves and leggings over her wrists and heels. Leaving it unzipped so she wouldn't get overheated before she had the rest of her equipment assembled, Iris connected the spare regulator to one of the tanks and propped it against the side of the boat, wedging it firmly with a life vest so it wouldn't topple over and break a toe. She then fastened a 30-foot line securely to the tank's neck, lifted it over the edge of the boat and lowered it carefully into the water, playing out the line until it was fully extended.

She fitted the BC to the second tank, then attached the regulator with its hoses and mouthpiece. She checked her gauges, inflated the vest slightly, then quickly donned the weight belt, gloves, and boots. Hoisting the tank and vest up onto the boat's gunwale, she eased herself into the shoulder straps of the vest, turning and sitting as she did so. As Jaid steadied the tank, Iris adjusted the vest, then donned her fins while still in a seated position on the boat's edge.

Jaid shook her head in bewilderment at the preparation. "It all seems so complicated. Do you ever get tired of all the work involved in diving?"

Iris continued her tightening, checking, tapping, all techniques she completed without deviation each time she dived.

"The time I spend up here getting ready gives me a safe, wonderful experience down there. Jaid, it's more beautiful than words can explain. It's another world completely. The weightlessness, the light, the sound. Each time is different. Maybe it's the temperature, or some fish I've never seen, but there's always something new to discover…" Her voice trailed off and her hands became momentarily still. "I wish you'd go down with me and experience it yourself."

Jaid looked at her friend tenderly. "Not just yet, dear. I'm still working on my claustrophobia. I'll be waiting here for you."

"I'll be down about an hour," Iris said. "We're right over the wreck, so I'll be within fifty yards or so and just forty feet down."

"Ten feet down would be too deep for me." Jaid said, frowning. "Iris, I know I've said this before, but I'm concerned about you diving alone. Especially since that dreadful storm."

"I know, Jaid," Iris said. "but there's no real danger here. My spare tank is down below in case of an equipment problem, and this time there's no danger from the weather."

"Well, I'm not crazy about it, but…" she smiled, "I hope you find your dolphin."

Iris returned her smile. "Yes." She carefully put the mask on, slipping the band over her braided hair, then inserted the mouthpiece and motioned to Jaid to do a final check on her air valve. She rolled over backwards off the edge of the boat, her right hand holding her mask and mouthpiece in place while her left held the free-swinging gauges and kept them from getting entangled.

There was the moment of surprise as she entered the water, when her mind told her she ought to be holding her breath and it took an effort of will to draw the first deep breath of air through the mouthpiece. The practiced rhythms of diving took over, and her breathing became slow and regular.

Iris checked her air pressure one more time and began her descent, impatient to be down in the blue depths. She loved this part of the dive, as her body gradually relearned how to be weightless, free of the constraints of gravity. As her breathing became regular and unconscious, Iris became more aware of the beauty around her. The water was translucent, laced with the minute air bubbles that accompanied her from above as well as those that naturally found their way here from the depths. Looking down, she saw gradually deeper blues, larger fish, gently waving greenery. An upward look revealed an array of brilliant blue melding into white, which coalesced into the blinding rays of sunlight that pierced the water.

The slightest movement changed her direction. A soft kick directed her wherever her shoulders pointed. Waving hands could propel or counteract the movements of her feet or the gentle currents. The water was an unlimited arena for dance—slow, easy, rolling head over heels if she desired, or doing barrel rolls counterclockwise. The body was utterly free to respond to the most subtle nuance. Natural. That was it. This was where she felt natural, free to think or do or feel anything. This expanse of water felt as though it were her own private home, her own place, inviting her to come and explore freely.

The old barge was directly below, sitting on the sandy bottom at fifty-five feet, its deck fifteen feet higher. It was one of the more interesting features in the sand flats off the coast of the Florida Panhandle, a gathering place for sea life that would not have congregated here if not for the barge's protective hull. They were too far north for living coral to flourish, so the wrecks, both accidental and intentional, formed an artificial reef that encouraged the permanent residency of myriad sea creatures.

This particular wreck was one of Iris's favorites, and its denizens seemed like old friends. From the starfish and sand dollars on the sandy bottom to the tiny neon-colored fish clustered near the barge's forward hull, she felt a kinship with all the sea creatures.

Iris circled the barge once, then kicked toward the wheel house positioned about two-thirds back on the deck. The wheel house had been damaged, and had a roomy hole on one side that was home to one of her favorite creatures, a green moray eel she had nicknamed Mort, who always poked his head out long enough to see if there were any handouts forthcoming, and, if not, would withdraw grumpily into the dark recesses of his artificial cave. His expressions were so like those of a grouchy old fisherman Iris knew that they always made her laugh.

From a net bag attached to her wrist, Iris obligingly brought forth an offering for this old man of the sea, a small piece of bait fish she had brought for the occasion. He took it with surprising delicacy, then puffed out his leathery cheeks and seemed to nod as if to say, "You may now pass." Iris bowed her thanks, and continued her tour of the barge.

As always, she was entranced by the play of light in the water, the morning sun slanting in to dapple the surface of the rusty barge and the white sand bottom. Surrounded by the soft blue-green water, it was easy to visualize herself in flight, moving freely in three dimensions like a bird soaring into the high atmosphere, unfettered by gravity and unworried by the concepts of "up" and "down." It was this feeling of physical freedom, of leaving gravity behind, that had first attracted Iris to diving. Then, once she had experienced the richness of life in the sea, she was hooked.

Although she had been here many times before, she never tired of exploring the area and searching for whatever new treasures she might find. Today, she discovered a blue glass bottle, its precise color uncertain against the blue of the water, but its shape interesting and worth saving. There were also a few shells that she slipped into her bag, after checking carefully to make sure they had been vacated by their former occupants.

Something caught her eye on the deck. She drew nearer, reached out and grasped a plastic neck-ring from a six-pack of canned soda or beer. Shaking her head in disgust, she dropped it into the net bag.

Iris moved leisurely through the water, kicking slowly toward the bow of the barge. There, at the very front, hung a rusty old bell, the clapper intact but the pull-rope long ago rotted away.

Standing beside the bell, Iris slowly turned full circle, her eyes straining to see through the blue depths surrounding her. Seeing nothing but small scattered clusters of fish, she pushed off gently from the barge's deck and matched her movements to those of a dolphin, just as she had imagined doing that evening on the beach. Arms at her sides, feet together, her body pulsed rhythmically as she curved and looped and soared. *Dear One,* she called mentally to the friend she sought, *am I going to see you again?* Her heart soared with her body, and she lost herself in her sensations. *I love this world. Your world...* she thought. *I want to share it with you.*

Once again she circled the barge, this time as a dolphin, losing all sense of time. It seemed to Iris that her vision was more intense, as if, looking at a shell in her hand, she could see beyond its surface and sense the secret chambers within. Then another dimension opened to her, and the hand holding the shell was not just a hand. She suddenly was aware of the bone and muscle beneath the skin, the tiny ridges on the fingernails, the pulsing of blood in veins that radiated over the back of the hand and down the underside of the wrist. She knew she was seeing herself as a dolphin would, not looking *at,* but seeing within.

Iris had been at depth for nearly fifty minutes before she checked her gauges and began her ascent. Breaking the surface, she inflated her BC. The water lapped around her. She closed her eyes and floated, enjoying the rhythmic motion, reluctant to return to the world above.

"Ahoy there, mate."

Iris reluctantly opened her eyes. Jaid stood on the boat, waving. She returned the wave and slowly made her way to the boat.

The boat rocked gently as Iris held onto the dive platform at the rear. She pulled off her mask and fins and handed them to Jaid. Iris detached the net bag from her wrist and set it on the platform. Still in the water, she unfastened her BC and slipped out of it. She boosted herself onto the platform, reached down and hauled the vest and tank aboard. A little breathless from the effort, Iris secured the tank and collapsed into a deck chair.

"Well?"

Iris looked up at Jaid.

"Did you see your friend?"

Iris shook her head. "No, but she's out there, Jaid." She stood up and moved toward the anchor. "I thought I would do my next dive over near the old lighthouse. We were in that general vicinity when the storm came up."

Jaid nodded and sat as Iris pulled in the anchor.

The boat cut smoothly through the water as they headed to their destination. Iris's thoughts were of the dolphin. Absentmindedly she pushed at loose strands of hair, forcing them back into the braid.

Jaid picked up the net bag and held it toward Iris. Iris nodded and Jaid opened it and began pulling out Iris's finds. She held the bottle up to the light. "Pretty. It's almost the blue of your eyes." Next she found a shell, creamy white with traces of rust and blue dotting the edges. She turned it over in her hand. "Interesting design."

Iris motioned to her. "Keep it."

"Thanks. I do like the play of color."

Reaching into the bag again, she pulled out the plastic rings. She looked up at Iris. "Manmade marine artifact?"

Iris shook her head in fury. "Don't people know it can strangle sea life?"

Jaid nodded in agreement. "It's scary to think what all is being dumped into the water."

Iris shuddered at the thought.

The trip took nearly twenty minutes. When Iris was satisfied with their location, she brought the boat around, cut the engine and lowered the anchor.

"It never ceases to amaze me how you can tell one spot from another. Water all looks the same to me."

Iris grinned. "We sailors have our secrets."

The preparation work for the second dive was much easier, and within minutes Iris had switched air tanks and was ready to dive. Jaid once again double-checked the air valve. "Okay," she tapped on the tank. Iris gave her the thumbs up sign, then entered the water from the platform.

Surfacing, she pushed stray hairs out of her face, readjusted the mask and began her descent.

The area she had chosen was typical of most of the Gulf dives, sandy bottom with few attractions.

Leveling off at thirty-five feet, she used the compass to head due east. As she moved through the water her thoughts returned to the dolphin. She could see the penetrating eyes. Eyes that inspired trust.

Pausing in the water, she removed her gloves and stuck them in the pocket of her BC. She slowly rotated, looking about the filtered blue environment for signs of her friend. Sand churned up to her knees, disguising her feet and tinting the water before it gradually regained its composure and returned to the floor of the sea.

Dear friend, come today. I am waiting for you now. I have so much to say to you. I know you will hear me. I know you know where I am. You are important to me. I will wait for you here, in your world. Please come.

Turning north, she pushed off ever so gently from the sand, arms freely gliding next to her body. Keeping her feet and legs relaxed, she bent her head and waist, scooping through the water, dolphin-like. Softly, she propelled herself over the sea grass with such gentleness that it barely moved at all. This time, no sand was disturbed.

Taking her own heart beat for the tempo, she undulated through the water in a large, lazy circle. Soon her heartbeat, her breathing, the pull of her head and the push of her bent knees became a single action, centered on the one thought of being with her dear friend, the dolphin. LUB-dub, rest; LUB-dub, rest. Her heartbeat filled her ears and regulated the motion of her body.

How cool it is where she lives. How silent. It is forgiving here, within this world. It is easy. I am suspended, supported, freed here, where she lives. Dear one, be with me, here, in your world.

The water, cool and soothing, enveloped her in a blue-green reverie. Translucent aquamarine graduated into green, royal blue and even navy, as she took in the view beyond her mask. The sea grass danced a slow-motion ballet for her as she passed, carried by currents she could not see or feel.

Bump. Iris's heart leapt out of the reverie. Bump. Then, a bump against her buttocks. Iris smiled, letting bubbles of air escape the corners of her mouth and rise in celebration to the surface. *She's here. She heard me.* Without turning her head or moving her arms, Iris slowly scooped her way back up from the grass where the last gentle bump had pushed her. She continued her circular path.

The large fast-moving creature swam by her so quickly she couldn't focus on it. Iris circled, her eyes trying to track. The dolphin passed again, coming within inches of her leg, close enough for Iris to see the healed scar that now formed a nick on the dorsal fin. *Because you helped us.*

When it passed yet a third time, Iris reached out her hands, palms up. The dolphin turned and caught her eye. For a moment, Iris was suffused with a sense of love and welcome that astounded her. *Such gentleness. Grace. So powerful, yet completely restrained and giving.* Iris slowly reached her hand up to touch the dolphin below the snout, letting her hand caress her throat. The dolphin moved a little closer and mouthed Iris's elbow, nudging her side. *Amazing. How can she do this without scaring me? How does she know it's okay? She wants to touch me. She wants to be touched. She's doing this on purpose.* As time stopped, they stayed there, immobile, transfixed.

Floating away from Iris, relaxed and moving freely through the aquamarine waters, the dolphin swam in enlarged graceful circles around her, seeming to beckon Iris to waltz with her in their still world of muted blues and filtered light. All around them the bubbles from Iris's air tank added to the ethereal environment.

They swirled and twirled together, now swift, now stately. They would brush together, and at the sweetness of the touch, Iris felt her heart beat, full and alive. *We could do this forever.* Finally, the dolphin's circles became larger and larger. It rose to the surface, then plunged back down to where Iris floated like an open anemone, arms out-stretched to bid her friend good-bye. The dolphin swam toward her embrace, then slowly moved away in beautiful curved patterns.

Iris's vision blurred with grateful tears as she watched the dolphin depart. More than ever, she felt embraced by this world, mind and heart open to the miracles she experienced here. And, more than ever, she knew she would keep coming back.

Iris surfaced about ten yards from the boat on the seaward side. She could see Jaid stretched out on a deck chair, her sketchbook in her lap, head swinging up toward the shoreline then down to her paper, arm furiously sketching. She had discarded the blowing caftan in favor of the sun suit she wore underneath.

"Jaid!" Iris called, waving an arm.

"There you are!" Jaid exclaimed, turning around in her chair.

Iris climbed up the small ladder and onto the dive platform. She laid the tank and BC on its side and leaned against the rail.

Jaid searched her face, eyes questioning. Iris could see her own joy reflected in Jaid's slowly-spreading smile.

"Jaid, she found me," Iris said, happy tears mingling with the salt water on her cheeks. "She found me."

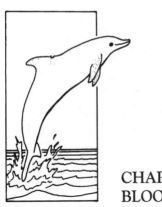

CHAPTER THREE
BLOOMFIELD, IOWA

Stephen woke up his favorite way that morning, eyes fluttering open and shut several times before focusing on any one thing. He wasn't sure whether or not he was still dreaming. Yes, one of his favorite ways to awaken. He could hear them talking in the background, clearly spoken sentences. They made no effort to keep their voices low, but rather than make him mad, he felt a special kind of happiness, knowing they were both in the house doing something together, being happy with each other. He knew he would be able to pad downstairs to them, still in the well-worn pajamas with the feet attached, and receive a warm, cuddly kind of welcome for his breakfast.

He stayed in bed another minute to play his special game, the guess-what-they're-up-to-just-by-the-sounds game. First he heard the sound of the coffee grinder, screaming its high-pitched warning to the ears before the nose got a chance to get the right answer. The water ran a long time, making a full pot of coffee. That meant there would be company coming, or else both Mother and Jack, the new stepfather, would be home together today. They loved their coffee and would savor it the entire morning.

The gurgle of the first few percolations began.

Now it was the silverware's turn to join in the morning symphony. The drawer squeaked. His stepfather softly swore, "When did this damn thing start up?!!" and he heard the silverware drop to the table with three distinct rings. Stephen knew that somehow he would have to tell Jack about the silverware drawer. Several weeks ago he'd noticed that it was sticking.

He noticed lots of things like that. It was his special assignment. There were things he saw around the house and at school that the adults didn't seem to know about, like how much the tadpoles had grown in the creek next to the bus stop, and when the buds on the trees first opened. And how much traffic had crossed the road overnight, revealed by the amount of dirt and slurp in the snow along the side. Sometimes it was so much that the snow was more slurp than snow.

Stephen released the pillow from his half-Nelson and slipped out of bed onto the floor with a slight slide away. The pajama feet were worn slick, so he had to stabilize himself momentarily. By the time he reached the first stairstep he was coordinated and almost alert. Stephen took a second to stiffen his feet enough to glide over the edge of the carpet from stair one to stair two. He slid off step two all the way to step four. Step five he took normally, otherwise the parents could hear both feet hit the living room floor, and they would yell about it. Stephen had already figured out what he could do, when—and now was NOT the right time to practice hitting the living room floor by sliding off the last step. Stephen scurried into the small dining room and greeted his mother by laying his head in her lap.

"Good morning, Pumpkin," said Mother, stroking his fine blond hair.

"Hi, Mom. Any frosted flakes left?"

"Let's see what we have here. Well, you're in luck, Mr. Wizard, because look what just happens to be hidden at the bottom of this box—just enough for a sweet five-year-old boy."

Stephen's heart warmed, not only to the words, but to the tone of her voice. Sometimes he thought his heart would jump out of his chest when she talked to him like this. She could look at him with those big brown eyes that looked like melted chocolate, and when she said something, her voice was exactly the same sound as her eyes looked—smooth milk chocolate, softened by the heat of her love, and poured all over him. It was delicious to hear and to feel. He warmed up all over. He loved how she hugged him with her voice like this. It was her special, private Mother voice, just for him.

He heard a throat clear, and looked over at his stepfather, reading the morning paper.

"Mornin'," he mumbled.

"Oh, morning, Stephen," came his response, deep and booming, too loud for five-year-old ears so early in the morning. Stephen secretly adjusted the gauge inside his ears that he had installed when his stepfather arrived. His Space Buddies had helped him design and install it, and he could call on them anytime for technical assistance. The Ear Gauge was like something he had seen in some of the Star Trek reruns he always watched whenever he had control of the TV set. Yes, an Ear Gauge that could translate foreign languages or could allow you to understand creatures from other planets—a category which fit the stepfather. The Buddies helped him learn how to adjust it without using any hands, just a discreet toss of the head in one direction or another, depending on whether he wanted the volume lower or higher.

Unexpectedly, the stepfather spoke again. "Happy Thanksgiving."

Stephen jumped up from the table, ran into the kitchen, and looked around. The signs of the holiday meal were everywhere. There was a huge, naked, pimply-skinned turkey resting on the draining board in the sink. The oven was on, heating up the kitchen to a comfortable toasty feel, especially nice since he was still in his pajamas. There were the big bowls on the counter top, not the usual medium-sized ones Mother used for meals. Sweet potatoes were sitting on the counter, next to the bowls. Pieces of bread which were now dry and hard were lying in a metal baking pan; these must have been broken up after he went to sleep last night. The ingredients Mother used for her special Jell-O salad were laid out too—lime Jell-O mix, broken pecan pieces, coconut, those special miniature oranges that he liked to nibble on, celery stalks not yet diced.

This would be his job—to help with the mixing. He was especially good at getting all the lumps out of things being mixed. He would ask if he could help with this part of it. From the looks of things, it would be either lots of food or lots of people, maybe both. He turned on his heel and went back to his breakfast.

Mother spoke again. "So, what do you think? Can you help me with some of the cooking? Maybe help me do some of the mixing today?"

Stephen was pleased beyond belief. Anticipating the pleasure of being with Mother while she cooked and hugged and talked to him all day was better than dessert at breakfast. He made a low growl to Tony the Tiger to express his joy.

"I'm gonna get dressed now," Stephen announced to the parents. The stepfather looked over his newspaper and blinked at him, scanned his breakfast dishes, and muttered, "Mmm-hmm."

Then Stephen finished breakfast, gave Tony a secret good-bye wave with his eyes, and headed back upstairs. It was time to check the Orders of the Day, secretly delivered to his room in the green metal tackle box kept between his bed and the wall.

It was clear that Mother would require a part of the day; perhaps it would be necessary to assign some of the day's orders to one of the sky lab assistants. The engineers would be glad to hear of the Ear Gauge success.

The door creaked open. Stephen held his breath atop the bed, wondering which alien would cross the threshold. There was always the chance they would intercept his messages and invade the Transmission Zone. Whoever had come in was cloaked—invisible—except for a strange drag and thump.

Moving ever so slowly, Stephen slipped one foot, a leg and then the other leg under the covers. A second more and he too would be cloaked, ready to meet this invader on equal terms. He was absolutely still. They would have to make the first move.

The thumping came closer, dragging past his laced-up tennis shoes with the socks stuffed in them, past the camouflage backpack and wooden crate, past the red enamel desk and all his colored markers, past the poster of Captain Kirk and the Starship Enterprise, past the encoded drawings of space cities, underwater habitats and space vehicles. They would find out everything if he didn't stop them soon! Abruptly they stopped, and the thumping was replaced by strange air noises; they were regulating the oxygen cylinders, changing over to mechanical breathers. The noises moved to the edge of the Zone and stopped again. *Now* what?

Stephen stiffened. The alien had placed the first probe

just inches from his face. He had been located by Sniffers! Capture was seconds away! Escape!

Stephen wriggled to the right just in time to escape the first pounce! Left, and he escaped another! This time he grabbed the forearm of the Sniffer, scoring with a low growl. Another pounce just barely missed his shoulder. Its body was now menacing above him! Pounce, a direct hit on the wrist. Pounce, another on the arm! Suddenly collared and dragged from under the covers to the top of the bed, Stephen went for the jugular, and wrapped his arms fully around the neck of Spock, his fifty-pound invading Labrador, who whimpered and thumped his tail ecstatically as their game came to an end.

Spock was his best friend and fellow traveler. He and Spock had completed many missions together in space. They were only a few million miles from being certified by the Mother Ship.

Stephen sat up abruptly, suddenly serious. Tilting his head, he slipped out of bed and padded his way to the large crate at the end of the bed. Spock whined as Stephen stepped into it and sat down.

"Want to go? I could use a copilot. Must be a pretty important assignment for them to change the Order of the Day." Spock inched in next to Stephen.

Stephen studied the instrument panel before him. Reaching to the spool of green thread, he turned it to the take-off mark scribbled on the panel. Turning various sized aluminum pie plates, he sat patiently while the thrusters warmed up…

"*Oxygen, one-niner-five.*"

"*Rrr-roger,*" *said the co-pilot.*

"*Altitude holding at zero two-hundred.*"

"*Rrr-roger*" *again.*

"*All engines on go.*"

"Rrr-roger, rrr-ready for take-off."

Stephen carefully pulled the wheel toward him, simultaneously adjusting the oxygen intake. The copilot monitored and threw switches in perfect coordination as they lifted smoothly, out the bedroom window, above the house and neighborhood, and through misty clouds pierced by mountain tops.

"Thrusters at zero, zero. Disengage!"

"Rrr-roger, sir. Disengaging number one, and... numberrr two. Cleared."

The two space travelers relaxed back into their contoured seats and lifted the visors of the helmets.

"Perfect take-off, Spock."

Spock beamed and thumped his tail, always so grateful for a compliment from his superior officer.

They approached a large body of water. The Mother Ship came into view, blinking and flickering.

"Right on time," Stephen affirmed.

"Rrr-roger." A shaft of light suddenly enveloped their ship. Spock growled.

"It's okay, Spock. They've cloaked us so no one else can see."

"Arrr-re they to be trusted?" Spock asked.

"Totally."

Spock relaxed, letting the hair settle back down on his neck. Stephen released his seatbelt and stepped into the beam of light. Spock leapt to his side.

"It's okay. I have to get my orders." Spock sat at attention, alert and ready for action.

A high-pitched clear voice came from the Mother Ship. "Welcome, Earth Ling."

Stephen leaned over to Spock, whispering, "That's what they call me. Because I'm from Earth and a cadet, a ling." Spock nodded.

The Mother Ship spoke again. "You have come in time. A

giant seameer is destroying our ships. We have lost many of our Lars. Your help is needed."

"We will stop it before it hurts anyone else," Stephen affirmed. Spock raised his ears and allowed the neck hair to rise again, in his most fierce presentation. Stephen turned to return to his ship.

"Do you have the croma?" asked the Mother Ship.

Stephen touched the Ear Gauge in acknowledgment.

"The seameer is very loud. You will need it to be able to approach him."

Stephen bowed his acceptance of the mission. The light withdrew and the Mother Ship moved out of sight.

Spock was full of questions. "Seameer? Lars??"

Stephen laughed. "Sea monster, and a lar is a, uh, hero. Now, let's go get him."

They returned to their ship and darted high above the body of water. Spock turned on the ultrasonic viewer and in moments they located the writhing body of a huge, snake-like monster moving along the ocean floor, leaving destruction in its wake.

"On screen, sir," reported Spock.

"Lock-on. Descend. Battle stations!"

Just as the monster shot to the surface of the ocean, Stephen and Spock zoomed past. They were engulfed in an ear-shattering roar, momentarily making them unable to communicate with each other. The ship teetered dangerously before Spock regained control. Stephen reached for the croma, and within seconds the roar diminished to a whimper. With a mutual nod, they returned to the attack, straight toward the monster's eyes, pulling up as it blinked, then around its ears, under its chin, back and forth, up and down without pause. The monster snapped viciously, vainly trying to destroy the annoying little space craft until it had tied itself in knots! With a final roar of rage, it sank slowly into the sea, leaving a surge of foam and steam.

Stephen and Spock high-fived and circled home. Just above

the misty clouds, the beam of light engulfed them. This time Spock thumped his tail expectantly. Stephen readjusted the Ear Gauge.

"Well done, men. You have made our colony safe. Earth Ling, because you are brave, the Council decrees you Sky Lar, Courageous Friend. Our people honor you."

The light dimmed as the Mother Ship departed at warp speed, leaving a delighted space captain behind. Stephen beamed with pleasure as he and Spock landed the ship effortlessly back in the bedroom, at the foot of the small twin bed.

"Sky Lar…Sky LAR," Stephen tasted the words gleefully. "Did you hear that, Spock? I'm Sky Lar now." Spock woofed his excitement.

Mother was calling from the bottom of the steps as they disembarked.

"Stephen, time to get started with the cooking, sweetheart," his mother said. "Are you dressed yet? Where are your shoes? Ready to cook now?" Mother sometimes got so many questions going he forgot to answer the early ones. Stephen turned around to put on his tennis shoes, answering over his shoulder, "I'll be there in a minute." By the time he gathered them up she was next to him, bending to help unknot the laces.

"How do you get these on and off like this?" she asked, pretending to be irritated with him.

"Like this," he said, and wriggled his left foot into the grubby shoe in less than three seconds. He reached down to pull the back of the shoe over the heel and adjust his foot.

"You're going to tear these things up before you grow out of them, doing that. Here, put this one on the way you're supposed to, okay?"

Stephen stood up, flattened the toes inside the tennis shoes, one with a clean new knot, the other with a three-day-old one, stuffed his favorite blue and yellow Trans-former into his pocket, and followed her down to the kitchen, saying, "I'm ready. I've cleared everything with my Space Buddies."

The morning was filled with the duties Stephen anticipated—opening cans, pouring them out, mixing one thing with another, smashing together chunks of things with buttery mixtures. Mother told him how to make the entire green bean casserole, which he completed with the exception of pouring the mixture into the long glass pan. He particularly enjoyed covering the sweet potatoes in softened margarine, accomplished by squeezing bits of margarine in his palms until they were softened by his heat, and smearing the potatoes several times each.

Reaching around from behind, Mother washed his hands in the sink afterwards to remove greasy traces. She turned the entire event into an elongated hug by snuggling next to his left ear and whispering loving secrets they shared. Her touch was warm, soft, strong enough to be safe.

Not so much fun was preparing the bread. He grew tired of buttering the zillion pieces Mother had sliced before she wrapped both loaves in foil. Stephen was relieved when Mother announced she could continue with the bread by herself, and suggested he go rest up.

On the way to his room he peeled off his dirty shirt and pants, and kicked off his tennis shoes. Once in bed, he completed the ritual by pushing off his socks to join the several others which lived at the foot of the bed until each week's laundry revealed their hiding place as the sheets were taken off. Within minutes, he was far away from the sounds of final preparations going on in the kitchen, in another world, climbing into his spaceship and taking off in a whirlwind to meet the Space Buddies.

Stephen was awakened by Mother's call. He quickly dressed in the clothes his mother had laid out for him and went down to the living room. "I'm here," he announced.

His stepfather said, "Great, now all we need are the other three and we're ready to eat. You look very nice, Stephen."

Stephen was surprised at the praise. "Thanks," he said, and looked down at his Sunday shoes. "When's dinner? I'm hungry."

"Ask your mother that one. She won't let me near the food. If you get near the turkey, grab me a sandwich full, will you?" Stephen was amazed at his friendliness. His stepfather normally didn't have any reaction to him at all, other than to glance at him when he spoke. The doorbell rang. His stepfather got up from the recliner to answer.

Through the front door came Grandma, arms full with a casserole dish wrapped in a dish towel, Grandpa toting several pies on a large tray, and Aunt Iris, carrying a green bottle with a yellow label and a red bow. Stephen eagerly danced while they made their way to the kitchen, anxiously awaiting the pick-up hug he was sure to receive. No sooner were the dishes placed on the kitchen counter than he was swallowed up in Grandpa's arms, feet leaving the floor. Grandpa's hugs were just the best—huge, big circular motion up from the floor, held tight in the strong, muscular arms, face scraped against beard and the smell of pipe smoke. All the while Grandpa talked to him, often unintelligibly, while Stephen was engulfed in the arms. Stephen just smiled and nodded his head, and answered whatever questions he heard after his ears were cleared.

Meanwhile, Grandma lectured Grandpa about being

too rough with the boy, saying, "Don't make him sick now, Carl. Maybe he doesn't want to be swung around like that." Grandma leaned over to him, kissed the top of his head and rubbed his back affectionately. "How've you been, boy?" she said. He basked in the glow of their love and attention.

Iris stood back from the grandparents. She waited for the commotion to settle, speaking to Mother and Stepfather, then leaned over and gave Stephen a warm hug.

"Rose, can we get started?" Jack bellowed out. Stephen readjusted the Ear Gauge.

"We're ready for you now," Mother responded.

Next to Stephen's usual place was Aunt Iris. She helped him scoot his chair up to the table, then touched his hair and said, "I'm glad you're sitting next to me, Stevie."

Grandma called for the blessing, and everybody bowed their heads. By squinching his eyes up and tilting his head slightly, Stephen could look around the table at the somber faces. But when his secret inspection had made a complete circle and reached Iris, her laughing eyes were looking back at him. He jumped, embarrassed at being caught, but felt better when Iris winked at him and smiled.

After Grandpa finished the blessing and Grandma had closed it out with an emphatic "Amen," Mother picked up Stephen's plate and began heaping it with food. Everyone began talking at once.

"Isn't it nice to have Iris with us again?" Grandpa ventured.

"You know I always love to see her. I just wish it didn't take so long between visits." Grandma dropped a spoonful of mashed potatoes on her plate.

Iris stiffened. She looked steadily at the cut-glass dish of cranberry relish before her, carefully spooning out a small helping with one hand and gesturing for Stephen's plate with the other.

Jack shredded the first slice of turkey into a stringy mess. "Honey, you brought in the wrong knife," he said to Mother.

Mother rose, saying, "I'll get the other one," and went to the kitchen.

Iris dropped a spoonful of relish onto an unoccupied part of Stephen's plate. "Cranberries, anyone?" she asked coolly.

Mother returned with the serrated knife and motioned to Jack to cut across the bottom and then down from the top. As Mother took her seat, Jack called out, "Who wants white, who wants dark?" and the serving commotion began again. Stephen's plate returned to him with white and dark meat, gravy to the side, blending in with the green bean casserole and making the French bread soggy.

"Iris, it's good to have you with us," Mother said. "This is a very special Thanksgiving. Stephen helped me a lot in the kitchen today, didn't you, Stephen? And you did a great job, too." Stephen looked at his mother and nodded his thanks, since his mouth was filled with soggy French bread and green bean casserole.

"So, what's new, Stephen?" asked Grandpa. "I want to hear all about your latest missions." Stephen noticed that Grandpa had already dropped turkey gravy onto his shirt, and a small droplet was stuck in the lower right side of his beard. Grandpa loved food and didn't always pay attention to where it went. Stephen thought for a minute before answering.

"My name's not Stephen anymore," he said. "Starting today, my name's Skylar."

There was silence around the table, as the grown-ups looked at each other. Then Grandma retorted, "Goodness gracious, Stephen, why in the world would you want a new name? You can't go around with two names—it'll just confuse everyone! Besides, you're named after Great Uncle Stephen who gave his life in World War II!"

"Aw, leave the boy alone, Edna!" said Grandpa, striking his knife against his plate for emphasis. "It's a great name for the country's youngest astronaut. Welcome aboard, Skylar! How about passing some of those vegetables this way!" He could always count on Grandpa.

Mother looked at him the entire time and then ventured softly, "Skylar is a very interesting name. Why did you choose that one?"

Apparently Jack had heard none of this, because he started talking before Stephen, now Skylar, had a chance to answer.

"They're going to add two new manager positions at the office," he said. "I'm up for one of them. One would take me out on the road more, but either way, I get a good pay increase and an extra week's vacation. And if I do good, we'll be moving to Texas in a year or so. That's where the home office is, you know. Kileyville, Texas."

"How wonderful, Jack!" Grandma chimed in. "Rose, you certainly have a fine man. I was afraid for you, you know, getting older, with a child and all, no college, just a secretary's job. No place in today's world for a woman in that condition. Jack here has just been a blessing, that's all, a real fine blessing to you and all of the family, isn't that right, Carl?"

Silence fell. Skylar saw Mother flush and look into her plate. He froze, fork midway between turkey stuffing and mouth, wondering what was wrong. But then Mother asked Iris if she'd pour some wine for those who wanted it. When the glasses were filled, Mother spoke again.

"I'm glad that Iris brought wine. Jack and I have more news that deserves celebration." Skylar studied her face and then his stepfather's for any sign of what the news could be. Mother looked down at him with eyes that were filled with meaning, a meaning he didn't understand.

"We're expecting. I just got it confirmed last Monday. I'm seven weeks pregnant. Stephen, you're going to have a baby brother or sister in the spring!"

Grandpa and Grandma both exclaimed their congratulations to Mother and Stepfather.

"This is just wonderful!"

"I don't believe it! Aren't you excited?"

"We're so very happy for you."

The voices ran together in Skylar's ears until he couldn't hear a thing. Glasses were raised in a noisy "Congratulations, hear, hear!" but Skylar couldn't make sense of any of it. He saw only a blur of green and white and orange and brown and yellow on the plate before him, running together in front of his eyes. Under his breath, he began the soft whirring sound that was the emergency control for the Ear Gauge, hoping it would dim out the confusion in the room. His slight shoulders began rocking rhythmically back and forth, to boost the Ear Gauge to its maximum screening power.

"You didn't know, did you, Skylar?" he heard Iris whisper. He shook his head. "I guess that's hard on you, not knowing." He nodded woodenly.

He let Mother give him a little hug, but felt strangely distant from her. The meal continued with the constant chatter and too-loud laughter, which he managed thanks to the Ear Gauge.

Why didn't I know about this? Skylar wondered. *What else is going on around here that I don't know about? Why hadn't the Space Buddies sent reports on this? The Flying Eye Spies missed this by a mile! Where will the baby sleep? Do I have to give up my room? Is it going to mess up my stuff? Will she still have time for me??*

He decided to shut down the information processing centers until he could talk to the Space Buddies, and concentrated on eating. Conversation went on around him while he kept his eyes on his plate. Soon the big plate was replaced with a small one containing a narrow wedge of pumpkin pie, topped with a white mound of real whipped cream. He ate it hurriedly, knowing dessert signaled the time he could ask to be excused. Then he escaped to his room to think about the new development.

The door shut solidly behind him. He sat down next to his bed, near the headboard which concealed the Transmission Zone. Here in the Control Tower, entered through a special air lock, was the secret room for important planning. It was a great place to rest and figure stuff out.

As feet pushed dress shoes off each other, hands reached for familiar toys. Sandy, his favorite stuffed toy dog, leaped right out from under the pillow as Skylar reached up for him; they hugged. Out of his left pants pocket came the Transformer that had helped him make the dinner. The entire Committee was here; the meeting could begin.

"Control in."

"Transformer in."

"Sandy in."

"Roger. What happened? Why didn't you guys tell me? Did you know about this baby stuff, or what? Why didn't any of you guys tell me?!!"

Transformer was completely baffled by it all. "I can't believe it myself. I've been completely in the dark! No one said a word to me about any of this!"

Sandy was looking straight ahead, expressionless except for the tiniest bit of pink tongue that hung out just beyond his teeth. "*I didn't pick up any scent of this at all. No one's said anything that I heard.*" *Skylar noticed that in fact Sandy's ears had not perked up from their usual flopped-over position.*

"*Well, what do we do now?*"

Transformer said, "There's nothing we can do right now. Let's just see what we can find out."

Sandy chimed in. "Yeah, I think there's nothing to get excited about yet. We'll find out more when everyone starts talking about it." *And with that he went right to sleep.*

"*Well, okay, guys. But just pay attention, okay? Roger, out.*"

He stood. There was a knock on the door which startled him.

"Skylar, it's Iris. May I come in?" Silence.

Skylar returned Transformer to his secret hiding place in the left pants pocket. Sandy was gently returned to his home under the pillow.

"Coming," he called as he checked these two friends before approaching the door. He pulled it open and there was Aunt Iris, alone, waiting in the hall outside his doorway. She smiled.

"Do you mind if I visit with you a little?" she asked.

He shook his head. "No, I don't mind," he said, backing up to let her step into the room. She turned and closed the door behind her.

"This'll keep their noise out," she explained as he heard the door click. "Do you mind if I sit on the floor?" He again shook his head, so Iris removed her Sunday shoes and sat on the large oval rug in the center of his room, making them the same size.

"They're down in the living room talking about baby stuff. I thought it would be a good time to slip out and talk with you instead."

Skylar nodded his permission for her to continue.

"I guess the news at dinner was pretty surprising, wasn't it?" She waited for his response this time.

"Well, yeah. I mean, where is the baby supposed to live? Am I going to have to share my room with it? I hope Mom doesn't want to give it my closet. I have all my stuff in there."

"I'm sure you have lots of questions about it all. You'll find out more about it in the next few days, I think. You can ask her what you want to know, too." Iris surveyed the room and smiled. "So what's in the closet that you like so much?"

He opened the closet door, disappeared for a moment and returned with plastic milk crate. He studied it briefly, then withdrew a clipboard with drawing paper and a set of design markers, army surplus binoculars, a toggle switch with loose wires dangling, a jeweler's eyepiece with the small rim missing and a length of twenty-four-strand telephone cable.

"This stuff came from Grandpa's last time I was there," he announced soberly. "Which would you like to see?"

Iris looked over the array and pointed to the binoculars. Skylar picked them up with both his five-year-old hands and handed them to her. She thanked him as he placed them in her open palm.

While she looked around, Skylar drew out a Space City transportation system where vehicles floated just above a magnetic power strip. He made sure the power strips were far away from the areas where children played. Iris began carefully scanning the room. Occasionally she "ooh'ed" or "ahh'ed" aloud. Within a few minutes the sketch was in place, details filled in with different colored markers.

"Ooh, Skylar, I hate to interrupt you, but this is just great!" Iris whispered. "Let me show you this." She reached out and positioned him to sit in her lap. "Tell me when." When Skylar nodded she leaned over next to his left ear, cheek touching cheek, and guided his head to look across the room to the highest window pane. She whispered.

"Do you see it yet?"

"Not yet."

"Look for movement."

He shook his head. "Wait, what was... yes," he nodded.

"Is it still moving?"

"Yes," his cheek nodded against hers.

"Okay, now just a little more... this way... tell me when you see it."

His head stopped its movement. He inhaled. Fingers adjusted the lens. "Wow!" escaped from under his breath.

"What colors do you see?" she asked.

"Gray, and sparkly—no white, and brown... and... orange... there's orange!" His breathing quickened. Iris nodded this time.

"Now, listen; what do you hear?" she asked in a voice just loud enough for the two of them. They sat completely still in the dimly lit room.

"Breathing, I hear breathing."

Iris nodded again, a slight chuckle escaping her. "That's us," she said. "What else?"

"I hear... wind. There's wind... outside, in the trees?" She nodded again. "What else?"

"I hear... whoooo, whoo! Whooo, whoo!"

Iris's cheek changed position as she smiled at his discovery. Skylar was completely hypnotized by the drama occurring just beyond his window pane in the twilight of early evening.

"It's an owl, Skylar. They're great to have around. They eat mice and things like that. You want to know what it was saying to you?"

Skylar put the binoculars down and turned to look at Iris with astonishment. He nodded yes, transfixed. Iris looked at him directly.

"It said 'Who cooks for you? Who cooks for you alllllllll…' " She had given a perfect imitation of the sound he'd just heard. She repeated it.

"Who cooks for you? Who cooks for…" Skylar joined in. They repeated this twice more, time enough for him to capture the growly, descending pitch at the end exactly right. Iris looked at him in triumph.

Skylar reached out across his own knees and maneuvered the clipboard and sky blue marker into reach. He bent low over the clipboard and carefully began to write. A shaky, misshapen S appeared first, revealing an intention that exceeded his skill at penmanship. He began to write the next letter, but stopped with a frown and erased what he had written.

"Aunt Iris, how do you write Skylar?" he asked.

"Hm-m… We'll figure it out together, okay?" she said. "But first, tell me how you got your new name."

Skylar eagerly related his adventure, how he and Spock had slain the seameer, and how he had been awarded his promotion and become a Sky Lar.

Iris nodded seriously when he finished his story. "Let me see your clipboard," she said as she motioned for Skylar to sit in her lap. Placing her hand atop his, she gently guided him in forming an S.

"That's the same letter that begins Stephen. Skylar starts off the same," she said softly as she began the next letter. "K is next, then Y and L…" She whispered the letters as they printed out Skylar's new name across the top of the page.

"There's my new name," he said happily, turning to

look at Iris. "Aunt Iris, I want to give this to you. How do you make your name?"

"You start with an I, then R, another I, and end with S," she explained. "My name ends the way yours begins."

Across the bottom he printed out the letters she had shown him, whispering aloud "IR......IS......" He bent low over the paper for a moment, giving his work a final review. With a blue marker he made one final correction. Without a word, he pressed open the clip, withdrew the picture and handed it to her.

Iris took it from him carefully, examining the complex cityscape with several kinds of vehicles, parks, children, flowers and people with grocery bags and briefcases. At the top in block letters was SKYLAR. And across the bottom, where Skylar had dedicated the drawing to her, she saw that he had dotted the 'I' with a sky blue heart.

CHAPTER FOUR

The empty bedroom echoed as Skylar tapped his feet on the hardwood floors. He'd never noticed that before. Now, with all his stuff gone, it was just a room that echoed. Sandy stayed close, as if fearing to stray too far.

The two of them surveyed the room one last time. Everything Jack had let him keep was downstairs in cardboard boxes. No more posters on the walls, no desk. No clothes in the closet, no more shelves with markers and papers. The rock collection and the special coins, even the arrowheads, would have been lost if he hadn't hidden them in socks. They had allowed him only one clipboard and a set of mechanical pencils to keep in the car. The faded wallpaper looked old next to where the posters had been.

He climbed to his feet to get a final look out the bedroom window. This was the window where Aunt Iris had shown him the owl. It was the window where he and Spock had launched uncounted missions into space. It was going to be hard to find a window as good as this one. Through the glass, the ripening stalks of corn stood at crisp attention, brilliant in green uniforms with hints of golden plumes. He whispered a secret good-bye to those cornstalks in perfect diagonals, to the elm tree where the owl lived in the crooked branch, to the campfire place in the woods, and to the creek that giggled.

He looked down below to all that wasn't going with them. What was a neat pile just a few days ago had grown to a mountain of some of the best stuff in the whole house. Dozens of empty shoe boxes, a lifetime of magazines from the basement shelves, out-of-date blackberry jams Mother had found in the cellar, the broken sump pump that had made the basement flood last spring. All their ice skates were goners, even his first pair. Mother would have kept those if Jack hadn't been so mad about the trailer being too small. He decided they had to throw out everything that wasn't "Texan," so the ice skates went on the pile, along with winter boots and the sled. What the neighbors didn't get, Grandma and Grandpa had tried to sort for the Salvation Army, but they couldn't keep up these last two days. Lots of really neat stuff was going to the dump, and there wasn't a thing he could do about it.

Down below, Jack was putting odds and ends in the trailer. Well, actually, he was throwing odds and ends in the trailer. He had been mad all morning after mashing his fingers on Mother's old sewing machine, the one Grandma had given her. No one had been able to do anything right since then. Grandpa was tying things down with sturdy cord, using his Swiss army knife to cut the ends. The station wagon was so packed, it looked like it would explode.

Noises drifted up to him from the kitchen. He moved down the steps and sat on the bottom one, out of the way, yet able to listen. Mother and Grandma were finishing last minute packing and cleaning, even though they had done about everything there was to do. Grandma was singing "See the U-S-A, in a Chevrolet" for the millionth time.

Each time she sprayed cleaning solution, she would stop singing, then start singing again after she wiped it dry. The kitchen, and her song, were squeaky clean.

Skylar walked through the empty living room to the front yard. Spock was having his last romp around the yard, chasing squirrels and birds he had known for a long time. He wheeled in the long grass and came galloping up to Skylar, looking for mischief.

"Not now, Spock. Gotta stay clean. Mom said." Spock was not convinced. He leaned forward and washed Skylar's face in a kiss.

"You are so bad!" Skylar said lovingly and grabbed him for a quick wrestle. Skylar had Spock pinned for the first point when the kitchen window opened and Mother called out, "Skylar, honey, not in your clean clothes! That's all you've got to wear in the car!" The window squeaked shut on their fun.

"Not in your clean clothes!" Skylar intoned in his Mother's cranky voice. "That's all you've got for the car," he whined as she had.

"Cause everything else got packed or thrown out!" he whispered angrily to Spock as he brushed the grass off his knees. He looked over his shoulder to brush his back, and couldn't believe his eyes.

There in the junk pile, next to the garbage cans and old clothes, empty paint cans and snow boots, lay Mapmaker One. Without a word, Jack had thrown out the spaceship. It was bent almost in two. The steering wheel hung sideways, and the doors didn't close. It was only cardboard and pie pans and two-by-fours—*Jack had been too rough this time. Too rough.*

He stumbled through the grass toward the junk pile. He needed his communicator, the one Grandpa had wired so the Space Buddies could reach him. Fumbling it from his shirt pocket, he coded emergency and whispered "MAY-DAY! MAYDAY! MAYDAY, Grandpa!!" Tears choked his words and stained the shirt he'd kept clean for the car. Before him was the carcass of the spaceship. Putting one foot in front of the other he pulled himself up high enough to reach the door handle and gave it a mighty tug. Nothing budged. He grabbed it with both hands and heaved himself backwards. The door tore off the body of the craft, dumping him into the grass and landing on top of him.

Skylar lay defeated, vanquished by the very machine he had tried to save. End game. A captain without a ship. In dirty clothes. Mother would kill him.

There was rustling at his feet. Sniffing. Smell of cherry tobacco.

"Attaboy, Spock! Emergency rations to the rescue!" Grandpa's muffled voice was very close.

Beneath the wreck, Spock bellied up to him. He stood on all fours, lifting the cardboard spaceship door off them both, and triumphantly dropped his cargo on Skylar's chest. Against the daylight Grandpa's silhouette provided a shadow. Spock was poised over him, wagging his tail ferociously.

"Good boy, Spock, good boy!" Grandpa affirmed. "How ya doin', there, Cap'n? You okay?"

In Grandpa's shadow, Skylar's eyes adjusted to the light. He looked down to his chest where Spock stared. There sat a new roll of Lifesavers, a little gummy, with two marks by dog teeth. Grandpa and Spock had rescued him. He couldn't contain the giggles. Grabbing the candy with one hand, he let Grandpa help him up with the other.

"Good boy, Spock! A real hero you are!" he chuckled. Grandpa took the roll and peeled off the first candy, tossing it up into the air where Spock gleefully snatched it. "Tangerine?" Grandpa offered him the next one. Grandpa ate the third one, and, between noisy crunches, brushed him off and straightened his clothes.

"Okay, let's see what we got here…" Grandpa mused. In a moment the spaceship was at their feet.

"Hmm, braces are fine, needs a little duct tape…Here, Skylar, hold this." Grandpa handed him the loop of cord and the Swiss army knife. "Let's settle this once and for all." He marched over to the laden station wagon and carefully placed the spaceship front and center on the trailer.

"Over here, boy, gimme some of that line." Skylar spooled out the cord and handed him the knife. "A couple of sailor's hitches will hold her. Now, go in the house and get me three of your mother's plastic bags. Gotta keep her dry, you know."

By the time Skylar reappeared, Jack was arguing with Grandpa.

"Who do you think you're talking to, old man…" Jack was madder now than he'd been this morning. "You think I'm going to haul that piece of junk a thousand miles?"

Grandpa politely took the plastic bags from Skylar and carefully wrapped the damaged spaceship. Jack looked as though he would explode.

"I said, who do you think you're talking to, OLD MAN…" Jack moved toward Grandpa and reached to pull the spaceship off the trailer. With lightning speed Grandpa intercepted Jack's forearm and moved between him and the trailer. Nose to nose, still holding his arm, Grandpa walked Jack backwards to the far side of the trailer, out of sight.

Jack was blustering. "You must be craz…What'ya mean?…Leggo my arm…You're outta yer…Okay, already…yeah, yeah…" Skylar couldn't make heads or tails out of what the two of them were saying.

Jack reappeared, massaging the arm Grandpa had held, still muttering to himself. He stopped a few paces from Skylar and glared at him. "Get that thing tied down good. We got a thousand mile trip to go." He stomped off to the house, rolling down his sleeve over a reddening arm.

Grandpa cleared his throat, and brushed off his shirt. "I think Jack understands how important it is to get this to Texas, Skylar. Let's get her wrapped real good." Two minutes later they finished. Grandpa reached into his pocket. "Watermelon? No, no, you want the pineapple." Skylar popped the yellow Lifesaver into his mouth. The two of them leaned against the trailer in silence.

"I'm going to miss you, Grandpa," he whispered.

"Me too," Grandpa replied hoarsely.

"I don't want to go to…" Skylar was in tears again.

"I know, I know," Grandpa said softly. "But it'll be okay, boy, because you can always call me. Telephone or otherwise." Skylar understood. Grandpa's heart could hear too, better than his ears, usually. Like this afternoon.

"Hug?" Skylar asked, and before he knew it, he was scooped off the ground and into the air just like in the old days. Burying his face in Grandpa's neck, they twirled and circled and Grandpa talked a mile a minute in words that Skylar could not make out except that each one of them meant "I love you." "I love you" wrapped in cherry tobacco, Lifesavers, clean flannel shirts and arms that held safe.

Then he was on his feet again. Grandpa steadied him and looked him in the eyes a long time. "I love you, Skylar."

"Me, too," Skylar mustered through tears.

"Heard your mother calling us. Time to get moving. Ready?"

"Guess so," Skylar lied.

"Let's go round up that hero," and with that, the two of them called Spock to the leash and got him settled in the car.

Jack checked the front door for the third time while Grandma got Rose and the baby into the car. Good-byes, last minute kisses, and important reminders crossed in every direction.

The car groaned out of the driveway, leaving behind Grandma and Grandpa and everything Skylar knew. In the front seat he heard his mother humming softly to the baby "See the U-S-A, in a Chevrolet."

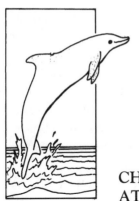

PART II

CHAPTER FIVE
ATLANTA, GEORGIA

The movements were slow, powerfully controlled and beautifully graceful, flowing with precision as the shadow on the dining room wall turned the man's solo ritual dance into a duet. The room had no furniture and was lit by a single overhead fixture, its opaque cover chipped in one corner. The man's well-toned body glistened with the exertion. His muscular thighs and full, defined calves flexed with each subtle shift of weight, long sinewed arms fluid as he formed and reformed each movement. Naked except for a pair of blue nylon running shorts, he breathed with deep concentration. His bare feet lifted and aligned themselves into the final movement and his outstretched palms slowly lowered to his side with an exhalation.

Alexander Greenleaf reached for a towel, feeling refreshed and centered after his early evening t'ai chi workout. The precision and control of this ancient discipline appealed to him greatly. It distracted him from the stress and pressures of academia as a tenured physics professor at Atlanta's Southeastern Tech.

Wrapping the towel around his neck, he walked into the kitchen. A large orange tabby with big yellow eyes jumped in through the window over the sink, intentionally left ajar for him. The cat stealthily walked across the counter, his movements slow and purposeful, as if he too were a master of t'ai chi.

"So, Muon, let's see what's in the fridge," Alexander said, giving his pet an affectionate scruff. The light of the refrigerator illuminated a single beer, a crusted container of plain yogurt, a half-filled carton of skim milk, a bowl of mysterious green mold, a box of brown bean sprouts, and two chocolate-iced doughnuts.

"Looks like slim pickings tonight," he muttered, taking out the milk and checking the expiration date on the label. He reached for a bowl and some cereal, adding just enough milk to moisten the contents.

"Muon, I know you're wondering why I haven't been able to pull off these experiments with cold fusion," Alexander said as he spooned sugar on top of his cereal. "You're probably thinking, 'Pons and Fleischmann had some successes, so what's wrong with you?' You're not realizing, however…" Alexander paused in mid-sentence, went very still for a moment, then left the cereal untouched and moved to his study, where his computer and office were set up.

He sat down at the keyboard and began to study his monitor intently. *What role is the lithium playing in the cell? Could contamination of the palladium rod affect results? How about tritium… Our calorimeter… I don't think it's sensitive enough—can we afford a better one?* "Yeah, now there's something to pursue...the calorimeter," he muttered.

After a while Muon joined him, jumping up to sit in his accustomed spot on the desk to lick and wash himself. Alexander came out of his concentration momentarily to ask, "Oh, buddy, you hungry? Must be—it's eight o'clock. Give me another five minutes…" He went back to his computer, losing track of time in his absorption with the work. Reaching for the phone, he called the lab to get the latest readings from his assistant. When the phone rang repeatedly with no answer, Alexander looked at his watch and was startled to discover it was nine-thirty.

Alexander returned to the kitchen to feed Muon and finish his dinner of cereal. He was surprised to find only a few dry flakes remaining in the bowl. "I honestly don't remember eating this," he said to the cat, as he absently opened a can of cat food and dumped it into the cereal bowl. Alexander headed for the shower, still focused on reading a printout he'd brought home from the lab.

The bedroom of his bachelor cottage was cluttered and comfortable, dominated by a king-size platform bed. Beside the bed was an ironing board, piled high with weeks of unopened mail, computer paper and stacks of newspapers. The bed's bookcase headboard overflowed with books, notes and odd pieces of paper. Its edges were marked with overlapping rings, the legacy of forgotten drinks.

Before Alexander stepped out of the bathroom, he ran a brush through his thick, black hair, noticing the abundance of gray, especially at the temples. *Not bad for a guy of thirty-eight, he thought. But I sure could use a hair cut. When did I last have one? Better make a note to get one before the big meeting with Blankenship.*

Out of the corner of his eye, he noticed the message light flashing on his answering machine. When he played the tape back, it was the voice of his friend, Tom Hawkins.

"Hey, Zan, it's nine-thirty and I'm at Melvin's Diner. You were supposed to be here at nine. Where are you?" said the voice.

"Damn," muttered Alexander under his breath as he reached for the phone. "Did it again, didn't I?" he asked sheepishly when Tom answered.

"Guess I'm used to it by now," Tom responded.

"Can we reschedule? Promise I'll show. How about tomorrow?"

"Can't," said Tom. "I'm flying out first thing in the morning to Florida—got a big real estate deal cooking."

"Well, call me when you get back. I'm sorry I stood you up tonight—maybe I can train Muon to remind me of my appointments."

"Hope you have more success with him than I've had with you. You're untrainable."

Alexander laughed. "See you when you get back."

He returned to his study and tuned the radio to his favorite classical station. *Perfect*, he thought, as the familiar sounds of Glenn Gould playing a Beethoven concerto filled the air. He settled at his desk, which was cluttered with paper and journals. A framed picture of Muon in a rare Atlanta snow fall peeked above the stacks. There were three pairs of tortoise-shell glasses, a jar of pens, most missing their tops, scribbled notations on Post-Its attached to almost every surface, and a ten-inch bust of Einstein with the ironic inscription, "God does not play dice."

Alexander pored intently over the computer print-out. *The answer is here somewhere*, he thought. *I've just got to find the key*. He began to put a folder of materials together, noting the date on his calendar. *A week from tomorrow I have my next meeting with Blankenship.*

He reached for his pipe. A non-smoker for three years, Alexander still retained the habit of chewing on the stem of the empty pipe when he felt anxious, or just wanted to think. He spent long minutes staring into the empty tar-black bowl, mulling over the cold fusion puzzle.

A gnawing in his belly brought him back to the present. "Guess that bowl of cereal didn't fill me up," he said, standing to stretch.

Muon roused himself from his nap, knocking his

photo over against the Einstein bust.

"You're right, my man, I don't like that picture there, either." He studied Einstein as he leaned over to rescue the picture. "You know, Muon, I marvel at Einstein's resistance to some of the theories of quantum physics." He paused. "That's true. I guess everybody has their blind spots."

Muon yawned, arched his back and extended his front paws in a huge stretch.

Alexander turned his attention back to Einstein. "Professor, my father preached me into believing that everything was preordained. While you don't go quite that far, you want me to believe in a cause and effect world. Well, pardon the disloyalty, but I prefer to challenge that belief—and I've got the whole of quantum physics to back me up. Heisenberg, thanks for your principle of uncertainty, my friend."

Muon's purr was clearly audible, like a small, powerful motor. Alexander listened to the cat's hum, unintentionally mimicking the half-closed eyes. His mind drifted through possibilities theoretically open to him.

"Maybe if I... Muon!" he suddenly cried. The cat leaped instantly out of reach. "I hadn't thought of that before!" He turned again to his computer, losing himself in the exploration of a new way to refine his experiment.

Alexander rummaged through the dresser drawers, muttering under his breath.

"A-ha. Success, Muon." He proudly turned and displayed a matched pair of brown socks.

At the sound of his name, Muon let out a "Mrow" and

leaped onto the ironing board, sending pieces of mail tumbling to the floor.

Alexander reached over and scratched his friend's head. "Sorry you haven't seen much of me this week, buddy, but I've been getting some promising results at the lab. I can't wait to see Blankenship. His expression will be worth all these sleepless nights."

Muon nonchalantly scratched behind his left ear, then settled in the squat position that Alexander referred to as his "ready on a moment's notice" stance.

"I know. We'll celebrate tonight. I'll stop at the store on the way home and get tuna for you and steak for me." He looked into the large, yellow eyes staring at him. "Oh, what the heck, I'll get steak for both of us, with a bottle of champagne for me and cream for you."

Spying his shoes across the room, he stood, his movements fluid and graceful from his years of t'ai chi. He whistled slowly, glancing at the clock. "Eight a.m.! Think I'm impatient to be there? Come on, Mu. I could use a cup of coffee." He strode toward the study, Muon trailing after him. He retrieved his pipe, patted Einstein on the head and moved on to the kitchen.

"Muon, this is going to be a red-letter day," he said, preparing a pot of coffee. "Blankenship, my cohorts—even the budget committee—can't refute these printouts." He thumbed through a stack of computer paper. Relaxing with his coffee at the little table, Alexander smiled. *I can't wait to see Blankenship's face. His support has been so important. Finding grant money, sticking by me while others scoffed at the idea of cold fusion. This might even be the very thing that gets him that appointment.*

Muon had quietly climbed onto his lap and lay curled in a ball. Unconsciously, Alexander stroked his fur as he talked. "If he's appointed dean he'll be better able to secure additional funding for my project. I need a new calorimeter. For all we know we could be getting more heat than that antiquated thing we've got can measure."

Alexander's mind ticked off pieces of equipment that would be welcome additions. He stood abruptly, dumping the startled cat unceremoniously onto the floor. Alexander rushed into the study. He grabbed a pen and began to list the equipment he wanted to request. "I can give this to Blankenship while I'm there today. It'll save time." His head shot up. "Time. What time is it?" He peered at his watch. "Whew, I was afraid I'd done it again."

Minutes later, Alexander sat impatiently in his old Volvo station wagon wishing he had changed the blades on his windshield wipers. He pulled his pipe out of his coat pocket and started chewing on the well-worn stem. "Wouldn't you know," he muttered to himself. "A little rain and the expressway comes to a complete halt." He shook his head in exasperation. "Of all days. Come on, dammit! Move! I'd like to be early for a change, so Blankenship will get a double surprise."

Alexander had seen Blankenship change as the department chairman's responsibilities had grown. When the project had first begun, he'd been totally supportive of the experiments with cold fusion. He had come by the lab almost every afternoon to see if the cold fusion cells had produced any heat or radiation. They would sit there for hours, drinking coffee and talking excitedly about cold fusion's promise of limitless, low-cost energy. They delighted in imagining new ways that cold fusion could enhance the quality of life and alleviate the looming environmental crises facing the planet.

But Blankenship's excitement had given way to skepticism, then cynicism, as replication of the Pons and Fleischmann experiment eluded Alexander. Dr.

Blankenship had continued to exert his influence on the budget committee to keep Alexander's research funded, but he'd stopped coming to the lab, and now required only a monthly report. It seemed to Alexander that the closer Blankenship got to becoming dean, the farther he got from being a pioneer. *I think he's scared*, Alexander thought. *He now sees pioneers as the ones with arrows in their backs.*

"Finally!" he declared as he jerked the car to a halt in his allotted parking space. He stuffed his pipe into his coat pocket and picked up the stack of computer printouts that were evidence of the first positive results of the work that had consumed him for the past year.

As the elevator carried him up to the fourth floor, his excitement grew. His strides lengthened as he headed toward Dr. Blankenship's office.

"Good morning, Dr. Greenleaf," said Dr. Blankenship's secretary. "You certainly look happy today."

"Good morning, Sara. Yes, I am," he smiled. "I have something very important to show Dr. Blankenship. It's going to be a banner day."

Sara returned his smile. She looked around the room as if to confirm they were alone. "I agree." She glanced down at the lighted button on the phone. "I think they've finally decided to make him the dean. He's talking to Dr. Ackerman right now."

Alexander nodded at the mention of the university president's name. He set the printouts on a chair, walked over to the window and stared out at the campus quadrangle.

Sara called to him. "He just hung up." She picked up the receiver. "Dr. Greenleaf is here."

Alexander knocked once and walked into the spacious office.

"Good morning, Alexander," said a beaming Dr.

Blankenship.

"Good morning, Charles. From the look on your face you must have some news on the dean's position."

"Well, as a matter of fact, I do. There'll be an announcement later today. I'm to be appointed next week." He leaned back in his executive swivel chair and rested his hands on his ample stomach. It was obvious he was quite proud of the fact that he was to be the new dean of one of the most prestigious graduate schools for the physical sciences.

"That's great," exclaimed Alexander. "You deserve it, Charles. I'm very happy for you. Dean Blankenship—has a good sound to it."

"Thank you, Alexander. Thank you very much. I hope I didn't keep you waiting too long."

Alexander began enthusiastically, "Charles, we're on the verge of a breakthrough. I'm convinced that we've had several bursts of heat in the last week but I need a more sophisticated calorimeter to measure them precisely. Look at these computer printouts. Right here, where I've marked them."

Alexander looked up from the printouts to see Dr. Blankenship holding his head in his hands, elbows on the desk, fingertips massaging his graying temples.

"What's wrong, Charles?" Alexander asked.

Dr. Blankenship continued rubbing his temples, then, sighing, leaned back to look at Alexander.

"Alexander, you've made what I have to tell you even more difficult than it was going to be. I had almost hoped that when you came in today you would finally have gotten discouraged. Then you wouldn't take my news too badly."

Alexander looked puzzled. "I don't understand."

"The school has decided not to renew your funding."

Alexander stood, stunned, then slowly sank into the

leather chair opposite Blankenship's desk. Unconsciously, he pulled the pipe from his coat pocket and stared at it for several moments.

"But what about these fusion indications?" Alexander protested, pointing to the printouts. "This is what we've been looking for all along. Surely when they see this they'll change their minds."

"No. No, Alexander, they won't. When the committee was debating the funding, I posed just this possibility. They concluded that even if there were to be verifiable progress, their decision would stand."

"But now that you're dean," Alexander said hopefully, "the funding can be reinstated, can't it?"

"Alexander, I would like to say yes, but I can't. Becoming dean doesn't mean I can start reversing committee decisions just like that. No. I'm afraid this decision is irreversible. You'll just have to live with it," he said with finality.

For a moment Alexander was silent. He thought about the budget committee members. He could just hear them, sitting around the table, talking.

"Greenleaf's got us way out on a limb with this cold fusion project."

"No reputable institutions are interested any more."

"It's too controversial."

"There are rumors now that it's all a fraud."

Alexander looked up with a start. "Charles, do you believe the cold fusion work is a fraud? Do you think we're making this stuff all up?" Alexander's face reddened as his anger grew. "What's going on? You used to be as excited as I was about a breakthrough like this. So what if we can't explain why it works? So what if it's hard to replicate? We used to laugh at the scientists who refused to believe what their eyes told them just because they couldn't explain it.

This was the essence of science to us, the challenge and the adventure of it... to find some new phenomenon and figure out how and why it is, even if it doesn't fit the old models."

Blankenship stared as Alexander continued. "So what's happened? Is this deanship so almighty important that you would turn your back on what we're supposed to be doing at this university?" Alexander worked himself up to a full standing shout and leaned over on Blankenship's desk, looking down at the roly-poly little man.

"Alexander!" Blankenship said, rising from his chair. "You have no right to speak to me that way, and I must advise you to cease immediately." In a less severe tone he added, "For fourteen years I have worked to become dean of this school. It has been my goal. Now that I am to be dean, I have the responsibility for a much broader range of concerns than just the obsession of one professor with a project that could bring embarrassment to this entire institution. You've had ample time to work on this, and your results have been meager, at best. I did not decide to end your project—the committee did. I have always supported you, but I will not overrule their decision."

Alexander took a deep breath. He knew he must control his anger. "I'm sorry," he said, more calmly. "You're right. You have been my friend through all this and you deserve my gratitude, not my anger. It's just that I'm very disappointed." He began chewing on the pipe as his pacing resumed. Suddenly he turned and pointed the pipe at Blankenship.

"Listen, Charles, we only have three more weeks before the summer break. I know you can't buy a new calorimeter or continue the funding for my lab, but I can't just give up on this project, not after I've begun to see some results. Would you ask the committee if I can continue to use the cells I've built and my other lab equipment? It's not needed anywhere else, and I'd like to continue on my own for as long as I can."

"Alexander, I don't have to ask the committee. Until further notice, you may continue to use your lab and the equipment. I don't know what you will be able to do about any new equipment, but rest assured no one will interfere with your continuing your work on your own. I'll see to that."

Quietly, Alexander said, "Thank you."

"Look, Alexander, I understand," said Dr. Blankenship. "I know you're disappointed. I wish there were more I could say, more I could do, but there isn't."

Alexander straightened his computer printouts and picked them up. The phone on the big wooden desk rang. Reluctantly, Dr. Blankenship answered. "Yes, Sara? All right. Thank you." He hung up the phone as he stepped around from behind the desk. Alexander looked at him.

"I know you're busy and I won't take any more of your time. I really am very happy they made you dean," Alexander said quietly. He extended his hand.

"Thank you, Alexander," said Dr. Blankenship, shaking Alexander's hand firmly. "And I am sorry."

Once out in the hall, Alexander stood, staring into space for several minutes. The elevator doors opened, revealing several of his colleagues engrossed in conversation. He turned abruptly toward the stairwell. As he walked slowly down the echoing concrete steps of the old building, he tried to reach through the numbness, to remember what Blankenship had said. He stopped and sat down on the landing. He had to get some order to his thoughts.

Maybe Blankenship did what he had to do, but at this moment Alexander could only see his lips moving, hear the words that seemed to be an echo from his childhood—give it up, don't try unless you know you can succeed. *Damn! I hate it! My father never believed in me, either.* Alexander cradled his head between his hands.

He had to think. He tried to put this setback in perspective, but nothing seemed to make sense. He remembered his grandmother. She had been a high school science teacher. When he visited her, she would show him her butterfly collection, telling him their Latin names, and her nicknames for them. She took him to her school and showed him another world under her microscope—a world of living, moving things. She gave him books and pictures, and then a microscope of his own. He had looked forward to these visits eagerly.

She was always proud of him when he won the blue ribbons in the science fair, and then would ask him what he had discovered, what he had learned and how much fun he had had. He loved his grandmother—and he had learned to love science.

It had been different with his father. He was fourteen, sitting at the dinner table with his parents. He recalled it now, so clearly...

"What's the matter, Zan? You've hardly eaten a thing. Aren't you feeling well?" Alexander's mother looked concerned and reached across the dinner table to feel her son's forehead.

"I'm fine, Mom. I'm not sick," he said, ducking away from her outstretched hand. Alexander hated it when his mother fawned over him like he was still a little boy, especially when his Dad was there.

"Well, what is it then, dear? Isn't your chicken good?"

"No, it's fine," Alexander said. "I'm just thinking."

"What could possibly be of such dire importance in your young life that you would worry your mother by not eating the fine dinner she has prepared for us?" As his father delivered this question in his deep baritone pulpit voice, Alexander picked up the golden brown thigh from his plate.

"Sorry, Mom. I didn't mean to worry you. I just can't decide what to do for the science fair." Quickly, Alexander took a bite of the fried chicken.

"So what's the big dilemma, son?" his father asked. "Whatever you do, I'm sure your efforts will reflect well on the family name."

Alexander furrowed his brow as his father spoke. It was true, he had always gotten a blue ribbon on his science fair projects. He knew his father expected no less. *But,* Alexander thought, *I've always just done the project my teachers suggested, and they always picked something that was sure to go over well with the judges.*

"Dad, I've always done what my teacher wanted me to do. I mean, it's always been fun, but there wasn't anything really adventurous about it. Everyone already knew what the outcome would be. That just doesn't seem right. I want more than a blue ribbon. I want to do a real science project."

"Just what do you mean by a real science project, young man?" his father said sarcastically. "I would have thought all your projects were real. Besides, what's wrong with getting a blue ribbon every year? It won't hurt your chances for a good college scholarship."

"Oh, I know," said Alexander, realizing he was venturing into dangerous territory. Already, for several years, his father had been speaking of the importance of his grades and activities in getting a scholarship to a good college. It was never a question of whether Alexander wanted to go to college or not, but in truth, even at fourteen, he was already looking forward to going, somewhere far away.

"I like winning the blue ribbons. It's only… I don't feel like a real scientist when I do a project just for the sake of winning the fair."

"Oh," said his father, tilting his head and peering at his young son over the top of his bifocals, "and just what does a real scientist feel like?" The stinging sarcasm made Alexander mad enough to stand his ground.

"I don't know for sure, but it's got to be different from building some model to show how gas engines work or something like that." Alexander went on, angrily. "Grandma says a real scientist looks at something in the world that nobody understands and figures out how it works. They explore. They ask why. I want to do a project that explores, that's designed to really discover something."

"I might have known my mother would have her hand in all this," his father exclaimed in disgust. "She's always filling your head with these unrealistic notions. Look, son, you're not a real scientist. You're an eighth-grade student. You are going to make good grades so you can get a scholarship to a good college, get out and get a good job, and so your mother and I can be proud of you. The more blue ribbons you pick up along the way, the easier it's going to be for you to get that scholarship. My mother may have taught science for thirty years, but she doesn't know about the real world like I do. There's an old saying. Them that can, do—them that can't, teach. So do the project and forget all these notions about real scientists."

Alexander bit his lip but the tears came anyway. He looked over at his mother, seeking the comfort he had spurned earlier, but she wouldn't even look at him. She stared down at her plate and buttered her roll, a bite at a time.

Later, Alexander told his grandmother what his father had said. Much to Alexander's surprise, she laughed. Putting her arm around his shoulder, she said, "'Them that can, do—them that can't, teach.' And them that can't teach, preach! It figures that your father would forget that last part."

The slam of a stairwell door two levels up, followed by the sound of footsteps, brought Alexander back to the present. Not wanting to see anyone, he quickly got up and hurried down the stairs. He reached the main floor, then charged through the heavy metal doors and out to his car.

The boxy, gray station wagon took him home, and soon he was safely sprawled on the worn brown tweed sofa in his living room, unaware of the habitual movements that had brought him there.

His head throbbed. He couldn't get his father's face out of his head. *Maybe you were right, Dad,* he thought. *Maybe I shouldn't be pursuing new, innovative ideas... Maybe cold fusion isn't feasible...*

The tabby climbed into his lap. "Dammit, Muon, I want to pursue cold fusion. It's become my life. And I know it can work. It's not easy though, is it? I need a lab and equipment. In short, I need money. How do you think I can get the green stuff, my feline friend?"

The cat stretched its front paws out and purred sonorously as it began to knead Alexander's leg. "You don't care to worry yourself about the mundane things of life, do you? I can't say that I blame you, but I've got to do something..." He rubbed the furry head. "It's almost time for summer break. What say we get the hell out of here?"

Alexander snapped his fingers. "Of course!" He reached for the phone.

CHAPTER SIX

Alexander surveyed the car as he finished loading his luggage and equipment. Surely Tom wasn't bringing much, since he'd only be staying for the weekend. Everything Alexander needed in the way of clothes was in two small suitcases, but the lab equipment filled most of the back of the station wagon. The last thing to be loaded was an unhappy Muon in his travel box, which Alexander placed on the seat next to him.

"Sorry, man. I know you don't like being in this thing, but just wait until you see the litter box at your new home. It's as big as all outdoors." He stuck his finger through one of the holes in an attempt to rub his friend's ears, but Muon moved to the far side of the box. "Guess I'm getting the cold shoulder."

When Alexander arrived at Tom's house, Tom was on the phone. "Just a few minutes and I'll be off," he said, his hand over the mouthpiece. He motioned Alexander to sit, but instead Alexander picked up Tom's suitcase and took it to the car.

"Hey, Zan," Tom called as he came bounding out of the house a few minutes later. "Sorry 'bout that, but I had a few details to tie up on a fantastic deal I just pulled off. I'll fill you in on the way."

Alexander felt himself beginning to relax for the first time since the meeting three weeks ago with Dr. Blankenship. "Would you rather drive, Tom? Since you know the way…"

"It's not the Jag, but sure," Tom winked.

Alexander felt good, sinking back in the passenger seat, his arm on Muon's box. "Tom, this is going to be great. Thank God the quarter's over. I can't wait to get to your beach house. You were right about that being the place to set up the lab."

Tom nodded sagely. "Most people come around to seeing the wisdom of my ideas."

Alexander feigned disgust. "Muon, how could I have doubted you? You did say Tom was only backing this project so he could be king of the world when it succeeds. Well, I doubt you no more, my friend."

"So I'm ambitious," Tom laughed. "Can't fault me for that. Listen, let me tell you about the latest acquisition of Hawkins Enterprises. Remember my golfing buddy, Paul Brisco? We've known each other for years…"

Alexander's mind drifted. *I wonder if the house is the same as I remember it, he thought. If the rec room is available, I'll use it. Of course, I'll need to hang some fluorescent lights and get some tables…*

"…buy some prime real estate together. I felt Paul was about to pull a fast one on me, so I got the word out I was cash-poor. Then, Paul said he needed to sell our property now, for cash…"

I can set up the computer, printer and modem on a small table. The box containing the microprocessing units, power supply transformer, and a terminal strip…

"…our agreement was that we each had first refusal if the other wanted to sell, so for a mere one and a half million I could have it, but it had to be cash."

Did I bring that box? Damn, it's important! It's the interface between the temperature and pressure-sensing probes of the cells and the computer.

"You should've seen the look on his face when I called the bank and told them to get a cashier's check ready. He was in a state of shock. Really, he was helpless..."

I'll need another long table for the cold fusion cells, calorimeters, and neutron detector. Where did I pack the water containers?

"And yesterday, I sold that same property for eight point two million—just wait 'til ol' Paul gets a load of that. Alexander? Zan! Man, the least you can do is pretend to listen."

"Huh? Oh, sorry. I was thinking about setting up my lab at the beach house."

"If I had people working for me who had your intensity, I'd be a rich man," he laughed, enjoying his own joke.

"Blankenship said I was obsessed," said Alexander. "I guess he was right."

"Well, as your only investor, I guess I should encourage that."

"You don't fool me," Alexander responded. "I know you're not worried about the money. Funding my work for the summer is a lot less risky—not to mention cheaper—than a lot of the deals you've been involved in."

"True, but usually I know a little more about what I'm getting into. You must have been a salesman in a former life."

"Come on! You weren't that hard to convince. All it took was the idea that you'd be in on the ground floor of something that could make you embarrassingly wealthy."

They drove on in silence for several minutes. Alexander looked at Tom. "I really appreciate the use of your beach house."

"Well, it was either that or listen to you rant and rave all summer."

"Thanks, friend." Alexander reached for his pipe. "Is the house basically the same as it was?"

"It's got a new roof and a larger deck, but other than that, yeah, it is."

"So you still have that big rec room?"

"Sure. It's not used for much, but it still has all my old stereo equipment, and the old upright piano, stuff like that. You want to set up the lab in there?"

"Yes, it's probably the best room."

"Go back to your dreaming, Einstein." He grinned.

"Tom, I may be crazy, but I just know cold fusion will work. I'm so close, I can feel it. There's… I don't know, some little something—some key will turn and I'll be getting energy consistently. I have the nagging feeling it's something obvious, something I already know."

"Okay, I believe you. I do know if anyone can discover it, you can. You have the glue to stick to something like this."

After their lunch stop Alexander tried to coax Muon into a better mood with a bite of his hamburger. "It's not much further, fella," he wheedled. "Come on, you know you like hamburger."

Tom chuckled. "I don't think even fish would tempt him at the moment. He is one mad cat. If things don't change, you'll have to find someone at the beach to listen to you. He certainly won't." They both laughed.

Alexander's mind went back to his project. He suddenly twisted around to look in the back seat.

"Whew, there they are."

"What?"

"The temperature and pressure probes. I need them to…"

Tom cut him off. "You mean you still haven't finished assembling your lab?"

"I know, I know, I need to lighten up. It's just… but I guess I've told you how important this is to me."

As the car pulled into the gravel drive, Alexander picked up Muon's box. "Look, guy. It hasn't changed a bit since I was here twenty-five years ago. Tom and I used to store our collection of horseshoe crab shells under those steps over there."

The house had gray shingles with white trim and a dark, shiny red door. Low, fragrant shrubbery filled the yard between the house and the narrow road.

They parked in the three-car garage adjacent to the house. In the past the garage had always been full of vehicles, one of them Tom's old Jeep. The salt air from the Gulf laid a thick film on everything, and the Hawkins family had always taken great care to keep their cars in the garage unless they were in use. Strange how little details came back to him after all these years.

"Do you come down often, Tom?"

"No, I seem to be too busy all the time," he said, as he unlocked the door.

"If you don't use it, why don't you sell it?"

"Well, it's going up in value every day. And I keep thinking I'll have more time to spend here. But it bothers me that it stays vacant so much now. Not good for a house."

Alexander put Muon's box in the middle of the room and opened it. The cat didn't budge. Alexander shook his head. "Take your time, fella." He left him to find his own way out, and headed toward the rec room to see if the lab could be set up there. *This is perfect!* he thought, just as Tom walked into the room after him.

"I'm not in the mood to work, but I sure am hungry," Tom said. "Let's go to the Sand Dollar. I'll introduce you to Iris. Her specialty is seafood, but everything there is good." He playfully punched Alexander's arm. "And she's easy on the eyes, too."

As they walked they could see the water off to the right, calm, soft waves breaking on the beach, depositing foam on the sand. A pelican was quietly hovering, and with a sudden swift dive hit the water, quickly swooping up again with his catch. No wasted motion. Just pure efficiency, accuracy.

Totally focused, Alexander thought. *Some people seem to be that way—no hesitation, no doubt, just precision and results. The antithesis of scientific research, where you try and fail, keep repeating and trying again. You know what you're seeking, but often you get something completely different. Not at all like the pelican's search—definitive, fast and productive. The budget committee expected me to be a pelican.* He chuckled at the thought.

They arrived at the wooden building, walked past the "Shoes Required" sign and entered the cool darkness of the bar. The rough-hewn wooden walls were seasoned to a golden-brown richness by the years. Almost every inch of space available was covered with notes written on dollar bills.

Alexander saw a tall, slender blonde behind the counter. *This must be Iris*, he thought. In some ways Tom would never change. Even in high school, Tom had talked a lot about all the good-looking girls they were going to meet.

Alexander hadn't had much success with women,

good-looking or otherwise. His marriage had lasted only three and a half years. Fortunately, there were no children. Since then, he had had several comfortable and convenient relationships, but nothing even remotely permanent.

His thoughts were interrupted by Tom. "Alexander, this is the fabulous Iris I've been telling you about."

"Good to meet you, Iris."

"Hi, Alexander," she replied. "Welcome to the Sand Dollar."

"What are the dollar bills for?" Alexander asked.

"Oh, that was started by Joe Kaminski," Iris replied in a friendly tone. "Joe is the one who opened this place, back in '61. According to him, a customer once wrote him a love note on the back of a dollar bill and left it as a tip. He attached it to the wall for luck. Before long, his customers were leaving their own notes, some just wanting to let people know they'd been here. I always suspected the woman was Sally, Joe's wife, but I never asked. The smile on her face every time Joe told the story to a new customer was enough evidence for me."

Tom tried to engage Iris in his typical flirtatious banter. "Iris, I've been chasing you all these years. Maybe I should leave you a love note on the wall—would a ten-dollar bill get your attention? One of these days, or better yet, nights, I'm going to win this one. You can bet on it."

Alexander watched Iris. Instead of the usual flirtatious response most women threw back at Tom, her face became blank, as if a shade had been pulled down. Completely without malice, she simply walked away toward another customer. *Tom's charm, good looks and money didn't dent that regal bearing,* he observed with admiration. Tom's eyes dropped, and his face took on the sheepish look of an adolescent boy, caught behind the barn ogling a girlie magazine.

Alexander was pleased he had been left out of that exchange. He turned his attention to the food. The fried shrimp were good, the best he had ever tasted. He slipped one in a napkin to take back to Muon.

CHAPTER SEVEN
KILEYVILLE, TEXAS

Skylar stood at the far corner of the dismal yard, looking up at the western sky. Low, dirty clouds tumbled and rolled toward him even as he watched.

"Texas people call that a Norther, Spock. See? Clouds coming in from over there, past the school." Spock sniffed the air, which had kicked up considerably since morning.

"There's a storm behind them that might come this way. It started way up in Kansas or someplace, maybe even Wyoming. It goes so slow you can watch it come down the street. By dinner tonight, all that dust will be at the bus stop, and by the time we go to bed, it'll be right here, at our house, you watch." Spock leaned against Skylar's knee for no reason at all. Skylar sneezed, already feeling the effects of the storm that had rumbled over hundreds of miles on its way to his yard.

He turned his back to the chain-link fence and slid against it into the brown, prickly grass. From here he could see the back yard of every house in their horseshoe-shaped subdivision, plus out to the street sign and bus stop. Every fourth house repeated the pattern: split-level, split-level, split-level, ranch, split-level, split-level, split-level, ranch. To make it even worse, their colors followed the same pattern; green, blue, yellow, gray, green, blue, yellow, gray.

Theirs was blue, with seven live trees and three dead ones.

No one lived on either side of him. Two doors down, there was a junior high girl he didn't know, who lived with her parents, a grandmother, and their cat. The other three houses with people had no children his age, just babies, and no pets. When the school bus roared up to their stop, the junior high girl jumped on first and sat in the back. He got on last, and sat up front. She never told him her name.

Everyone had been cranky today. Jack let the side door slam on his way to work, and woke Jack Jr. an hour early. Mom put out the box of cereal for his breakfast, but had no time to check his homework while he ate. The new baby was going to be born any time now. Mom had worn the same faded house dress three times, even though it had carrots smeared on the front. This morning, oatmeal had dried on her forehead where she had pushed a few strands of hair away from her eyes. Jack Jr. was busy pulling pots and pans out of the cupboard next to the stove. For a few minutes, he and Mom almost had a nice talk about school, and the playground.

"All the equipment is brand new, isn't it Skylar?" she asked. Her eyes were soft and smiling. He nodded. As soon as he swallowed, he told her what he'd discovered.

"Know what I found Monday? Down by the far end of the soccer field, almost near the creek, there's a big hole. I bet it goes on forever! Bet it's for a gopher or a snake or something…"

Mom was immediately alarmed. "You saw a snake? Lord have mercy, all I need is for you to get bitten by a snake, on top of everything else!" she scolded.

"Naw, Mom, I didn't actually SEE one, except for that dead one the janitor got from the parking lot.…" Before he could tell her of the janitor's bravery, Jack Jr. scraped his hand on the sharp edge of a pot lid and started crying, and she was up and taking him out of the room. Skylar finished breakfast alone, stopping by her room long enough for a good-bye kiss on his way out the door.

"Be careful, Skylar," she called as he headed across the yard.

The day had been unbearably hot, too hot to move. What greenery there was had withered. Grass grew from runners, not seed. Trees stayed low to the ground. Plants blossomed after rainstorms, then quickly dropped their seeds and went back into hiding. Everything had a leathery cover. Skylar missed the fresh, cool mornings when frost gave everything its deepest color, and let you leave footprints.

Jack had planted trees and bushes halfway across the back fence. When they withered and died, he blamed Spock. "Damn dog's been killing my trees again, Rose," he threatened at dinner. "Keep that mutt away from my trees, boy, or it'll come out of your hide." Jack never once noticed the white scaly bugs on the leaves. He kept watering those trees for weeks after they died, then he left them there as mute warnings.

The heat drove both Skylar and Spock inside, down the steps to the basement, to the secret fort in the middle of the moving boxes. Skylar had arranged it so the boxes looked casual outside, but inside was the beginning of one of his greatest constructions. The entry way was L-shaped to keep out the light, like Eskimos built their igloos to keep out the cold. Spock went in first to sniff for intruders, and Skylar held his tail at the "L" so he wouldn't wag the tunnel loose. The main cubicle was a double-strength washer/dryer container, with Styrofoam glued in the corners, a perfect place to stick pins, and a spare compass and a mechanical pen. Even using a flashlight, no light escaped from the fort.

Plenty of gauges and dials were attached to the back wall, below a great star map from one of the National Geographics he had found when they moved. Two empty paint cans made seats. This was the first fort that had a storage shelf, a thirty-inch piece of hardwood flooring carefully salvaged from one of the new houses, and fitted into precisely-cut slots in the Styrofoam corners. On it was Grandpa's special communicator and the tin container Grandma had used to send him fudge last Christmas.

Skylar opened the tin container and pulled out an Oreo, his favorite. He carefully pulled loose the top, licked off the filling, and ate the bottom half, giving the top to Spock, who thumped his tail contentedly.

"Know what time it is, Spock?"

Spock most assuredly did. He sat up and privately woofed, so soft his lips barely moved, much like when he was dreaming of great adventures.

"Good boy! You sure do know, don't you!" Skylar reached for the communicator and another Oreo. He punched in the secret code with his thumb while he separated and shared another cookie. Static filled their ears. He used another code, then boosted the transmission power.

"Lifesaver One, this is Mapmaker. Come in, Lifesaver One." Interference continued to plague them. He switched to alternate power.

"Lifesaver One, acknowledge. Acknowledge, Lifesaver One. This is Mapmaker. Come in, roger." A faint signal stabilized. Skylar leaned close to the communicator and covered his mouth to focus the sound.

"Yes, yes, it's me, Grandpa! Me and Spock!" Skylar moved the communicator to Spock who promptly gruffed another private woof for Grandpa.

"Look, uh, Grandpa, just wanted you to know that, uh, well, we miss you. Spock and me wish you could come visit us." The line crackled.

"I'd really like to see you, Grandpa. To talk about stuff. You know, stuff. Nobody around here…"

There was a sharp pop, followed by a steady whine. Skylar quickly lowered the volume, and checked the transmission code. No use. They'd been disconnected. The line was dead.

Rose carefully lowered her very pregnant self to check the oven. No matter which way she bent, she was three inches too high to check the pot roast. Opening the oven door meant another thirty minutes before the kitchen cooled down, another thirty minutes of sweaty torture as she cleaned it up for the night. Jack was going to have to get that air-conditioning man out if she was to have this baby. The air conditioner had been broken for three days and the house was like a steam room, even with all the windows and doors open. She cleaned the counter top angrily. It was just too much, waiting for this baby to come, with hundred degree heat all day. There was no relief from the backaches, and the way her ankles swelled, she couldn't even lace up shoes anymore. Any time, the doctor said, only days now.

She absently opened the macaroni for dinner and

poured it into the boiling water. She hadn't slept well in days, getting up at least every hour with her small bladder. The varicose veins behind her knees hurt, making her wonder about blood clots. Nobody knew how hard it was to get through a single day. Nobody knew, and nobody cared. The screen door slammed against its frame.

She caught herself. No more crying. Jack didn't know what to do when she cried, so he usually ended up yelling. No more crying, no more yelling, not before dinner, anyway. She dabbed at her eyes with the kitchen towel.

The telephone jangled and made her jump. She'd forgotten she'd adjusted it loud so she could hear it from upstairs. She sank heavily onto the step stool positioned against the wall near the telephone.

"HELLO? HELLO?" she said, matching its volume.

"Mama? What in the world? Are you crying?" Rose inhaled sharply. "Oh no, oh no…" she continued, much softer. She leaned against the kitchen wall and closed her eyes. "When? Oh no…" Her voice trailed off into sobs. "Not now, not just when…" More tears. She was silent for a long moment. She wiped her eyes and blew her nose. "Are you all right? How did it happen?" She continued listening, crying little sobs and noisily blowing her nose through the conversation.

"…any day now. The doctor says any time soon. I can't possibly go anywhere… I just can't believe it's now…" She broke into a fresh round of crying.

"I guess I won't be able to be there, can't even wear shoes now…" Silence again. "I don't know how you'll manage alone. Are you okay there? Who's with you now? Really? Do I need to call anyone? Yes, yes, let me talk with Jack, and I'll call later tonight."

Rose hung up the phone and slumped against the wall, heaving quiet sobs to herself. When she was through, she slowly straightened, and lifted herself off the stool. At an unusual noise she turned toward the screen door.

Skylar was slumped against the door jamb, crying into his sleeve to mute the sound. *Had he heard it all, from the first moment the telephone rang?* Rose reached out and tenderly pulled him to her awkward body. She smoothed her hand over his hair, instinctively rocking them both from side to side.

"Skylar, I'm so sorry," she said quietly. She let him sob and cough, and hold onto her.

"You know, honey, he's been sick a long time. Still, you're never ready…." Her voice trailed off again as Skylar came to the end of his tears.

"We'll both miss him a lot." She hugged him tightly, and gave him her last tissue.

She held his face in her hand a moment longer. "I've got to go tell Jack now," she said softly.

Skylar turned off the forgotten burner and slowly climbed the steps to his room.

The storm arrived early, whipping dust and papers and dead leaves in swirls through the yard. The shutters banged uselessly against the house as sharp, bitter rain pelted the windows and darkened the sky.

All through the long afternoon, while Mom entertained Jack Jr. and the new baby upstairs, Skylar worked quietly in the basement. Jennifer was just about a month old, and it was good that she slept most of the time. Mom seemed to cry easily now, especially if anything reminded her of Grandpa. Taking care of two little ones was hard for her. Jack was away at work most of the time, so it was up to him and Spock to look out for Mom. She needed something really special to cheer her up, something that would give her back her smile, maybe even a little laugh.

She would be so proud of him by the time she saw his special project. It was really going to be something. This would definitely make her feel better, and when he saw that look she saved just for him, all the extra work would be worth it. He had fixed his own lunch and was out the back door before she finished warming up Jack Jr.'s vegetables.

The basement had a small concrete floor, rough-surfaced, with a ceiling just high enough for grown-ups to stand up in. Around it was a crawl space with banks of musty-smelling, fine brown dirt about three feet high. There were stairs to the kitchen, and on the side a nine-step stairway leading to the backyard. It was fun to watch the dust float in the patch of daylight at the foot of the stairs. Texas sun was a lot sharper than Iowa sun, and if either door opened, you could watch the dust sparkles turn into a tornado.

On one side of the basement Jack's grimy workbench was piled high with tools and a jumble of motors and parts. Nearby lay the pile of moving boxes that secretly enclosed the fort. In the center was the small cleared area where Jack would strip a piece of furniture or work on his projects. Lately, he had been too busy with his job to come to the basement, so Skylar could work long hours alone.

Opposite the work bench was the metal octopus of the hot air furnace. It was about five feet in diameter and equally high. Big round ducts snaked out of the sides, reaching across the ceiling to the rooms above.

Dim light filtered in through high windows at each end. Two old fluorescent shop lights flickered and hummed as he and Spock completed the final details of the magic world at the base of the furnace.

For days, he had carried bucket-load after bucket-load of soft brown dirt down the steps and piled it around the furnace. The only dirt he had found soft enough to dig was at the far end of the parched back yard, where Jack had been planting shrubs. Each bucket-load required a long journey—forty-seven steps out, kneel and dig, forty-seven steps back. Finally, there was enough to begin the process of shaping the hills, valleys, roads and cities that lived in his mind's eye. Using the buckets of dirt, he had constructed a mountain spaceport. Toy soldiers peeked out of bunkers. Lego spacemen defended rockets which had been carefully aligned on their pads, ready for launching.

It had taken forever to dig small holes in the hard dirt bank for the road's support posts. But each was exactly right to hold up the yardsticks for the miniature roadway extending from the top of the bank to the floor. Discarded floor molding created a superhighway from the bank to the top of the furnace.

Twin ranges of mountains cut diagonally across the realm, running up to the cliff at the furnace. A river valley, dotted with trees and houses, ran down between the mountains.

Too bad the river wasn't real. Each time he added water it soaked through the brown dirt and disappeared. Finally, it oozed out beneath the bottom of the city's guard wall and gummed all over his sneakers. The best he could do was lay Christmas tinsel in the gullies, and, when the light was right, it twinkled almost as if water were running.

But the houses and trees were real. The trees were tiny branches broken off the shrubs in the back yard. Outside, those shrubs were nothing much, but here, in miniature, they turned into a lush, inviting forest.

The houses were some of the best yet. They were built from bright red Lego blocks, cereal box cardboard, Mom's party toothpicks, and other supplies from his own toy box and Jack's hardware collection. And there were simple farmhouses, with outbuildings and corrals. The center-piece was a ten-inch castle with towers, turrets, and a moat with pretend water made of carefully-positioned shards of broken mirror he had found in the crawl space. Old Lincoln logs buried on end made the castle walls.

He leaned back on his heels. Grandpa had given him those Lincoln logs. Grandpa had watched when he tore the gift paper off the tube and had laughed when he spread them all over the living room to see how many there were. Then they had spent the day putting them together and taking them apart over and over again. Skylar rubbed his dusty hands against hot tears. Mom wasn't the only one who cried. He still missed Grandpa. Grandpa had shown him how to build his first Lincoln log house. He pretended Grandpa was helping him again with this very important project and it made him feel a lot better.

He spun life into his creation, moving quickly from one section to another as he completed the spaceport. With the slightest thought, vehicles moved, people transported from place to place and soldiers marched.

"Almost ready, Spock, almost ready for Mom." Spock opened his eyes at the sound of his name and thumped his tail agreeably.

"Move over, boy, so I can get to the highway." Spock dipped into a delicious stretch, moved three lazy steps and curled back up to continue his nap.

"Sleepyhead," Skylar complained as he stooped to nuzzle his best friend. He got up, stepped over Spock, and leaned to reposition the strut below the superhighway. Satisfied, he was putting the finishing touches on the castle garden when he heard footsteps overhead. As the basement door opened, his mother's voice called down to him.

"Skylar? Are you there?"

Skylar ran to the foot of the stairs, wiping his muddy hands on his tee shirt. "Hi, Mom!" he said, his excitement spilling over. "Come on down. I've got something to show you."

"Oh, a surprise?" she said, a smile in her voice. "That'd be nice…"

As she reached the bottom of the stairs, Skylar could see the little crease in her forehead that seemed to appear whenever she was worried. "Skylar, how… did you get… so… grubby? I thought you'd been playing in your fort all afternoon."

His moment was at hand. "Mom, look!" Skylar led her by the hand to the magic land. "Look what I built for us. Here's the castle, and this is a farm where pigs are raised, and there's the forest, and this is the spaceport where the starships land…"

Spock had awakened for the presentation and was reinforcing each of Skylar's points, dancing excitedly and barely able to restrain himself from jumping into the middle of the space city.

"Oh, Skylar!" breathed his mother, her voice barely above a whisper.

He continued full speed. "…the water for the moat is shiny 'cause it's more of a lake, but this is a river, so it's skinnier, and see, if you stand just right you can watch the water move…" Skylar turned to position her to see the river move. He stopped dead in his tracks—the worry crease was deeper than ever.

"What, Mom? What is it?" Skylar asked, frantically wondering if the castle was wrong, somehow, or if she'd rather have horses than pigs.

"Skylar, honey, it's ...it's beautiful, dear," his mother whispered. Skylar released a deep breath of relief, even though her face still looked worried. "Where did you…"

"Rose? Rose!?" came the booming voice of Skylar's stepfather. "Dammit, Rose, someone's been digging back there where I planted those shrubs. Rose?"

Skylar could hear his heavy footsteps overhead, and hoped he wouldn't come down to the basement. The space city was for Mom, not Jack. Jack never had fun, and Skylar knew he would try to ruin everything for them. So Skylar closed his eyes tightly, and imagined his mother and himself safely behind the walls of the magical castle, far from the reach of his stepfather.

When he opened his eyes, Mom was still staring at the magic land, as if she couldn't move. Then, more footsteps, and Jack's heavy tread descended the stairs.

"Rose? Who tracked all this dirt in here?" His stepfather stopped short at the bottom of the steps, his mouth dropping open in amazement as he took in the scene.

"What in the hell has this kid done now?" Jack exploded. "I can't believe it!" He turned to Skylar and shouted directly at him, within arm's reach and even louder than before. "Where in the hell do you dream up things like this? You've ruined my shrubs and you've wrecked the basement. Damn it! How can you be so stupid?" He was shaking with rage.

Skylar cowered under Jack's wrath. Never before had Jack been this mad and this close. Rose was frozen in place, and looked frightened too. Again, Jack lashed out at Skylar.

"I'd like to give you a whipping for this. I ought to make you go cut your own switch—a good, thick one!"

Skylar didn't move. He knew that Jack was working

himself up into a full frenzy now, and anything he said or did would only make matters worse.

"Aw, forget the goddamn switch," Jack hissed. He approached Skylar, his arm raised.

Terrified, Skylar squeezed his eyes closed, all at once afraid of the first blow and wildly wishing himself out of this place. When he opened them a second later, everything moved in freeze-frame slow motion. Jack's face was monstrous, contorted. The vein across his forehead bulged and pulsed. The cords of his neck were taut. His mouth stretched open in a weird way, saliva flew, and it closed with a sickening sneer. Rage burned right out of eyes too black to be human. Skylar was deafened with fear, but the smell of Jack's sweat paralyzed him, engraving the sight of every grimace onto his brain. He was trapped like a deer caught in the high beams of a speeding pick-up truck.

As Jack moved to strike, Spock leapt from the floor. With a throaty growl, he snapped at Jack's coiled fist. The dog crashed against Jack's chest, and knocked him off balance. Jack's blow missed Skylar. Skylar saw Jack steady himself and reach for a shovel leaning against the basement wall. Spock stood his ground in front of Skylar, hunkered low, with hackles raised and teeth bared.

Skylar found his voice. "Run, Spock! Go! Now!" he commanded.

Spock hesitated, torn between his duty to obey and his duty to protect.

Focused on the dog still guarding the boy, Jack's eyes were pure hatred, as the shovel began its vicious arc. A loud thunk stopped it mid-stroke as the sharp blade of the shovel slammed into the joist over Jack's head. Stunned, Jack lost his grip and shook his hands as though they were on fire. He folded over and groaned in agony. He sank to his knees on the muddy floor, trying to reach around to his lower back with hands that still burned.

Cautiously, Rose approached him. "Jack, Jack? What is it? What's wrong? Is it your back again? Did it go out on you?"

Silently, Skylar signaled Spock the sweeping motion to go. Still hesitant, Spock finally bounded up the steps and out the door.

Jack groaned. He staggered slowly to his feet, still hunched over, fixing Skylar with a glassy stare. Using the shovel as a crutch, he gingerly straightened up, brushing away any help from Rose.

"Boy. Come here."

Skylar heard the hoarse command, but did not move.

"Jack, now he didn't mean..."

"Woman."

Rose stopped in mid-sentence.

"Come here, boy. Come over here. NOW." Skylar stepped in front of his stepfather and looked down at his feet. Jack grabbed the back of Skylar's head.

"Look at me when I'm talking to you, boy. You hear me?"

"Yes, sir," Skylar responded quietly.

"Speak louder, boy. Speak so I can hear you."

Yes, sir," Skylar said louder, trying to keep his voice from cracking.

"Now here's what you're gonna do. First, you go get that dog and tie him up out back. Then you come back down here and you clean this place up, and I mean clean it up. If I come down here and find one clump of dirt, or one thing out of place, you will learn what sorry means. You understand me?" Skylar tried to look away, but Jack shook him. "I said, do you understand me?"

"Yes, sir."

Jack loosened his grip and repositioned himself against

the shovel-crutch. Skylar turned to his mother. Rose looked at the floor, fidgeted with her apron, then stepped back from both of them.

"After you've cleaned this place up, you go to your room and you stay there. You got that?"

"Yes, sir."

"Come here, Rose. Help me up these steps." Rose turned away from Skylar and positioned herself under Jack's free arm. Jack hobbled and moaned and grumbled the two of them up the steps, leaving little cut marks across the linoleum with each punch of the shovel.

The sun had gone down hours ago. He lay on the bed, already out of his bath, but nowhere near sleep.

It had taken forever to clean up the basement. Buckets of dirt were a lot heavier going up steps than coming down them, but each one was removed and put back around the puny trees and shrubs Jack so loved. With any luck, every one of them would die.

He had hid all his houses and cars and ships in a secret box. He had carefully cleaned Jack's supplies and returned them to the filthy, greasy work bench. He had shoveled and swept until he could do no more, then had swept again. It was the only way to keep Jack from inventing some problem to complain about. Finally, the basement looked cleaner than when they moved in, and Jack had come down the steps and said he was through.

"Go get your bath," he had growled, and that was that.

The bedroom didn't feel right without Spock. Spock was supposed to be on the rug, right off to his side, so in the middle of the night they could cuddle. Or play aliens in the morning. Now, Jack would probably never allow Spock back in the house.

Mom never did see what he had made for her. She had gotten that worried look all over her face, and before they could even talk, Jack had come down and ruined everything. And almost hit Spock! Then she had been so worried about Jack that she never saw....

A tear rolled out of the corner of his eye and dropped into his ear. Mom never saw. She never saw the mountains, or the river that moved, or the rocket pads, or how the soldiers were hidden so only their eyes showed. She never saw how the farm had a red barn the same color as Grandpa's. When he looked for her, when Jack scared him and he needed her, she never saw him. She never saw.

There was arguing in the kitchen. The hollow doors between the rooms did nothing to stop the noise.

"What are you doing, Rose?"

"Fixing a little plate for Skylar."

"The hell you are. Put that down. I'm not breaking my back to have that kid of yours tear up my yard and flood my basement with mud and junk from God knows where."

The baby started crying. "There, there, now, Jenny... Jack, he needs to eat something."

"The back of my hand is what he needs. My dad would have busted me right on the spot if I'd have pulled something like that. If that damn dog hadn't thrown my back out, I'd be giving him a good whipping now."

"Well, I'll give it to the dog, then."

"The hell you will. That damn dog just tried to kill me, or have you forgotten. Jesus," Jack moaned as he moved his chair away from the table. The chair squeaked. Silverware dropped onto plates.

"Oh, Jack. Spock didn't mean it. He was protecting

Skylar. He thought you were going to hurt him. He made a mistake, that's all. That's a good girl, Jennifer, that's right. It's okay." The hutch squeaked rhythmically as Mother rocked the baby back and forth.

"Once a dog turns on you, you can't trust it ever again." The chair pushed back from the table now.

"Ever again," Jack repeated, and his heavy footsteps moved toward the bedroom.

Skylar feigned sleep as the footsteps approached the bedroom door. They paused. Skylar held his breath. He shivered as the shadow of his stepfather moved past the bottom of the door. The footsteps marched back down the hall, fading in their off-balance cadence.

From the silence of the bedroom, Skylar listened to the chirp of crickets and the cacophony of the cicadas in the hot summer night. Spock howled dolefully.

Skylar crept from his bed to the window. Peering into the moonlit night, he saw Spock, sitting as close to the house as the short rope would allow. Spock, too, knew where he really belonged. Skylar was pretty sure Spock saw him through the window.

The carport light came on, stretching into the back yard just past Spock. A screen door squeaked open and banged shut. Against the yellow light, Skylar saw Jack raise the rifle to his shoulder.

A single shot shattered the night. Spock, still on the rope, jolted backwards, and down.

Silence fell in splintered shards around him.

CHAPTER EIGHT
BRYSON BEACH, FLORIDA

Iris sat in her overstuffed chair, gazing out at the waves. She was cocooned in stillness, only her fingers moving as they caressed the small shell she held in her hand. The sound of the telephone caused her to jump, leaving her momentarily uncertain as to where she was.

She had long ago decided that telephones hated ringing almost as much as she hated hearing them. Why else would they sound so irritating? Yet the shrill ringing persisted. Iris picked up the receiver to stop the noisy intrusion into her solitude.

"Hello," she said distantly, still lost in her thoughts.

"Well, I can't believe you're really home. Are you busy?" questioned a familiar voice.

"Oh, Rose, no. I've been sitting here thinking. I treasure my quiet time."

"Sounds like a coffee commercial to me, Iris. Having three kids and a husband who needs catering to doesn't give me much quiet time, you know."

"Guess not, Rose. So, what's up?" Iris interrupted, eager to get to the crux of the conversation. She considered telephones to be a necessary instrument for business or concise messages, but she did not enjoy extended conversations.

"Well, Iris, you know the way Jack is. He works so hard, and I've got my hands full with these three kids, like I said. Moving out here to Texas was hard for all of us, especially Skylar. You know, I just don't know what to do. He's such a dreamy boy, so different from Jack... and Jack doesn't understand him. Jack tries to be a good stepfather to him... he's got a bad temper, though, and things just aren't good between them."

What does she want? Iris thought. *My sister has always had a hard time getting to the point.* Besides, it had been a long time since Iris had spent any time with Rose and her family. The last time she had seen them, she sensed that Rose's husband Jack and Skylar were having trouble getting along.

Rose rambled on about her family and life in Texas. "He was so attached to Daddy. I'll tell you, I think Skylar talked more to him than to us. But on the other hand, what options did Jack have? He had to think about his new job responsibilities, and I didn't realize just how homesick Skylar would be."

Rose's voice had a peculiar tremor in it. Iris realized that she needed to talk to someone she could trust, to air some of her worry.

"Nothing Skylar does seems to sit right with Jack," Rose confided. "I feel so caught between two people I love so much. Jack has our little Jennifer and Jack Jr. now, you know, his own flesh and blood. Skylar is a loner, always wrapped up in some fantastic space story or something. But, you know, he's my first baby. I love him. He's a good boy, just a little different."

Iris listened to her sister, resigned to the fact that, whatever the purpose of Rose's call, she would disclose it at her own pace. She remembered the Thanksgiving she had spent with Skylar several years ago, having recognized then that he was a little boy who didn't feel comfortable with adults. *Of course*, she laughed to herself, *I didn't like Jack that well myself. Rose obviously loves him, but I'm not sure how much of it is for him and how much for what he provides.*

Rose continued. "I was thinking about sending Skylar to camp this summer. I just don't know how we can afford it, what with the new baby and Jack Jr.'s allergy medicine. Seems like there's always something," Rose sighed.

"Yes, I've heard camp's expensive," Iris agreed, primarily to move the conversation to whatever its conclusion might be. Remembering the little boy she'd spent time with, Iris couldn't imagine him as an outdoorsman—he was so absorbed with his drawings and his gadgets. He wasn't a very social kid, either, *but*, Iris thought, *there's nothing wrong with that. I can appreciate someone who is comfortable with his own company.* She wondered if Rose was going to ask for a loan.

"Well, the two of them are driving each other—and me—crazy. I try to keep Jack happy, but I never know what's going to happen next. I'm afraid sometimes…" Rose lowered her voice conspiratorially. "So I was wondering, Iris. Do you think Skylar could come visit you this summer?"

The request came out of left field for Iris. This was one favor she hadn't anticipated, and she was silent for a beat too long while she mulled over the alternatives and implications.

"Iris? I know it's a lot to ask, but . . ."

"Well, this is a bit of a surprise. I think Skylar is a very special nephew, but I've never been around kids much. I'm not sure I could keep him entertained."

"Just give him a chance, Iris, and you'll love him like I do," Rose pleaded. "I promise. We just need some time here. A little distance would really help. Besides, it could be fun for both of you. Skylar is pretty good at taking care of himself, you'll see. Please say yes!"

A nine-year-old boy? Iris thought to herself. *Twenty-four hours a day?* Then she heard herself respond with a single word: "Yes."

"Great!" Rose exclaimed. "I'll make arrangements for his flight and call you back. Is next weekend okay?"

Iris played with the damp sand, squishing it between her toes and fingers as she sat on the deserted beach. Totally absorbed, she watched as the first rays of sunlight played across the dark water. The widening streaks of blue, gold and pink colored the morning sky in a remarkably different way than the familiar pinks and reds of sunset.

She watched a sandpiper playing its never-ending game of tag with the ocean waves. With head down, it would chase the receding wave in hot pursuit of any edibles the water might have uncovered. As a new wave broke the tiny bird would scurry away as if on tiptoes, the small legs moving rapidly, only to stop and begin the process anew. "Bird, you sure don't want to get your feet wet. Here, have some of my breakfast." She tossed a piece of bran muffin toward the bird. The sandpiper delicately stepped over it in search of tastier goodies hiding just below the surface of the sand.

"What a pleasant surprise."

Iris turned, "Good morning, Jaid. Morning, Natty." She reached over and scratched the pig's head. "You look mighty fine today." Miss Natasha grunted with delight and flopped over on her side.

Jaid's rich, infectious laugh echoed off the beach around them. As though drawn by the sound of her voice, hordes of pelicans and seagulls filled the air, circling overhead. "Good morning, dears. That's right, Jaid is here with your breakfast." She began scrounging through her purse. "A-ha, here it is." She pulled out a plastic bag filled with bread. "Would you like to walk to the lagoon with us? The crew is waiting for their breakfast."

"I'd love to."

Jaid gave Miss Natasha's halter a gentle pull and the three of them headed toward the water. As they waded through the shoreline foam, Jaid glanced at Iris from beneath the large brim of her hat. "When is that nephew of yours coming?"

"His plane arrives this afternoon."

"Well, I can't wait to meet him. Anyone who has the imagination to change his name from Stephen to Skylar is my kind of person. Maybe he'd like to attend your middle-aged friend's art camp?"

They both laughed, sharing their joke about Jaid's definition of middle age. At sixty-four she still didn't think she had reached it.

"Jaid, you'll outlive us all."

"I hope we'll all grow ancient together. Can't you see it now, plastered on billboards all up and down the highway: 'Quarter mile ahead: The Woman Artist Who's Older Than Dirt!' " They laughed.

"You know, Jaid, I've been thinking that Skylar might like your art camp."

"That's wonderful. Well, if he's interested, there's definitely a space for him."

"I'll talk to him about it."

Iris stopped and stared out at the breaking waves. "Wish there was time for a dive today."

"Did you go out yesterday?"

"I did, but I didn't dive, I just swam around a bit."

While talking, they had arrived at their destination, and now stood facing the lagoon. "Oh, Jaid, this place is always so lovely."

"Particularly at this time of day, when it's so isolated." Jaid agreed. "There isn't a prettier sunrise anywhere. The colors are so vivid. I guess it reminds me of the Aegean." As Iris watched, the air was suddenly filled again with dozens of pelicans and seagulls. "They nest on the other side of that dune. It's secluded enough for them to feel safe from all the curious people."

Jaid opened the bags containing bread and began tossing small pieces into the air. The birds competed noisily for each morsel, swooping down and catching them in midair. Iris watched their game for a few minutes, then joined in, as Jaid began to speak.

"Did you see Dear One?"

"Eventually. She looked like she'd been playing rough with another dolphin. I thought, at first, that she'd gotten into a fight with a shark or something. There were some striped marks, like scars, on her back and part of her melon, but other than that she seemed fine. We had a great swim."

"You have a wonderful relationship with that animal." Jaid smiled as she lifted herself up off the sand.

"Come on, Miss Natasha." Turning to Iris she said, "I'm off. Remember, I'm flying out to New York in the morning, but hopefully I'll be back by Wednesday." She waved as she turned and headed toward the dune.

Iris glanced at her watch. "Elmore, I'm leaving to pick up Skylar."

Elmore nodded.

The screen door slammed behind her as she descended the steps and climbed into her jeep. She headed the vehicle down Highway 93 toward Panama City.

It had been almost four years since she had last spent time with Skylar, at Thanksgiving dinner at her sister's house. It had been a difficult day for Skylar. She remembered his room, an artful collection of spare parts, drawings of space cities and old junk. She had been deeply moved that Skylar, a child of few words, had trusted her with his private world.

Her thoughts wandered back to her own childhood and her neighbor, Mrs. Mitchell, the old woman who had been the guardian of her childhood dreams. She remembered the daily visits, and Mrs. Mitchell's garden. There was a path of once carefully-set flagstones covered with cool green moss. Pale blue forget-me-nots spilled over the edge of the walkway. An old cement bird bath stood under the gnarled apple tree so fragrant in the spring. Often she found the old widow stooped over one of the multitude of flower beds, cultivating the well-tended soil. It had been her refuge, this garden, and she still remembered the nurturing warmth of the old woman's smile and embrace. She'd felt safer there than in her own home. So vividly she remembered . . .

It was her first duty each afternoon to walk to Mrs. Mitchell's house and bring the mail from the roadside box up the long, graveled driveway to the house. When she came home from school, she carefully hung up her dress and put on her favorite flannel shirt and blue jeans.

Aside from feeling soft, comfortable and cuddly, the jeans and flannel shirts were just the right combination to keep out the brisk fall wind. She loved the contrast of cool wind blowing against her cheek while the rest of her was just exactly warm enough. The bright sun, cutting through the gray sky, warmed her skin. The cool wind commanded her attention. Even the leaves were fun to be around. She noticed a remarkable number of colors, especially in the sugar maples. They moved through the most delicate changes, from greens to yellows to oranges, reds and finally earth brown. It was a challenge to move down the road silently, what with all the dry leaves underfoot. But by carefully lifting her toes, and lifting her foot high enough not to stir up the excess leaves, she found she could place her foot on what appeared to be moist areas, and, if she really concentrated, she could move effortlessly and quietly, like the Arapahos she had read about.

Mrs. Mitchell lived exactly three houses, two pastures and three dogs away. In the spring, crocuses, which lined the driveway from the road to the front porch, would poke their heads out from under the snow, looking like a floral version of tutti-frutti ice cream. But Iris knew that Mrs. Mitchell had her *real* treasures inside her house—it was a museum of glass figurines, porcelain ornaments, special glassware and painted dishes which covered the walls, tables, the mantle, and even the little ledges dividing the tops and bottoms of the windows.

The back yard was a secret garden, secluded behind a stone wall. Mrs. Mitchell had climbing rose bushes, honeysuckle, hibiscus, even a grape vine growing against the wall. Iris marveled at the impossibly tiny trees growing in squat little rectangular pots off in one corner. The trees couldn't have been more than five inches tall, yet Mrs. Mitchell assured her they were older than many of the trees nearby that were taller than her house.

Iris knocked on the door—knock, knock, knock-

knock-knock—their secret code. Iris had suggested this so that Mrs. Mitchell would know it was her and not have to peek through the gauze curtains.

"Hello, my dear, how pleasant to see you," Mrs. Mitchell welcomed her, standing back in the house out of the bright sunlight.

"Thank you ma'am." Their carefully polite greeting assured them both that whoever might overhear would have not the slightest idea of what they really shared with each other. Iris stepped through the door and into the cool, dark living room.

"Here are your letters, Mrs. Mitchell. And I have something to tell you about school today." Mrs. Mitchell approached, gave her a gentle pat on the shoulder, and received the mail Iris placed in her hand.

"Yes, dear, in school? Tell me everything." They proceeded to the kitchen, Iris trailing behind the wizened old woman with the slightly bowed knees and bent back. Mrs. Mitchell left in her wake a faded scent of rosewater. Iris sat at the small clawfoot table while Mrs. Mitchell prepared their refreshments.

"I listened to a very famous and old story that Mr. Burroughs, my teacher, read to us. Today was the first chapter. He promised that each day he'll read one more chapter. He said it may take the whole year to finish just this one story! We all sit at our desks and we wait until he's through with his lunch, and then he starts to read. It's called "The Tale of the Ancient Mariner," and it's a story about a man who goes to sea and gets in a terrible storm and is left without any way to get back to shore! You want to know how I know he's ready to read to us?"

"Why, of course, dear, how can you tell?"

"Because he always eats a green apple as his dessert. And you know what he does with it?"

"What?"

"He eats the whole thing—first the regular part, then he eats the core, and all the seeds and that part that sticks between your teeth. And he saves the stem for the last. Mrs. Mitchell, HE EATS THE STEM, TOO!"

"My goodness, dear! What an odd fellow! And you say he does this every day?" Mrs. Mitchell, still working at the kitchen counter, was gifted at hearing conversation behind her. Iris was never forced to alter her storytelling for the old woman.

"Yes, ma'am, every day, right in front of our whole class. Frederica and Anna think it's disgusting. Even Allan and Dale think he's nuts. He does this right in front of everyone. And no one says a word about it. All the kids think he doesn't know what he's doing. But I think he knows exactly what he's doing and I think he does it on purpose. Isn't that just the best joke in the whole world!"

"Why, yes, dear, it is quite clever of him now, isn't it!" And they both laughed delightedly, sharing the joy of Iris's story, eyes laughing together. Mrs. Mitchell placed two glasses of lemonade on the table before them.

"You know, Iris, I so enjoy your visits each day. And I'm glad to have you for a friend. You know, a lot of my other friends have gone on before me. I miss Mr. John the most," she sighed wistfully. "We were married fifty-four years ago, next February, you know. But I talk to him sometimes anyway. And sometimes I just sit and remember about us. Sometimes I forget he's not still here."

Despite the seventy-three years between them, Iris somehow knew that Mrs. Mitchell appreciated their quiet moments together as well as the words they shared.

"Can we go look at the glass animals now?" Iris asked. She put down the lemonade, still half full.

"Let's just put these in the refrigerator to keep them

nice and fresh, shall we?" Mrs. Mitchell carefully accepted Iris's glass, using two arthritic hands to maneuver the slippery glasses, allowing Iris to open the refrigerator door for her. Iris walked to the living room coffee table where the glass figurines had been placed. She waited for Mrs. Mitchell to motion her to sit.

On the table sat blown-glass unicorns, a horse, two dogs, a dolphin, a wolf, a chicken with three miniature chicks trailing behind, and several giraffes. Iris never touched them unless she was invited to do so.

"And which would you like to visit with today?"

"I'd like to take the unicorn for a long ride." Iris was sitting at the very edge of the faded, green brocade wingback chair. Her hands were on her lap, holding each other clear of the figurines, yet trembling with excitement.

"And so you shall," said Mrs. Mitchell quietly, gently retrieving the smallest unicorn of the three, the one which was crystal clear except for a deep gray forelock. She handed it to Iris.

Iris bent low and held the tiny crystal unicorn close to her mouth. She closed her blue eyes. An almost imperceptible furrow appeared between her eyebrows. When she and the unicorn finished their conversation, she opened her eyes and looked at Mrs. Mitchell.

"And so, where shall you two go?"

"To the sea this time."

"And will you be traveling alone, just the two of you?"

"We'd like you to come with us if you would. Do you know how to swim?"

"That would be just lovely, dear! Don't worry about me, I'm an excellent swimmer! I'd like to sit behind you on the unicorn, if that's all right with you both." And with that Mrs. Mitchell sat back in her chair, wrinkled hands resting comfortably on the arms, and closed her eyes. Iris scooched back on the chair, feet lifting slightly off the carpeted floor, carefully holding the unicorn between left thumb and forefinger.

Gently gliding off from their resting place, such worlds they visited! Iris's eyes adjusted from the bright daylight of the air to the soft, almost glowing presence of the sea. Near the surface, sunlight penetrated the water, making it sparkle around them.

"Hold on, Mrs. Mitchell, we're going to go in for a dive now!"

"Yes, dear, I'm ready."

And they broke the surface, gurgling their exclamations about the green-blue world around them, discovering they could breathe as easily here below as above. Iris turned to Mrs. Mitchell and they laughed through their teeth, sending up little trails of bubbles. They saw plants, ancient rock surfaces, corals, and fish in every color possible, from pale white-yellow to deep, almost-black purple. Their forward motion slowed to a delicate, effortless dance, weightless and graceful. Iris pushed the hair away from her face. Her jeans, filled with air from their swift descent, were faded blue balloons.

And everywhere there were friends. It didn't matter if they swam, floated above the surface of a rock or along the sandy bottom, or used thoughts to move instantly from one location to another. She could sense that they were gentle and curious.

Iris, with Mrs. Mitchell behind her, spent hours explaining her life on land. She explained how most creatures breathed air, and how some lived underground. How some used languages, others didn't speak at all, some used sounds, light, even temperature to direct their actions. They all were captivated by Iris's descriptions of moving around on the earth, and almost no one could understand how she needed help to move from one place to another if it was too far to walk.

Most of these magical friends got about by imagining themselves from one place to another. Iris laughed when they told her the funny places they'd sometimes found themselves in when they got distracted or started dreaming! And she was doubly surprised when they pointed out to her that she got herself to them in the very same way!

The unicorn pawed, wanting to return to his family. Rising toward the surface, Iris waved good-by to her friends. Hearing a splash and feeling cool wind blow across her damp clothes, she knew she was returning to her own world. She felt her hair dry in the wind. The last bit of water dripped from her rubber-tipped, round-toed tennis shoes. The tiny unicorn landed squarely back on the palm of her hand.

"Thank you," she said. Mrs. Mitchell lifted her head and cleared her throat.

"Well, that was just wonderful, my dear!" she said, patting her hair back into the neatly gathered bun in the back of her head.

"Didn't you especially love the colors this time!" Iris exclaimed.

"Oh yes, dear!" Mrs. Mitchell replied quietly. "And it was so warm and comfortable, it just made me feel young again."

As Iris handed the tiny unicorn back to Mrs. Mitchell, she noticed that the old woman's hands were warm to the touch, the skin soft and pliant.

CHAPTER NINE

"Okay, fella, this is your stop," said the uniformed flight attendant, after the plane had emptied its passengers past Skylar and into the blinding sun and thick humidity that was Panama City, Florida. He pulled his green tackle box from beneath his seat and followed her to the door nearest the cockpit, then down steep metal steps onto the blazing asphalt. It was so bright he squinted his eyes almost closed. Once inside the small terminal building, they walked to the receiving area where she turned to him once more.

"Whew! Feels better in here, doesn't it? Now, you just stay with me until someone comes for you." She looked at her clipboard. "Let's see, it's supposed to be, uh, Iris Sanders, right? Is she your older sister?"

Skylar, eyes not yet adjusted, directed his answer to where the voice was coming from. "Aunt, it's my Aunt Iris."

"Very well, let me know when you see her. I'll be finishing up my reports here at the desk. You can sit right over there." His vision returned. She motioned to the waiting area just a few feet to the left. He moved over and dropped his backpack onto the adjacent chair, resting the tackle box on his lap.

A tall woman approached. She stood just beyond arm's length, to his right. "Hello, Skylar. It's me, Iris," she said. "I'm glad you're here." She smiled and offered him her hand.

Skylar was stunned at how similar the voice was to Mother's. He saw the unmistakable Aunt Iris—tall, lanky, well-tanned, an explosion of hair pushing out from the ribbon which pulled it to the back of her head.

"Hi," he said as they awkwardly shook hands. Her smile caused her eyes to sparkle with the unusual blue he remembered. The flight attendant was moving toward them. Iris showed identification and the attendant bent to Skylar.

"I hope you'll be flying with us again." She pinned a plastic airplane on his shirt pocket, and gave him a handful of small bags of peanuts. "Have a good vacation!"

"Now we'll get your luggage, Skylar. What did you bring?"

"My tool kit and my suitcase."

"Okay. We'll get the suitcase at the baggage claim area."

In less than ten minutes they were on Highway 93 headed west to Bryson Beach. The roads were flat and smooth, like Texas, but the sky was much brighter. The road they were on was lined with dense thickets of low trees and broad-leaved bushes, interspersed with blotches of tall wavy grass and creeping grass on the ground near the road. Sand blew over the edge of the roads and flew up in swirls as they raced past. There were very few houses along this road, not at all like the organized and boring houses around him in Texas. White birds with long, droopy legs seemed to hang in the air far away, and short birds with long beaks perched on the posts along the fences.

Iris groped below the driver's seat for a moment and

fished out a pathetic-looking hat, which she handed to him. It had probably been a white canvas hat at one time, but now it was a dull gray, with two brass-lined holes on either side and long, shoelace-type strings hanging loose. The brim had been snapped up on one side. Skylar put it on and tied it under his chin. For the first time since he arrived, he was able to stop squinting. She smiled at him, then turned her eyes back to the road.

Finally, they moved through a small gathering of buildings, an ancient gas station that needed paint, a boat equipment store, and what must have been a grocery store. Outside was a portable sign that said "Milk, cigs, T-shirts, gas, beer." Only three bulbs still flashed on and off. As they passed the houses, several little summer-type places, it looked as though everyone was gone for the afternoon having left their laundry hanging on the front porches—towels, swimsuits, long-handled nets leaned up against the wall any old way. From under one of the porches, a large black dog charged playfully after Iris's jeep, barking in pursuit. Skylar jumped at the sound, then pulled down his hat to hide the tears from Iris.

They went a short distance down a very narrow road toward the beach, and into a driveway paved with broken shells and gravel, next to a weathered gray beach house with a screened porch.

When Iris cut off the engine, Skylar looked through the dusty windshield at the house where she lived. The screens which covered the entire porch were worn by the salt air. The bottom two steps had no paint at all in those places where feet had passed over them. Boat paddles were leaned against the steps, and tennis shoes were sitting, sole up, in the sun. It was very different from Texas.

"Come on in, Skylar. Let me show you where to put your things." He moved through the living room, noticing the interesting furniture and carefully-placed belongings, saying nothing.

He followed Iris into a small room off the living room. Pausing in the doorway, he placed his hand on the black glass knob of the plank door. A smell of clean sheets and soap filled his nostrils. He walked over to the twin bed, setting his things down on the nubby chenille bedspread.

The end table held a glass lamp whose base was filled with shells. Skylar studied it from all angles.

"The top unscrews," Iris volunteered, answering his unspoken question. "I found all those shells on the beach." Standing by a blue wooden desk with three drawers, she said, "This is your desk."

She turned and twisted the switch at the top of the arm lamp attached to the back of the desk. Skylar joined her, extended and retracted, turned, swiveled and adjusted the lamp. He nodded wordlessly.

Iris pulled the cord of the fabric-covered window blind and sunlight flooded the room, highlighting dancing flecks of dust.

"It's too hot to keep this up during the day. But at night—well, you'll see. You can see a million stars on a clear night." Iris's voice was so soft Skylar wasn't sure if she was still talking to him or just reminding herself. She loosened the rope and began carefully lowering the blind, shading the room to a normal light.

"This room is yours. Your bathroom is right through here." He peeked in and saw blue and red towels projecting their brilliant colors to him. "I'm going to fix our dinner. I think I know what you'll like."

Skylar carefully sat on the edge of the bed and took stock of his surroundings. He was tired. Then he moved the green tackle box, with "SKYLAR" printed on the top in block letters, to the desk. He closed the door to the room and withdrew the most important contents—note pad, colored pencil set, mechanical pencil—all of which he neatly arranged on the top of the desk.

Then he began to unpack his suitcase. He removed his most carefully-packed belonging, his stuffed dog Sandy. Sandy had been his dog before Spock, and now Skylar refused to be without him. As long as Sandy was nearby, he knew he always had a friend that Jack couldn't hurt or take away. He placed Sandy at the very bottom of all the pillows Iris had given him. Sandy was very shy, not good at meeting people, and Skylar wasn't about to disturb his need for privacy in this new setting.

He returned to the suitcase and removed the things Mother had packed—underwear, socks, shirts, shorts, a few pairs of long pants, a cotton sweater, pajamas, bathroom supplies. Then he pulled out his slippers, the ones with the vinyl soles and terry cloth insides, and put them on the floor, midway between the head and foot of the bed—right where his feet would be when he rolled out of bed each morning. He pushed the suitcase under the bed.

Opening his door, he heard it groan—it wasn't a spring-coil like the screen door, so he would have to investigate that later. He smelled coffee and heard something—was it bacon?—frying. His nose led him to the back of the house, through the darkened living room into a brightly lit kitchen area. Iris had two plates, toast, sliced fresh tomatoes, onions, cheese, lettuce leaves, and a few spoonfuls of mayonnaise and mustard set out. Coffee was dripping from a triangular funnel into a glass beaker.

"This is what makes Florida famous." With that, she opened the small refrigerator and withdrew a glass container filled with orange juice. "Squeezed just for you."

She poured Skylar a small sample. He tasted it, then drained the glass.

"More?" she asked.

He nodded and she refilled the glass, almost before he had finished swallowing. He licked his lips in appreciation.

Iris began preparing her own sandwich, gesturing for Skylar to do the same. "When I was a kid I thought the only people who had all their orange juice squeezed fresh every day were millionaires." She laughed softly at the thought. "I'll show you how to do this tomorrow. I always keep fresh oranges here."

She ate in silence, while he devoured his sandwich. Iris motioned for him to make another. He carefully prepared exactly one side of a sandwich and then folded it in half, doubling its contents. By the time he got to the bottom of the orange juice he was completely satisfied. He rose with his dishes to put them on the counter.

"Thank you, Skylar." She joined him at the sink, showing him where the silverware and glasses and trash were located. "Let me show you the rest of the house," she added, moving into the living room. Skylar followed her.

Skylar liked the fact that Iris didn't try to make him talk. He also liked what he saw. Everything looked like it could be touched, studied or used. Small shells, bits of glass, ornaments, and oddities sat on the middle of the window ledge, glistening and projecting light onto the ceiling.

He heard Iris's voice. "You can use anything you like here in the living room, Skylar. Be careful with anything that would break. The shells and crystals are very fragile—when you pick them up, take special care. They're very important to me." The look on her face told Skylar these were Iris's "treasures," just as the belongings he kept in his green tackle box were his. She smiled and rested a hand on his shoulder. "I hope you'll be very comfortable here."

Iris walked over to stand next to the wall on one side of the room. "Look, Skylar, you might find this interesting," she said, as she pointed to an acrylic painting in a rough-hewn wood frame. "This is one of the five or six paintings your Grandpa Carl did about fifteen years ago. He had talent, but didn't find much time for art. He did this when he was laid up for a couple of months with a broken hip. Grandpa fell off the old barn roof when he was installing a solar collector he had built."

"I know where that is," Skylar said, pointing to the gentle pastoral landscape. "That's on the back part of the farm."

Iris smiled. "You're right, Skylar. It's down by the creek where your Mom and I used to swim and find salamanders under the rocks. Did you used to play there, too?"

"Yeah," he choked, thinking about summer afternoons on the farm with Grandpa and Spock. For several minutes they stood looking at the painting.

After Iris left the room, Skylar wandered back to the living room and settled himself into a comfortable wing-back chair in the corner nearest the neat but tightly packed bookshelves. He looked across the room at the painting his grandfather had done.

Then he rose and went to his room, returning with his colored pencils and sketchbook. He positioned himself to draw, and began to lay out the lines for his own landscape, a bit more fantastical, with a cluster of domed buildings. They seemed to be inspired by soap bubbles within soap bubbles. Flying vehicles soon appeared over the tops of trees and spires, domes and towers. He drew a gateway to the cityscape, then yawned. The day had taken its toll.

Skylar sat looking at his drawing as the sky deepened in color from soft gray to dark purple. He shifted position, putting on an imaginary flight suit and adjusting a life-support backpack, then settled back in the chair and entered his landscape. He must have fallen asleep, because the next thing he knew, he felt a gentle hand on his arm and heard Iris's soft voice.

"It's nine o'clock," she said. "Looks like you're about done in. Ready to go to bed?" Skylar nodded, gathering his drawing materials. Iris hugged him goodnight and he shuffled off to his room.

Once inside with the door closed, Skylar peeled off his clothes, crawled between the cool sheets and withdrew Sandy from under the pillows. Turning to face the wall, the two of them quickly dropped into deep sleep. The stars would have to wait until tomorrow.

His first awareness was of the sound, a whispery roar that repeated itself, over and over. Then a brightness projected past his closed eyelids, quite different from the usual tone of his room. As he rolled over, his toes bumped into a cold wooden wall. Skylar forced his eyes open to see what this was. It was white—all white. This was not his room at all. This was not Texas....or Grandpa's. His vision cleared and he noticed lines and corners now, saw his clothes near the bottom of this bed. *Oh yeah, this is Aunt Iris's house. And I'm staying here. It's cold.* He rearranged the knotted sheets and cotton blankets, pulled the pillows back to the top of the bed and located Sandy, who'd been tossed on top of the blanket while he was getting organized. He settled back down, covers pulled up to his chin and fitted close, all the way to his ears. Sandy was resting on his chest. *Florida. I'll need sunglasses to wake up in, I think.*

He used all his senses to orient himself. Ears: no coffee grinder or television, just screaming birds, water noises, big, washing something. Nose: kitchen is going, something's baking. Cinnamon toast? Eyes: must be late, everything's sunny, everything's where I put it yesterday. Mouth: tastes dry and cinnamony in here. Dust too. He sneezed. *Gotta get up.* Feet swung from under the covers directly to the slippers, the result of lots of practice. The covers were thrown off with a single left arm swing. Sandy was stored back under the pillows. Skylar slid his feet across the floor, pulled open his door and walked quickly to the bathroom to wash his face. Now awake, he returned to find his toothbrush, made a second trip to the bathroom and went to find Iris. His nose led him to the kitchen.

"Good morning, Skylar. Breakfast? Orange juice is at your place already." Iris smiled and turned to open the oven door. He was washed in the powerful aroma of cinnamon raisin rolls. "I bet you'll like these," she said as she separated them one from another. She put two huge homemade cinnamon rolls in front of him. He could see the raisins bulging out of the folds in the top.

"Let them cool a minute," she cautioned. He watched their cinnamon juice and icing slowly mix together and drip down the sides. Seconds later Iris was laying a plate with scrambled eggs, link sausage and sliced cherry tomatoes in front of him. She moved salt and pepper to his half of the table, then fixed herself the same, heaping salsa on her scrambled eggs while Skylar observed, eyes wide.

"Salsa—tomatoes, green and red chiles, spices. Want to try it?"

"Uh-uh. This is fine. What time is it?"

"It's not quite eight in the morning, Skylar. Did you rest well?"

"Okay."

Skylar finally put together what had been on his mind since yesterday. Iris had a voice a lot like Mother's. But where Mother always told more of an answer than the question deserved, Iris used only the most necessary words.

"After we're finished, we can go to the beach."

"The beach?"

She nodded. "Oh, and wear your sneakers—the sand gets hot. Better put on some sunscreen. You'll find it in your bathroom cabinet."

"Um-hmm," he replied, in between swallows of cold, sweet orange juice.

Iris was picking up her dishes. She excused herself, left the dining room and was skimming the newspaper when Skylar appeared in the living room properly dressed and basted with sunscreen. She handed him the ancient canvas hat and a pair of sunglasses. They both headed out the door, down the steps and across the scraggly grass area to the expanse of brilliant white sand.

Iris, in a visor and massive dark sunglasses, knew where she was going. Skylar moved as quickly as he could, doing his best to stay atop the sand, yet burying his feet with every step. It got to be a game between sand and feet. So far feet were losing, bad. Birds were hanging around, suspended in mid-air, it seemed to him, and yelling at them both about something.

Iris laughed and called to them. "Good morning, everybody!" With that, she reached into a net bag and threw bread chunks as far as the wind would allow. "Those are seagulls and terns—they know where the handouts are. Noisy, aren't they? They love to come steal from picnickers, too." Iris's tone told Skylar that she loved these birds, and that all her accusations were meaningless.

Skylar was dumbstruck when he saw the water up close. He stopped abruptly and looked at what was the largest anything he had ever seen. The gray-green water of the Gulf reached from the sand to the sky. At the sand's edge, it frothed and danced and swirled into creamy bubbles that stayed behind when the water washed back out. Grasses and seaweeds and various unidentifiable things got pushed up or pulled out from the sand with each sweep of the water.

This constant washing up and back took place the entire length of the beach, as far as he could tell. Far off, a few boats bobbed on the water's surface. Billowy clouds reached down to where the water disappeared into the edge of the sky. He noticed the wind was blowing at him, making him squint his eyes. He turned to where Iris was standing, watching him look at the water.

"Can I get in?"

Iris nodded. "Of course you can! Just don't go out too far."

He walked down the dune, noticing that the sand hardened as he got closer to the water. He stopped abruptly to study his footprints as he got close to the water's edge. The water first oozed out then quickly recovered its territory within the confines of each footstep. As he moved into the slushy area, the footprints themselves disappeared almost instantly.

"No one would know we were here, would they?"

Iris shook her head. "Just the birds. And no one believes them, anyway."

He high-stepped through the water's edge, splashing salt, sand and water well past his knees. Tentative at first, the explorer moved slightly faster with each step and then began an easy trot. Careful feet transformed into pounding ones.

Skylar ran down the beach, tracking Z's in the edge of the surf. He was completely involved in the feel of the water's tension against his ankles, the height of the splash, the sand's resistance and tug at each footstep. He was a scientist making a profound discovery, a joyful entrance into new territory. Skylar's former world of drizzling gray skies, Montgomery Ward and Chevrolets had suddenly exploded into eye-squinting sunlight, cool, frothy seawater that stuck to the skin—a world that would make the farmlands of Iowa and highways of Texas forever mundane. He lost himself in exploration, unaware of the passage of time.

"Skylar!" He heard his name being called. It sounded just like Mom calling him in for dinner back home. He came to an abrupt halt and turned back reluctantly. His head was sunk into his shoulders as he slowly walked back down the beach toward Iris.

"I hate to do this, but it's time to go," she said when he reached her. "I have to go over to the restaurant."

Skylar didn't want to leave, but as Iris headed up the shoreline back to the house, he followed, breaking into a trot to catch up.

"Lots of stuff on the beach," he said.

"What do you mean?"

"Four different kinds of birds. And it looks like the waves bring all kinds of stuff in. I found this."

Iris looked down to the nine-year-old's hand. Skylar carefully unfolded his water-wrinkled fingers.

"That's a small sand dollar," she explained. "Like the name of my restaurant. They're little creatures carried by the tides. When they get washed up past the surf line, they dry out. People collect them. The bigger ones have gotten harder and harder to find, so they're real special. If you like, we'll go beach-combing tomorrow. You can tell a lot about the ocean by the evidence it leaves on the shore. It's a new adventure every day. Would you like to do this again tomorrow?"

"Uh-huh," Skylar replied, as he moved ahead of Iris, back to the house.

When they arrived, Iris sat on the bottom step and said, "You'd better take off your shoes before you go into the house."

As she pulled off her own shoes, she held one out for him to see. Black, gummy lumps encrusted with sand dotted the sole.

"This is beach tar," Iris explained, as she reached for the can of solvent she kept under the stairs. "This'll take it off." She wiped the sole with a used, blackened rag.

"I keep these shoes just for the beach, but I still have to clean them. Otherwise, they'd be a mess. Let's see yours."

Skylar pulled off his own shoes and looked at them. "I didn't even see any tar on the beach," he said.

"It's mixed in with the sand so you can't see it." She handed him the rag.

As Skylar rubbed his shoe, he asked, "Where does it come from?"

"There are oil wells in the Gulf, and big tankers that come in to pick up the oil. Sometimes they spill some, and it winds up on the beach. When I first moved here, it wasn't such a problem. But now it seems to be everywhere."

"Someone should tell them to stop," said Skylar firmly while he scrubbed at the tar on his shoe.

"You're right," she agreed. "All done? Let's go inside and get cleaned up. I'll take you over to see where I work."

They rinsed the sand off their feet and legs with the garden hose at the bottom of the stairs, then went into the house.

CHAPTER TEN

I ris stood in the middle of the bar. She studied the room, scanning for anything that might have been over-looked after the lunch crowd. Her eyes rested on the dolphin sculpture. Walking over, she ran her hand gently over the glossy, polished finish of the silvery-stained wood.

Her fingers accurately anticipated each subtle curve. She loved its coolness, and allowed her sense of touch to fill her mind with memories of Dear One and their times together. A smile crossed her face as she thought of all the love that had gone into making this beautiful piece. Truly, Jaid had captured the essence of her friend. Whenever she touched it she could actually feel Dear One's presence. "Thank you, Jaid," she whispered as she caressed the dorsal fin, then walked behind the bar. Turning on the radio, Iris lowered the volume and located WBEA, her favorite classical station. Rich, melodious sounds echoed through the empty bar.

"That's nice," she murmured. "Three-eleven. Time enough to enjoy this for a little longer." As a rule the regulars started arriving around four. First the fishermen, stopping for a drink after a long day on their boats. Some stayed on for dinner, while others had a couple of drinks and headed home for their supper. The dinner crowd began to arrive about five-thirty, and by nine the last stragglers were served. The only exception to this was on Thursdays, when she introduced her newest special. Then the dinner crowd would start coming through the door before five, knowing from experience the latest gourmet treat would be in great demand. If Jaid was running late, Iris always saved a plate for her.

Comfortably involved with her thoughts, she moved through the preparations for the evening shift in time with the music, waiting for the name of the piece to surface in her mind.

The musky scent of Cinnabar filled her nostrils, and a crescendo of jangling bracelets overshadowed the music on the radio. "Welcome home, Jaid," she said with a twinkle in her eye, turning to watch her friend ease onto one of the bar seats.

Jaid shook her head and smiled. "How wonderful it is to be back," she said. "I missed you and, of course, your specials. I kept telling everyone I had to be home by Thursday, but alas, it wasn't to be."

Iris laughed. "Was your trip to New York successful?" She handed Jaid a Guinness Stout and a glass.

"Thanks." Jaid poured the drink into the glass, then took a long sip. "The best part for me is getting back home, but yes, it was very successful. After meeting with what seemed like the entire staff at the bank, I decided to do the piece for their seventy-fifth anniversary." She took another sip. "My, that's good. They served champagne and fancy wine but no Guinness Stout." Setting the glass down, she turned her attention to her friend. "You know, Iris, I do believe some of those employees have worked at Scarsdale Bank and Trust since Day One—they weren't at all stuffy, just dear. They acted as though the mural I'm doing for them is as important as the new building they'll hang it in." She fluttered her ringed hand against her breastbone. "They are so excited about it all! And the enthusiasm they generate is so contagious I have to bite my tongue to keep from doing it gratis." She winked at Iris, who laughed. "It was a fabulous trip." She took a long draw from her beer.

"And how are you? What about Skylar—is he here?" She half turned, glancing around the bar.

"I'm fine and yes, he's here. At this very moment, though, he's gone with Elmore to pick up a few things."

"I do want to see him. I haven't even been home yet to check on Miss Natasha. Why, if she had any idea I'd stopped here first...." Jaid threw up her hands and tossed back her head, rolling her eyes in mock horror. Iris laughed.

"I'm flattered. Hungry?"

"Maybe I'd better wait. They actually fed us a decent meal on the plane." She shook her head. "I forced myself to eat it, but all I've thought about today was getting home and having some of your wonderful delicacies." She peered around the room. "You here by yourself?"

"For now. Charlene called in sick."

Jaid grinned. "Maybe I should don an apron and wait tables."

"Thanks, but Elmore's youngest daughter, Jeannie, is coming to tend bar, and the regular dinner staff will be here." Iris laughed, "That's a great mental picture, though."

They laughed together. "So, tell me about Skylar." Jaid shifted her position on the stool and looked at Iris. Iris completed the liquor inventory and turned toward her friend.

"Where would I even begin? It seems as though he's been through a lot. You'll like him. He's constantly drawing—not doodles, but real drawings. I think he's talented."

Jaid smiled. "Well, I hope he's decided to join our class next week. There'll be all age groups and levels of ability. He'll be right at home."

"Yes, he told me he'd like to be there," Iris nodded. "Oh, and he's curious about my crystal cluster. I told him you would love to explain it to him."

"You know I'll enjoy that!" Jaid exclaimed.

Iris continued. "He discovered my shell collection. The truth is, Jaid, I've really enjoyed telling him about them. It reminds me…"

Jaid cocked her head, waiting for Iris to finish her thought. "Of what?" she asked gently.

"Mrs. Mitchell."

"Oh, yes. Your childhood friend," Jaid said. She paused and involved herself with her beer until Iris finished her thought. "By the way, you look wonderful. I can tell you're really enjoying his visit. It's hard to believe I haven't met him. Well, at least I'll be with him next week." She shook her head, moving to gather herself to depart. "If I don't get a move on, I'll be right here all evening." With a swish and a jangle she was gone.

Sounds of activity came from the kitchen, announcing the return of Elmore and Skylar. As Iris looked up, Skylar came barreling in through the service door, his face red from the heat, blond hair plastered to his head. He looked up at Iris. His eyes were as big as saucers, and a huge grin covered his face. It was one of the first smiles Iris had seen since he had arrived. *Elmore's influence*, she thought.

"Gee, Aunt Iris, you should've come with us. Elmore knows the neatest places. There was…" He stopped short, putting a hand to his mouth. "Lots of grocery stores."

She reached over and combed his wet hair with her fingers. "Uh-huh, looks like it was hard work. How about a drink?" Skylar nodded enthusiastically. "Make yourself comfortable on one of the stools." Skylar ambled around and sat.

"What'll it be, pardner?" she asked, executing a grotesque Texas twang.

"I'll have a…" he said with a sly look, "a longneck Lonestar."

"Comin' up. Will that be chocolate, homogenized or pasteurized?"

"Mm-m-m, I'll take chocolate."

After pouring the milk, Iris stood back and watched him. In the short time he had been here he had begun to unwind, to lower his defenses little by little. He still wasn't talking much, but his tense jaw muscles were more relaxed. Shoulders which had been held tight and forward had slipped back to the normal gangly movements of a nine-year-old boy. He was even making more slurping noises than he had dared to just seven days ago.

"My friend Jaid came in earlier to meet you." He looked up from his glass. "She just got back from New York."

Skylar blew through the straw, forming a tiny mountain of bubbles at the bottom of his empty glass.

"She's looking forward to having you in her art class next week."

His mission accomplished, he set his glass down, tipped his head to one side and looked at Iris. "Is she the one who made the dolphin?" He turned toward the sculpture.

"Yes. She's the one."

He slid off the barstool and walked over next to it.

Iris joined him. "See the nick in the fin here?" She pointed at the dorsal fin. "It's Dear One, the dolphin I told you about." She stroked the dolphin's beak.

"Does she let you touch her like that?" Skylar asked.

"Sometimes," Iris smiled.

Skylar's eyes were full of wonder. "How long have you known her?"

"You remember when I came to your house for Thanksgiving?"

"Yeah, I was just a kid then."

"Well, I had just met her a couple of months before that."

He continued to study the sculpture as he plopped onto one of the bar stools.

Iris returned to the bar, glanced at her watch, and realized the afternoon lull was about to end as the regulars started coming in for a beer and conversation on the way home from work. A silent observer, Iris joined in the conversation only when pressed, but she paid attention to what went on. The customers appreciated her quiet way and knew she could be counted on to lend a confidential ear when required.

Today, the first to arrive was Hank Taylor. He had a shop on Highway 93 that sold lawn mowers, boat engines, chain saws and mini-tractors. He was also a handyman who could fix just about anything. Since he'd rescued so many tools and mowers long overdue for the dump, saving his customers money, he was a popular man among the Bryson Beach residents. He was quiet, gentle and competent. Iris admired him.

"How's it goin', Iris?" Hank asked, slipping onto a well-worn seat.

"Just fine, Hank. Everything okay with you?"

"No complaints. Guess I'll have the same ole' thing." Iris was already placing a frosty mug of beer before him, completing their daily ritual. As Hank began to sip his beer, Red Calhoun lumbered in. A big brawny man with rough, ruddy skin, baked by hours in the hot sun, he gave off the odor of fish, sweat and tobacco. Iris assumed he'd gotten the nickname Red because his hair, now a yellowish gray with just a few faint steaks of red, had once been brilliant carrot orange. Loud, boisterous and opinionated, Red could spend an entire evening arguing a point on one of his many favorite topics.

Iris poured Red's beer and set it in front of him, wondering what this mismatched pair would discuss today.

Red opened the conversation. "What do you make of this weather, Hank? Kinda makes you think something's going on, don't it?"

"If we don't get some rain soon, a lot of my customers'll be going belly up," Hank said, nodding as he spoke. "They say it may not get any better."

"We don't need any more problems. Hell, man, fishing's been bad enough as is it. It's like there's something out there killing 'em." Red snorted and asked for another beer.

Iris turned to another customer, but she caught snatches of their ongoing conversation as they argued back and forth about bad weather and water. It kept reverberating in her mind. She shook her head and moved on to another customer.

"Whoo-whee, it's a scorcher out there today, ain't it?" the sweltering fisherman commented to the restaurant at large as he came into the bar. He eased his bulky frame onto a stool. "They say this hot spell's gonna last!"

Iris agreed with a nod as she wiped the counter.

"How 'bout a beer and a sandwich, Iris?" He turned to see several more fisherman walk into the cool restaurant and sit at the table behind him.

"How's it going?" he asked.

"Not so good," Ralph, the oldest one, replied. "Can't even catch a cold."

Ed, one of his companions joined in, "It's not paying

for the gas to get out these days." The fishermen com-plained good-naturedly among themselves for a while, trading insults and comments on the declining catches all were experiencing.

"Well, how 'bout this feller here?" Ralph asked as yet another fisherman walked into the restaurant. "Hey, Slim, c'mon over and tell us one of your lies." The lean, tall man with a weathered face and thin, limp, shoulder-length hair strolled over and languidly sat down.

He looked around at the expectant friendly faces of his companions and shook his head sadly. "You know, fellers, I've been putting out my nets here in these waters since my daddy taught me, back in the fifties. I've caught my share of just about everything, shrimp, crabs, mullet, even some sea bass and a grouper or two... heck, we all got by, didn't we? Dang if I'm making it these days... humph, it's a good thing that ole boat of mine is big enough to sleep on—I reckon it's a blessing I get along so good with my ocean critters," he said with a broad wink.

"Ocean critters?" questioned Ralph, "What guy who makes his living out there—or tries to, anyhow—makes friends with the fish?" Sensing a story in the making, the other fishermen began to elbow one another in the ribs.

"Oh, yeah," Ed added, "Slim here has had several experiences in the Gulf with fishy friends. Tell us about it, Slim." Signaling for a beer, Slim settled back expansively and looked into the expectant faces.

"Well, it was one of those days when the fishing was tolerable. I'd been out all day and had filled the hold with mullet, by myself, you know. I was ready to fire up and head back when my motor just burned itself out. Ah, she'd been on the fritz for a while, but I thought she'd be good enough for another coupla months. Well, sir, she was deader'n four o'clock... and I couldn't raise nobody on the poor excuse for a radio I had back then. So I was just sittin' there… all that money in my hold getting older by the minute… when I had this here idea."

By this time all of the occupants of the bar had quieted and turned their attention to Slim. Iris paused and stood still, waiting expectantly for Slim to continue, and even Red had quieted his ranting to listen.

"You know those stingrays that like comin' around when we clean our catch? Well, sir, just about the time I was kinda gettin' down, I saw this big ray—I'm talking big here—I'd say over fifteen feet from tip to tip—down below, a dark shadow right under the boat. I got me one of my trolling lines baited and put it just a little out from the bow. 'Ray,' I said, 'these are desperate times. You help me get back to shore, and I'll give you the best galdurned dinner you ever ate.' "

By now the circle of fishermen had begun to smile and lean forward, anticipating an unlikely end to the story. "Well sir, that big ole ray, he just up and took my bait and jumped up out of the water," Slim said, illustrating with a big smack against his knee, "and wouldn't you just know it? He started flapping those big wings of his and up he went, just like a big kite with a long tail—picking up the wind and pulling my boat along by the line as we moved inland. Every once in a while he'd swoop down to the water and get wet again, but in we came. Shucks, I went down and brought up two of the best mullet I could find and skinned 'em for him. I even cut those fish up for him. It was the least I could do."

The fishermen laughed and Iris smiled quietly to herself. As she walked into the kitchen, the delectable aroma of garlic and oregano surrounded her. Elmore looked up, wiping his hands on the oversized apron. "It's ready, and it's good," he grinned. Iris took a spoon and tasted the authentic Portuguese paella. She nodded approvingly as she helped herself to a second sample.

Returning to the foyer, she saw that Skylar had returned to the sculpture and was walking slowly around it, letting his hand trail over its smooth surface.

People drifted in and noise swelled in the restaurant. Iris returned to her duties, smoothly filling bar orders and handling the cash register. She had a perfect vantage point from which to marvel at Skylar's total absorption with the sculpture. She was almost disappointed when Jeannie came over to relieve her at the bar.

"Skylar, I hate to disturb you," Iris said as she approached him, "but it's your dinner time." Mesmerized, he turned to her with a blank look. Reaching across the dolphin, she pushed Skylar's unruly hair out of his eyes. With her touch he became aware of his surroundings.

"Dinner time," she repeated gently.

"Could I have a sandwich?"

"Let's go into the dining room."

He hesitated. "Okay," he shrugged, and turned to follow her into the small dining room. Iris seated him at the only two-person table near the door of the dining room and placed a glass of water in front of him. By the time he had settled in and arranged his napkin, she had returned with a serving of paella. On a small plate to his left she placed two slices of fresh homemade bread, still warm and yeasty.

"Your sandwich, sir," she announced with mock seriousness. "We call it the 'bread and butter house special.'" She lifted the top slice to reveal a slowly melting pad of butter sinking into the remaining slice. "Accompanied by paella." They enjoyed their meal together in an island of relaxed silence among the early dinner patrons.

When finished, Skylar retrieved his sketch pad and

pens from the pantry shelf where Elmore had stored them. He climbed onto his favorite bar stool and immediately lost himself in his drawings, glancing up occasionally at the sculpture.

Iris looked over at the young boy who, head over pad, hair hanging in his face, sketched away in total concentration. *Such intensity!* she thought. *The place could fall down around him and he would never notice.*

Around eight, as the main rush slowed to a trickle, Jaid appeared. Iris smiled a greeting and looked toward Skylar. Jaid followed her look and stood observing him for several minutes. She acknowledged Iris and proceeded to the dining room.

After her meal, Jaid came into the bar from the dining room. Her jewelry announced her arrival. The multitude of bracelets and bangles made her glint, dazzle and sing. Positioning herself in the center of the room, Jaid kissed her fingertips and tossed Iris a congratulatory "C'est si bon!" in her best throaty voice. Iris acknowledged her friend with a subtly raised eyebrow and a wink.

Iris saw Skylar, preoccupied with his paper and pencils, lift his gaze momentarily to the colorful woman dressed in royal purple, blue and red. Even though he looked in Jaid's direction, Iris noted Skylar's eyes were vacant, as if he were following the commotion around Jaid more than Jaid herself. Jaid must have noticed the same thing, because a moment later she exchanged greetings with several of her friends, then hefted her comfortable bulk onto a stool.

From her large, multicolored Guatemalan bag, she pulled a pad of paper and several colored pencils and began to draw. Iris suppressed a smile as she saw Skylar glance at Jaid discreetly, while Jaid herself kept her own eyes on the paper and studiously avoided direct eye contact with the boy.

After a few minutes, Jaid separated the top sheet from her pad and slipped it along the bar to Skylar's side, close enough to be tempting, but far enough away to give him the space to ignore it if he wished. Ignore it he did.

Jaid retrieved her paper and began altering it. Skylar gathered the salt shakers, pepper grinders, napkin holders and extra menus and carefully aligned them around his "work space." The only open space was directly in front of him, where he stacked the pens and pencils in order of size. He resumed his drawing, occasionally standing on the rungs of the bar stool to study the sculpture.

Jaid made her second presentation, moving the paper in his direction along with an extra salt shaker. Skylar paused, looked over her offering absently, took the salt shaker, and then made several marks before returning the paper to her without comment.

Jaid reviewed his additions, made several more of her own and passed it his way beneath a ketchup bottle. The third try was charmed. Skylar looked toward the paper, then put his pencil down and studied Jaid's piece carefully. He propped her paper up in front of him inside the wall of bottles and chrome-plated containers. Withdrawing pencils of several different colors, he detailed his reply, and moved the work back toward the woman who refused to surrender. As Jaid studied this response, Skylar cleared the obstructions from her side of the bar.

Jaid examined his drawing and nodded. She glanced at the sculpture, then gave Skylar another look of agreement. He accepted it with genuine seriousness and returned to his own drawing. Not a word was spoken between them.

A minute later, as Iris walked up, Jaid passed another piece of paper to Skylar, this one visible to Iris as he examined it. It was a sketch of the gallery with Jaid's studio above it. A sign hung over the gallery door with the words "Indigo Moon Gallery and Studio" printed on it. On the landing at the top of the stairs leading to the studio she had drawn a mat with the words "Welcome." On the stairs was a young boy, sketchpad and pens in hand. It was an invitation to her studio above the gallery on Forsythia Lane. As Skylar looked up, Iris said, "Skylar, this is my friend, Jaid." No further introduction was needed.

Later that night, as they walked into the house, Skylar headed for the big overstuffed chair and plopped down.

Iris stood near, looking down at him for several minutes, studying his motions, breathing patterns and position. She sensed he was so full of the day's happenings that he would need to unwind before going to sleep.

"Well, Skylar, you've had a long, busy day. First your shopping adventure with Elmore and all your discoveries…"

He sat up and began digging through his pockets. With a look of delight he held out his hands to her. "I found some great shells when we were down by the pier."

"Yes." She smiled. "You can tell all your friends about your treasures, when you get back to Texas."

He seemed to shrink visibly, responding only with, "Uh-huh."

Iris knew she had touched a sensitive spot. "Tell me about Texas, will you?"

Skylar stared out the window toward the dark beach.

"It's flat and hot and scratchy. Not like here."

"Scratchy?"

"Yeah. Here you can play or roll in the sand and it's fun. But there it hurts. The grass scratches you." Iris nodded in understanding. "It's not like home, either." Iris realized he was referring to Iowa. "We had snow for Christmas there. I could sled and skate and build snow forts and stuff. But it's all the same in Texas." He shook his head. "It never changes."

"How about your friends?"

He continued staring out the window, not answering. Not sure if he had heard her, she repeated the question. "Do you have any good friends in Texas?"

He shrugged. "Not really, not any more. Miss Taylor at school is okay, and Mr. Sanchez at the Ace Hardware gives me things that are broken. Sometimes I fix them or make them into my own machines."

She nodded. "Tell me about your little brother and sister."

"They're okay. Jennifer cries a lot. Jack Jr. is three years old, and he's a pest. He messes up my things, or loses them." He lowered his voice to confide in Iris. "I've even installed a 'Jack Jr. Alarm System' on my door. I made it out of parts from the Radio Shack."

"Are there any other kids in your neighborhood?"

"There's one girl who's bigger than me. She goes to junior high. And there are some babies about Jennifer's age. I had a friend at school but he lives too far away. I only get to see him when my mom can take me in the car."

"That's too bad. I guess you can't play together as often as you'd like."

Skylar leaned his head on the chair arm and draped his legs over the other arm, in a contorted position only a child could achieve or find comfortable. Several long moments passed before Skylar finally answered. "Uh-uh. Mom's pretty busy now." He closed his eyes and buried his head in the back of the chair.

Iris leaned over and rubbed his small back. "Well, I'm glad you're here." He peeked out at her.

"And Elmore's glad to have a helper. You two sure stayed gone a long time today. Were you shopping or exploring?"

A smile spread across Skylar's face as he sat up. "Both. We went to the market and the grocery and the pier." He added, in a whisper so low she could barely hear, "And the hardware store."

"Just as I thought," Iris said, feigning indignation. "The hardware store? What on the menu required the hardware store?"

He sucked in his lower lip as he thought, then he giggled. "That's where we got the noodles. They were with all the nifty rope."

Iris put one hand to her heart and the other to her forehead in a dramatic gesture of mock despair. "Oh, no, not rope noodles! My poor, unsuspecting customers. They'll never eat at the Sand Dollar again." From behind her hand she looked down at him. He saw her peeking, and soon they were both laughing.

Iris dropped her pose and stood smiling at him, wondering what Elmore had done to bring Skylar out of his shell. *I'm grateful, whatever it is*, she thought.

Slowly Skylar got up, looked at her with a shy smile and put his arms around her. She dropped down to her knees and encircled his small, wiry body with her arms. They hugged tightly. A smile spread over her face.

CHAPTER ELEVEN

Where is he? He ought to be coming along any minute now, Jaid thought, as she stood at the screen door of her studio atop the Indigo Moon Gallery, watching for a small figure to make its way down sandy Forsythia Lane from the main road. Skylar was due for a visit, and Jaid was eager to welcome her new friend to her home base, built on a twenty-four acre parcel facing a protected cove near the single road in and out of Bryson Beach.

Years ago, Jaid had discovered the original building which now housed the gallery and her studio. It was an airy, light, sturdily-built cotton warehouse built in the '20s, with high open spaces and seasoned heart pine floors. The building had been renovated to create a three thousand square foot, two-story structure, with the gallery below and studio above, connected by an outside stairway.

The Indigo Moon complex had evolved to include four covered work sheds for sculptors, a series of connected workshops for the artists and artisans who came to Bryson Beach for the opportunity to work with Jaid, four cottages used as artists' apartments, a lushly-appointed pen with a small wading pool for the incumbent Miss Natasha and her frequent litters of piglets, and a palm-roofed pavilion down at the water's edge, large enough for entertaining parties of up to a hundred people.

In the gallery itself the paintings, sculptures, weavings, ceramics and porcelains, photography and jewelry of the resident artists were displayed and sold. The entire top floor served as Jaid's studio and apartment, with a full open kitchen and king-sized platform bed at the far end, and a breezy screened porch facing the pavilion and cove at the other.

Jaid had minimal furnishings in the studio itself. There was a long sturdy pine table which served dual purpose as a work table and, with proper appointments, as a dining table. Occasionally, when Jaid reached an impasse in her work, she'd shift gears and cook for her family of artists and friends. She prepared wonderful aromatic Greek food to tantalize the taste buds and titillate the palate, reminiscent of her days as a young American bride in Mykonos.

When she saw Skylar coming, Jaid rushed down the steps and out into the yard to greet him. "Welcome," she said, with mock solemnity, and then, with a jangle of silver bracelets and her trademark laugh, she opened her arms to the wide-eyed nine-year-old. "I've been waiting for you!" Skylar responded with a shy grin and followed Jaid into the gallery. It smelled of dust and turpentine, oil, rust, wood, and canvas. The interior was brilliantly lit from the recessed lights and the midday sun flooding through the windows.

"This is a 'found objects' show, Skylar," explained Jaid as she began the tour. "What you'll be seeing will include mechanical, non-functional discards and discoveries used in new and exciting ways. I think you'll like what you see." Skylar had begun to move slowly from display to display, lost in his concentration as he examined pieces of jewelry and glass, weavings, drawings, and sculpture. The jewelry featured dolphins and other sea creatures in rich sea-colored enamels, or fashioned in pins and pendants of unusual green corroded metals rescued from the sea. Exploded watch parts combined with semi-precious gems in pins and earrings. Large, heavily textured weavings of rope, hemp, multicolored wools and metallics were suspended as room dividers for various pieces of sculpture standing on the floor or displayed on pedestals. Art glass pieces were featured in the windows. Incorporated within their leaded lines were bolts, nuts, pins and gears, gaskets, pulleys, fishing tackle and trap parts integrated into brilliantly colored pieces, completely unlike a traditional stained glass format.

Jaid was impressed with Skylar's careful, thoughtful inspection of the art. *This one could be special*, she thought, as she watched him examine intricate diagrammatic pencil drawings with connecting points of tension and lightly colored pencil tinting splashed with bold strokes of primary colors. Skylar got down on his hands and knees to examine free-standing sculptures that gently moved, and one that twittered like an early morning bird.

He seemed particularly fascinated with a sculpture built with bicycle handlebars, sprockets and chains that clicked gently as they moved some irregularly shaped gears and wheels through a series of levels, dropping them into a green reflecting pool with a plop and then picking them out of the water to travel the chain ride once again, clicking their way slowly along.

"I'd like to meet the kid who built this." Skylar turned to Jaid, speaking for the first time since they'd entered the gallery.

Jaid smiled and nodded. "Skylar, the 'kid' who constructed this is thirty-seven years old, and you can meet him this weekend if you want."

"Thirty-seven?" he asked. "Gosh, that's OLD—that's even older than Jack—that's my stepfather," Skylar's words were rushed together, "but maybe we could play together sometime when he gets off work."

Noting the admiration in Skylar's eyes and his obvious sincerity, Jaid gently replied, "Skylar, this is his work… this artist is becoming quite well known for his kinetic sculpture. That means moving parts, you see."

"You mean he makes money doing this?" Skylar asked.

"Absolutely."

Skylar shook his head slowly and looked up at Jaid. "He gets paid to have fun?"

Jaid laughed. "Exactly. The best kind of job to have. Tell you what. I want to take you upstairs to the studio for a tour. I've got some special chocolate chip cookies for us. You continue looking around, and I'll be right back." She left him standing near a permanent exhibit near the stairway door at the back of the gallery.

When Jaid returned, she found Skylar intently engrossed with a painting in the center of a series of canvasses that looked almost sculptural, with thick, glistening layers of brilliant oils, as if the paint itself captured the light and illuminated the paintings. He appeared entranced with a vertical canvas in which a rich forest green supported spire-like granite-colored and textured planes above which rose a brightly lit crystal city against a dark night sky. Beacons of light connected the city above to random sparks of light below.

Standing silently before the painting, Skylar lifted his hands and, careful to avoid its surface, traced the shape of the granite-like spires as far as he could reach. He opened and closed his hands as if throwing the sparks of light to the top of the spires. Jaid came to stand motionless behind him as he dramatized the painting. After a long silence, Skylar half-turned to her, his eyes full of questions.

"That's one of my paintings, Skylar," Jaid nodded. "It's called 'City of the Dreamers.' "

Skylar turned back to the canvas and softly repeated the name. As he stood captivated, Jaid gently rested her hands on the young boy's shoulders.

"Where is this, Jaid?" he whispered to her finally. "Is this City of the Dreamers far away?"

Jaid gave him an affectionate squeeze. "Oh, not so far. Sometime soon we'll set aside some time and I'll tell you all about it."

Skylar became a daily visitor at the Indigo Moon complex. First he'd stop by Miss Natasha's pen, rousing her from her nap to offer a tidbit and scratch her ears, rewarded by staccato grunts of appreciation. Then he would walk by the work sheds, occasionally stopping to watch works in progress. The resident artists greeted him with enthusiasm, enjoying the intense concentration and obvious delight the boy shared in their art as he would ask intelligent questions yet remain as unobtrusive as possible. Finally, he would make a winding tour of the gallery itself, stopping to examine new and familiar pieces, always pausing in front of Jaid's Dreamer Series paintings before climbing the stairs to her studio.

If Jaid was involved in her work, Skylar would usually paint or sketch quietly until she was ready for conversation. The two of them would talk about their favorite topics: art and the beach. Skylar sometimes asked for a story, and Jaid complied with a dramatic rendition of fictional or personal experiences.

"I declare, Skylar, I bet you've got the details of the Dreamer Series memorized by now. It's really quite flattering, and I'm not at all surprised that 'City of the Dreamers' speaks to you so," she said one day as they shared their daily ritual of juice and cookies on the screened porch, swinging in the bleached oak bench which hung from the ceiling rafters.

"You know, I promised to tell you a story of the City. So what do you say that today we take our shoes off, get comfortable and go back to a time long ago and far away?" Jaid looked down with affection at Skylar, whose eyes followed her every move as she reached into her skirt pocket to withdraw an object. Turning toward her on the bench, he hastily pushed his shoes off without bothering to unlace them.

"What's that?" he asked, scooching to find a comfortable position.

"It's a special crystal that was given to me by a very dear friend as he told me the story of the magical land of Lemuria."

Skylar moved close to Jaid's open palm and studied the crystal from several angles. "Why is it special?" he asked seriously.

"Because it holds the story of Lemuria."

With his two hands, Skylar took Jaid's hand and carefully lifted it so he could see sunlight glance off the facets. "Where? Where's the story?" he asked with a smile that told her at once he believed her and he didn't believe her.

Delighted, she knew now he would require an answer, no matter how long it might take them. Not one ever to miss such an opportunity, she took a long moment to gather her thoughts, heightening his anticipation.

"Ever use computers at school?" she continued.

He nodded immediately. "For English, math, too. And in the library…"

Jaid saw him wondering where she was going with this question. "Well, every computer has…"

"Crystals inside them!" Skylar interjected, forgetting his manners.

Jaid laughed and nodded her affirmation. "They're called computer chips and they hold information just like this one."

"Can I hold the crystal?"

"Sure."

As Skylar snuggled into the soft warmth of Jaid's ample body, the crystal clasped in his hand, his mouth opened in a wide yawn. He was becoming familiar with the feelings of safety that came with being close to Jaid. She was like a fortress, protecting him in a world he was still not sure of. As he relaxed his small wiry body, his mind opened to the imagination she always nurtured in him.

"Once upon a time," Jaid began, as she wrapped an arm around Skylar, "there was an ancient magical land. It existed so many thousands of years ago that most people can't even imagine it today. There are those people, though, who hold it as a seed in their hearts. Those who hold the seed can rediscover it through their love.

"In this land, no farther away than your own dreams, dwelled a people who lived in great harmony with themselves and nature." The corners of Jaid's mouth turned upward into a smile as she recognized Skylar's youthful innocence, so like that of those in the ancient civilization she had begun to describe. She continued. "Many thousands of years ago, this magic land of Lemuria was hidden by thick gray clouds. Black mountaintops jutted through the mists. From above the clouds everything looked black and white. But beneath the clouds was a great surprise — the earth was ablaze with light. The sun, instead of living only in the sky as it does now, also seemed to dwell within the earth, its bright rays shining through grass, and flowers, and trees. Since the earth itself was a source of light, the colors were more vibrant than you could even imagine today. Everything that grew on the earth seemed to glow from within. The landscape was lush and awesomely beautiful. Plants and trees swayed in the light that danced from their leaves. The flowers were so bright, with their deep tones of blue, red, purple, yellow and green, that they seemed to have been freshly painted each morning by the light fairies.

"In this bright and beautiful land, people lived in small villages. Clusters of about twenty families would live together in thatched-roof houses. Some were built on stilts, some leaned against steep hills, depending on the terrain where they were located in the outer regions of this huge land mass surrounded by water. Few people, however, lived in the interior. This was because the interior was thick and lush with tropical plants. Imagine it, Skylar, some of the plants were five or six times as tall as you and maybe four times as big around. The flowers that grew from the vines and trees were also huge. A single flower would seem like a whole bunch of flowers, glowing from within like a brilliant light. The trees were bigger and taller than we can even imagine."

Skylar said, "I've never seen any plants and trees that big, or flowers that bright."

"Nor have I. It must have been a sight to behold!

"As you can understand, it would have been very hard to traverse the forest, let alone live in it. Some people did, however, make their way deep into the interior. Those who did were awed by the most wondrous of sights. They discovered the true mystery of Lemuria. They came upon tall stone spires rising out of the jungle. The columns were so tall they looked like they could reach the heavens with just one more stretch.

"And guess what! On top of the stones were crystal cities—*cities partly made of ground-up crystal dust*. They sparkled throughout the land like huge beacons of light."

Skylar crossed and recrossed his legs. "Jaid, what were the cities of crystal like?"

"Well, there were different kinds of cities. Among them were cities of healing, teaching, scribing—that's recording knowledge—and dreaming."

Skylar asked, "Who went to the cities? How did they get there?"

"Boys and girls about your age, some younger, were called to the cities. They were called according to their special talent."

"How were they called?"

"There were many ways. Some were called through their dreams. Some just seemed to know of the cities, and would talk of them so much their families knew they had been called. Others would be told by those who came down the spires of stone in search of those who had heard the calling. Those who were chosen would travel for weeks, months, or even years over a range of mountains and through the thick, lush forest to the foot of the massive columns that supported the cities."

"Then what? Once they were there, how did they get to the top?"

"Well," Jaid said, clearing her throat, "they learned to teleport."

"TELEPORT? You mean like on Star Trek, when Captain Kirk says, 'Beam me up, Scottie.'?"

"Yes, and that's how people got to the crystal cities."

Skylar asked incredulously, "How did they do it?"

"They would sit at the base of the peaks, sometimes for several months, learning to change their energy from one form to another. They learned to imagine that they had become the earth. When they were one with the earth, they would travel up the stone to the city. Once there, they would then imagine that they were themselves again. Here's how it would look. You would see a burst of light as the person vanished. Then you would see another bright light at the top, and, *voila*, the person would reappear, just like Captain Kirk."

Skylar commented, as if to himself, "People really did teleport!"

Jaid responded laughingly, "People really did teleport. They became the earth, and then poof, they were at the top of the spires."

Skylar laughingly repeated, "Beam me up, Scottie." Then he asked, "Jaid, do you think if I had lived in Lemuria I would have been called to one of the cities?"

Jaid tenderly cupped Skylar's chin in her hand and replied, "I'm sure of it, Skylar." She silently mused that his calling would surely have been to the city of the dreamers.

"Jaid, what did the boys and girls do once they were in the cities?"

"They were taught by the teachers until they had mastered the skill that was their special calling. Then they would either stay and teach others, or they would teleport back down the spires to use their skills helping people. For example, the healers would travel around the countryside healing people. The dreamers would sometimes appear in villages or at festivals to dream people's dreams for them— but mostly they dwelled in secret places hidden deep in the forest, and they were very hard to find."

Skylar raised up, placing his palms on his knees, his face fixed on Jaid. "When Jack tells Mom I'm a dreamer, he makes it sound like there's something wrong with me."

Jaid patted Skylar tenderly on the shoulder and responded, "If you had been a dreamer in Lemuria, people would have searched high and low for you. They would have known you had a special gift."

Skylar leaned back against Jaid with a satisfied smile as he realized he could hop on his imagination and travel to a magic land where dreamers were not only wanted, but desired — a land where dreaming was valued.

With a knowing look in her eyes, Jaid said to Skylar, "Let's imagine you are in Lemuria and you are going on a journey to find the dreamer. You would start by searching far and wide. Maybe you would roam through the high snow-capped mountains of the Southwest, or along the meandering 's'-shaped rivers that ran through the shining bright corn and wheat fields of the Northwest. Perhaps your search would take you through the rolling hills that sloped down to the barrier reefs in the Southeast, or maybe you would climb among the lush tall pines and sequoias of the mountainous timber country of the Northeast.

"Whether your search took you through the natural terrain or into the small, clean villages of thatched-roof huts, you would never miss the opportunity to ask anyone you saw, 'Have you seen a dreamer? Can you help me find a dreamer?' Since all of the people were very friendly, they would usually smile, even though the reply was 'No.' But you could tell they were sorry they couldn't help. Once in a while, though, if you searched long enough, you would find someone, perhaps a very old man or woman, who could lead you in the right direction. They might take you part way and then tell you that you must complete the journey on your own.

"As you continued to search you might see streams in the distance that shone so brightly they looked like pure light, liquid light. A surge of excitement would well up in you because you were close. Once you approached the streams they would seem so magical you'd want to kneel down and splash your face with the sparkling water. Then, looking up from the stream, you might see a gazebo nestled in a clearing in the forest. Sitting in the gazebo would be the dreamer. It could be a man, or a woman, of any age or shape. But sometimes, they were very fat. Imagine it, Skylar. Right there in front of you would be the largest person you had ever seen. He would seem to have three or four stomachs and two or three chins. His eyes would be closed, and as his rolls of fat heaved up and down you would hear 'Hnh, hnh, hnh, zzzzzz...' coming out of his mouth.

"Although the dreamers were sometimes very funny-looking, they were the most magical of people, because if you asked them, they would dream your dreams for you and make them come true."

Skylar asked, looking up at Jaid, "Now that I have found the dreamer how do I get him to make my dreams come true?"

"Well, first you tell him your dream. Then the dreamer asks in a big booming voice, 'W-H-O-O-O m-a-k-e-s y-o-u-r d-r-e-e-a-m-s c-o-m-e t-r-u-u-e?'"

"What's the answer?"

"The answer is, I do."

"How can that be?" Skylar asked with a chuckle.

Jaid answered, "In Lemuria, what lived in your heart and mind was what you saw in front of you."

Eyes shining, Skylar asked, "Jaid, what do you mean?"

Jaid repositioned herself, thinking a moment, then looked out over the cove. "Have you ever wanted something so bad you could almost taste it?"

"Um, yeah, the microscope that Aunt Iris got me last weekend."

"Remember how you began to imagine all the experiments you could do?"

"Yeah."

"Then, when Aunt Iris saw you looking at it in the catalog, you just knew she would get it for you?"

"Yeah. Is that all there is to it?"

"No, there's a little more. It's important to choose what you want, and then to decide nothing else will do, as you did with the microscope. Then you started thinking about how much fun you would have with it. So your feelings of fun also helped you get it, as well as the fact that you really believed you could have it. And, my dear Skylar, that is the stuff of which dreams are made."

Skylar's eyes were wide, as if an electric charge had been applied to his thoughts.

"If they could make dreams come true, why did the Lemurians ask the dreamers to dream their dreams for them?" he asked.

"Once you knew you could dream your own dreams, and how to do it, you could ask for help. People who lived in Lemuria, both men and women, worked together doing what each could do best to make dreams come true."

"I wish my grandpa could have been in Lemuria. He could fix and heal just about anything. He fixed my spaceship, and he even healed Sandy's plastic eye when it fell off." *If only he had been there that night…*

Jaid continued, tenderly, "Your grandfather would have loved Lemuria. The oceans were so clean and beautiful that he would have rejoiced at the very sight of them. People thought of the oceans, streams, meadows and forests as a part of themselves. They loved the land so much that the timber cutters only cut the trees that were sick and ready to die. They never unnecessarily killed or hurt anything."

Slightly tilting his head as if sifting through potential questions, the curious adventurer turned to Jaid. "One more question."

"What is it, dear?"

"What happened to the Lemurians?"

"They decided that their work was done, and therefore it was time to leave. But before they left, they wanted to give a gift to the future. They were a very advanced civilization. Although they didn't have the technology that we do today, they didn't really need it. They could use their minds and hearts to create whatever they really wanted. They could focus their love to reach great depths of joy and creativity.

"The Lemurians wanted to share this knowledge with those who would come after them. They knew that at some future date this knowledge would be desperately needed. Since they understood that information could be packed in crystals, they stored all they knew in them. Then they scattered the crystals throughout the earth, to be discovered like little capsules of knowledge thousands of years later.

"After giving their gifts of wisdom and love to the whole earth, it was as if they said, 'Beam me up, Scottie,' then disappeared into the mists."

Skylar handed the crystal back to Jaid. Turning slowly, eyes wide, he said to Jaid, "I wish I could live in Lemuria."

"You can, Skylar. Imagine you're there, and always remember the dreamer's question: 'Who makes your dreams come true?'"

Skylar answered firmly, "I do."

Skylar leaped up the stairs to art class, tackle box swinging. The wood floorboards and porch rail glistened in the rain-rinsed morning light as he paused on the deck. Zheww-w-w-flap-flap-flaaapppp. He took note in his mental diary as his eye and ear were caught by the flash of a great blue heron lighting on the marsh grasses below.

As he swung through the screen door and into the huge white-washed studio, he counted six girls and four boys milling around.

He took a seat at the comfortably battered pine table and decided to get ready. Opening his tackle box, he unfolded the drawers and straightened the supplies inside.

"Hello there, Skylar!" Jaid called from the far end of the room. "We'll be introducing ourselves in just a minute."

Skylar, eyeing her brilliant tie-dyed dress, felt her warmth welcoming him.

His eye turned from Jaid to her immediate left where ribbons of color streamed through the large disc-shaped stained-glass window. A full spectrum of color fanned out from an opalescent pyramid design in the glass. It washed the wood floors, walls and ceiling in a rainbow of colored sunlight. *It's a rainbow and a pyramid gate we can pass through into outer space*, Skylar thought.

He carefully instructed his space team as they boarded the imaginary space-time converter for the voyage across the room. His tackle box became the control panel and Skylar was off into the launch procedure.

"Okay, crew. First we start at the red and fly up through to the purple then into the space gate of light," he whispered to the tackle box. "Remember to strap your projection gear carefully in place."

It was wonderful fun captaining the ship as it swept and dipped, first from the colors on the floor, then up and off the high white-washed ceiling rafters and over into another ray of colored light. The craft was moving smoothly along the last purple-colored ray leading toward the white light pyramid, where they would burst through into free space, when Jaid's voice startled him back to his seat.

"And this is Skylar. He's visiting here from Texas this summer. Skylar, will you tell the class a little about what Texas is like, or perhaps you could tell us what you brought with you in your box today?" Jaid asked with a flourish. She moved around to the back of Skylar's chair.

Everybody's been talking and I'm last and I can't get my voice to work, he thought hopelessly as he stood and turned his very private tackle drawers around to show everyone the pencils and his collection of some new-found shells, treasures from Grandfather and from home.

"Uh, I like to draw a lot," he half-whispered and sank back into the safety of his chair. A few of the girls smiled at him. The others were already looking beyond him to the studio display.

Jaid beamed and moved to lay out large poster boards, scissors, paste and stacks of magazines with lots of colorful photography.

"Today, we are going to begin by creating collages. Does anyone know the word 'collage'?"

The other kids' hands shot up as Skylar just looked at Jaid.

One of the girls explained that she had made a collage of pictures for her science class project and told how she'd cut out stuff that told a story and pasted it on the board. Then, Jaid showed how to cut out colors and make shapes in an abstract sort of way.

Neat! He thought, as he first cut, then tore out, colored shapes. *This paste is fun. I can make big lumps of it, make stuff like I do in the sand at the beach. Then I can put the colored pieces on top of it.* Skylar built up his board in three-dimensional blues and greens. It was like looking through the water to the bottom below and seeing an underwater station where his crew could land and live in a new life support environment. When he finished building up the layers, he started to carefully draw over it with details of the station. All the while, Jaid was watching and working with her own piece.

Skylar loved the big table, sitting with the kids like himself, tearing and working furiously with no concern for neatness or for what someone might say.

After Jaid stopped to pass out drinks and snacks, she walked around each child, most of whom were finished. She paused near Skylar. While the children were munching away, she stood for a moment, enraptured.

Skylar thought, *Oh, no. I'm not finished.* When that happened in school it meant trouble. But Jaid exclaimed, "Class, gather round and see what Skylar has done with his collage. Look at how he has crushed and crinkled the paper, built it up on the page with paste. He has torn some pieces, too! Very, very good…" She thought out loud as her voice trailed off, studying his work with fascination.

Skylar flushed red hot and sat poker-stiff in his chair, not daring to move. *It was fun a few minutes ago but now I want to get under this table.* Jaid seemed unaware of his embarrassment and continued making suggestions to his classmates.

She ended the class with a homework assignment: they were to think about dreaming before going to bed, then draw their dreams first thing when they woke up.

Skylar folded his tackle box and scooted out the door

while Jaid was preoccupied at the sink. He thought about the assignment as he scuffed through the sandy, sculpture-filled courtyard and out to the road.

Maybe that would be neat, but not so much fun if we have to turn it in, he thought.

Skylar stood and put the shell he'd been sketching back in its place on the shelf. He turned and looked at Iris, who was reading the newspaper. "Night, Aunt Iris."

She stood and hugged him. "Good-night, Skylar."

No sooner had he fluffed up the bed pillows in a fortress around and behind him and Sandy, than the wind started rattling the palm fronds outside the window. The sound became interstellar laser guns flying across miles of space in mere seconds. Soon he became one of the pellets and entered the rich blackness of outer space, the comfort of the night and his child world of dreams.

I'm an astronaut... I think. No, I'm not floating. I'm hanging up like a kite or my good shirt in the closet. Looking down at himself, Skylar saw a strange painted-on outfit. His feet were dangling. *This is a puppet outfit and I'm still in outer space, but we're slowly moving on a merry-go-round.*

He noticed he was turning on a circular overhead conveyor belt, suspended from strings along with his fellow space buddies. *We're puppets and my feet are very cold and very mad. I can't get off my hanger and I can't move my neck to see what I'm hanging from.* Eerie carousel music started playing in the background. *It's black and lonesome and I can't talk to my crew. We have been captured.* Skylar continued turning, staring straight out into space.

Then an eggshell-thin gray wall appeared to his right. *Here is my chance. I'll start swinging on my strings. Maybe I can kick through.* He started up the momentum by thinking himself in the direction of the wall. Then he kicked out, shattered the wall and broke through. *But, I'm not free. I'm still hanging and I'm twisted, twisted and knotted. I can't turn around. It gets tighter and tighter...*

Feverish, Skylar woke in a mound of covers. The sheets were hopelessly twisted and his mouth was open, throat dry. It was morning, but he was very tired and frightened. He lay there studying the rays of light playing across the ceiling. The sunlight cast a golden hue and Skylar gazed around the room as the furniture gradually came into focus. Then, remembering his homework assignment, he gathered Sandy under his arm and moved over to his desk.

He started to draw, but instead of using pencil, he outlined heavily in black crayon on the construction paper before him. What began as his usual, patient rendering of his private world, rich in intricacy, became an erratic page of black scribbling. Frightened and angry, he scribbled away furiously. He barely acknowledged Iris when she said, "Morning, Skylar."

Iris had just finished putting away the groceries when she heard the creaky board on the back deck, followed by Jaid's hearty voice.

"Hi, there."

Iris leaned over to the screen door and nudged it

open for Jaid. "Coffee?"

"Love some," Jaid said, and set her bag down on the kitchen table, reaching in, fumbling around for something. She pulled out a turnip, and said, "Let me just give this little tidbit to Miss Natty. I've been saving it for her."

Iris filled the coffee-maker with water, and turned as Jaid came back in.

"Have a seat. You seem preoccupied. You okay?"

"Oh, yes, yes. I'm fine, although you're so right." Jaid lowered her voice. "I really do have something on my mind. Is Skylar here?"

"No, he's gone down to the Sand Dollar to help Elmore prepare the crabs for the gumbo. Do you need him?"

"No, I really need to talk to you, but it's about Skylar. He did something unusual in class today, and frankly, I'm quite disturbed about it."

Iris got up to pour the coffee. "I think I might know what you're going to say."

Jaid shifted in her chair, leaning one elbow on the table, chin in hand. Iris could see her lips purse slightly.

"Good. Let me tell you what happened. I gave the children an assignment yesterday, one that, if I may say so, seemed especially exciting to them. Actually, to me, too. The idea just popped into my mind. I think it was inspired by Skylar, really. Anyway, they were to spend a few moments before falling asleep last night, thinking quietly to themselves, telling themselves that they would have wonderful dreams. Then, when they awoke in the morning, I asked them to remember their dreams and draw them, however they wanted, in any medium they chose. And you know, I was particularly interested in this assignment for Skylar. He's been telling me about his dreams, both sleeping ones and his 'daydreams'—quite wonderful they are. And powerful."

Iris said, "He told me a little about your story of Lemuria. He's been spending quite a bit of time sitting quietly, sometimes with that beautiful piece of quartz you gave him. He closes his eyes, but I can tell he's not sleeping."

"Yes. I think I've known since I first met him that he's a dreamer. A little different from what most people mean when they say that, of course. So, this morning, in class, the children had set the drawings out on the big table.

"Oh, Iris, their work was so exciting! Really, some wonderful images. I could see a new confidence in some of my old students. But when I asked Skylar which one was his, he shrugged, and said his wasn't there. I asked him why, and he just shrugged again. We just stood there for some moments, then, finally, he told me only that it was done. And that was all he would say. He just clammed up on me."

Iris sat quietly, eyes almost closed. She pulled her napkin through the napkin-ring and mused.

"I knew you had given him an assignment. He told me about it, and seemed very excited. He spent some time last night before going to sleep just sitting quietly. Then I saw him put his pad and crayons on the little table next to his bed.

"This morning I glanced in on him. I was curious about what his dream would look like, and I hoped he'd show me his picture before leaving for class. I saw him drawing, very intensely, working back and forth over the paper.

"When I passed by a little later, he seemed to be finished. He was putting some things away, and he had a drawing in his hand. He didn't show it to me, but I did catch a glimpse, a lot of short, black, heavy strokes."

"Do you know where it is now?"

"I think he has it with him."

"You said you saw lots of black. That concerns me."

Iris agreed with Jaid, but refrained from saying so. There was something in Jaid's tone that was setting off a little warning signal for Iris. She wondered what was happening between Skylar and Jaid.

Jaid almost echoed her thought. "I wonder what's going on with Skylar. I'm sure he knew I would want to show his work to the other students, and especially to the newspaper reporter who's coming in the morning. That reminds me, I've got to find Skylar and talk with him about that, too. I'm sure he's never done an interview before, and I'd like to give him a little coaching.

"You know, he's going to be my star student. I think we're good for each other's creativity! I can't imagine what might have gotten into him."

CHAPTER TWELVE

"Hey, anybody home? Zan, you here?" Alexander rose from his work and started toward the door.

"In the lab, Tom."

Tom sauntered into the room. "Jesus, Alexander. I love dedication but just once I'd like to catch you goofing off. This is the third time I've popped in here to find you like this, nose to the grindstone. Hell, man, you're still as pale as the day we arrived a month ago. You're really starting to worry me."

Muon responded with a loud "Mrow."

"Even Muon agrees."

"I'm all right, Tom," Alexander protested, giving the cat an annoyed glance.

"That's a joke. Look, as your business partner, it behooves me to protect my investment by making sure you don't burn out before you solve this riddle of the universe and make us both rich. As Chairman of the Board and, therefore, your boss, I order you to get out of this lab and onto the beach. Go for a swim. Go for a walk. Sunbathe. Do something fun."

"But Tom, I have a lot of work to do. There are so many permutations to the chemical components of the 'soup' that I can't afford to stop work."

"Look, Zan. All kidding aside. You can't keep this up. I'm serious. You're killing yourself. Your obsession with proving that Dr. Blankenship and all the others were wrong is eating you up."

"But..." Alexander started.

"No 'buts' to it," Tom interrupted. "I'm dead serious now. I won't stand by while you crucify yourself on the cross of scientific discovery just to make a goddamned point to a bunch of goddamned academics and a dead father."

Alexander looked up, startled.

"Yeah, that's right. I said it and you know it's true."

"Tom, you don't understand. Just like they don't understand," began Alexander.

"Hey, don't start in on me," Tom interrupted. "I understand a hell of a lot more than you ever wanted to give me credit for, and obviously more than you do on this particular subject. What do you think this is about, you working so hard like this? It can't be about deadlines, because I haven't given you any. It can't be about money, because I've agreed to fund you.

"It's not about any of that. It's about you wanting to be able to go back to Atlanta this fall and say to Blankenship and the rest of them, 'I did it. And you didn't think it could be done.'

"It's about proving them wrong. It's about trying to make them sorry they didn't support you. It has nothing to do with science or breakthroughs or all your ideals. This is petty anger and vengeance, pure and simple."

Alexander stood staring at Tom. The muscles in his jaw twitched and his breathing was rapid, but he said nothing.

"Look at it this way. So what if you slave away all

summer and solve the problem? What do you think Blankenship and the others will do? Do you really think they're going to bow down and kiss the hem of your lab coat?" Tom shook his head. "It'll never happen, my friend. Never. So you might as well forget it."

Alexander stood silently for a moment. He was furious, but he could see that his friend was truly concerned. Feeling ashamed, he loosened his clenched fists and looked down at the scuffed old linoleum floor.

"You're right, Tom. I've lost sight of why I started work on this project. But it really pisses me off. Those pompous assholes. They can just sit up there and decide whose work is valuable and whose isn't. God, I hate that."

"Of course you do. Nobody's saying you shouldn't. You just can't let them ruin the rest of your life. Now will you please get out of this lab? Go for a walk. I'll meet you at five at the bar, and we can review where we stand."

"All right, all right." Alexander conceded. "You win. I'll go."

Alexander walked down the beach. In spite of Tom's admonitions, he couldn't take his mind off of his work or what Tom had said about his reasons for working so hard. He was oblivious to his surroundings. Wind, sand and seagulls made no impression on his senses, nor did the sand construction that stretched from the base of the nearest sand dune across the beach to the waterline.

He heard a voice calling from a distance and then the sound of someone running behind him. Curious, Alexander stopped and turned to see a small, very excited young boy dragging a gallon bucket and waving a trowel, looking grim and determined. Alexander recognized him as the child who was staying with Iris, but couldn't remember his name. As the young boy reached Alexander, he set his bucket down, propped his hands on his hips and looked up at Alexander with disgust.

"Were you calling me?" Alexander asked politely.

"Yeah, I tried to call you but you didn't hear me. You didn't see my sign, either," the boy said now with a hint of despair.

"What sign?" Alexander asked.

The boy turned and retrieved a piece of plywood propped in the sand behind him. On it in bright red paint had been scrawled "THIS IS A CONSTRUCTION ZONE. OFF LIMITS. NO TRESPASSING. GO AROUND."

"You're standing right in the middle of my city. You've destroyed skillions of dollars worth of homes and factories." The young boy sat down in the sand with an air of defeat.

Alexander looked down and saw the wake of destruction he had left behind him. He appeared to be standing in the middle of the major highway going through the town, and he saw that, in his self-absorbed meandering, his shuffling gait had leveled almost one-third of a very elaborate sand construction. The boy explained to Alexander all the things that now lay in ruins, with an intensity that echoed through Alexander's head.

He surveyed the damage carefully and listened closely as the boy emphasized the seriousness of his transgression.

"I'm sorry. Listen, aren't you the boy staying with Iris?"

"Yeah, she's my aunt. I met you at her restaurant. You're Dr. Greenleaf, aren't you?"

"That's right. You have a good memory, but I'm afraid I don't remember your name."

"It's Skylar."

"Skylar. Okay, Skylar, but please call me Alexander. Look, I'm very sorry about your city. I've had a lot on my mind lately and I wasn't paying attention to where I was going."

"No kidding," Skylar agreed.

"Well, what say I help you rebuild it?"

Skylar looked at him, head cocked to one side. "Will you do it the way I say?"

"Sure, I'll do it just like you want. Then maybe I'll do my own section over there. If it's all right with you, of course."

"Okay."

"Great. Let's get started."

Alexander removed his shoes and socks and rolled up his pants. The two of them worked intently, repairing the damage he had caused. As the new structures went up, so did Alexander's spirits.

CHAPTER THIRTEEN

Everything he needed was there: an extra pair of
shorts, two clean tee-shirts, underwear, two fluffy
towels (Sandy was wrapped in one of them),
sunscreen, visor, sunglasses, binoculars, fish book, pad and
pens. He was sure of it, because he'd packed and unpacked
the small canvas backpack three times since he'd been up.
Twice he had put in the small blue face towel, and then
removed it. He was already dressed, having changed from
the green camp shirt to the yellow Bryson Beach one. He
had had the flip-flops on and off a half dozen times already,
putting them on when he thought he heard Aunt Iris
finally get up, and taking them off when he saw that her
room was still dark. The bed was made, the window blinds
adjusted, sunscreen was on his nose and forearms. There
was nothing to do but sit and wait. Well, okay, he could
check the backpack one more time.

*When will she ever wake up? I hope she hasn't forgotten
we're swimming with Dear One today.* Then it hit him. He'd
fix breakfast, and that would get them to the water sooner.
He placed the backpack on the neatly made bed, smoothed
the bedspread one more time and moved through the
darkened house to the kitchen.

Soon the table was set, the orange juice squeezed, the

cereal ready to pour. He sat down at his spot and had just begun reading the cereal box when Aunt Iris stepped into the kitchen and looked at him, surprised.

"Good morning, Skylar. Couldn't you sleep?" she asked, the look of nighttime still in her eyes. She had three little wrinkles on her left cheek from the way she had slept on her pillow.

"Oh, I slept great. I just wanted to be on time." He stepped to the refrigerator to get the orange juice as she ground the coffee beans and started the hot water.

"Oh, right. On time for our trip. Well, thank you. And thank you for all this." She motioned to the table he had set. Moving to her chair, she stopped a moment and gave him a nice hug. Her kimono was cool on his cheek and ear. Within another minute the kettle was screaming "Hot water!" and she poured it over the grounds in the funnel that fed into the glass beaker.

Skylar wolfed down his cereal and juice, hiding behind the cereal box so Aunt Iris wouldn't tell him he was eating too fast. When he was through, he looked up to see his aunt still slowly sipping her coffee. Impatient, he went to retrieve his backpack. In a flash he was out the front door, loading it into the Jeep.

"I'm ready when you are," he said, darting back into the kitchen.

Aunt Iris was ready in less than ten minutes by his watch, although it seemed like an hour. Soon they were readying the boat, and finally, he could feel the damp morning wind singing past his ears as they crossed the inlet.

In his fish book, the pocket-sized red one with detailed colored pictures, he had read that dolphins were really air-breathing mammals. They were members of the toothed whale family and could weigh five hundred pounds or more. They navigated by sonar and were thought to have a high level of intelligence. The little forehead part was called a melon. Aunt Iris had told him some of the stories about dolphins, like the one about sailors who were pushed into shore from burning ships, and the one about dolphins showing up to play with children swimming off the coast of Australia. He also knew that scientists were doing tests, and that dolphins could follow commands and answer questions.

The motor slowed as Iris brought the boat around. Finally she cut off the engine and dropped anchor.

"Are you ready?" asked Iris. For Skylar, it was not a second too soon. She picked up the fat inner tube and tossed it into the water behind the boat, where it bobbed, tethered to its line.

"I'll swim out to Dear One first. You can hold onto the inner tube and watch. Okay?"

"Okay." Skylar tingled with excitement as he watched his aunt step off the diving platform and disappear beneath the gently rippling surface of the water. The sun's reflection on the waves sparkled like holiday lights. This was better than any Christmas had ever been!

He waddled carefully over to sit on the edge of the platform, feet splattering in the blue rubber flippers. He dunked his dive mask in the water like Aunt Iris had shown him, and saw her surface about ten yards away. With a nod, she signaled him to come on in. Nervously, he put the yellow mask over his eyes and nose and tightened the straps. Now he had to breathe through his mouth.

He took a deep breath and held it as he slid into the water. His life vest buoyed him as he awkwardly paddled over to the inner tube. Bobbing in the ocean, he felt like a cork on a fishing line. Cupping his hands, he slowly moved them back and forth, testing the resistance to his movements. He checked his flippered kicks, enjoying a new strength and lift in the water.

Holding tightly onto the inner tube, Skylar lowered his face into the water. He felt the mask press against his face as the bright blue sky and dazzling light transformed into another world. It was like entering a dream. He became all eyes, totally focused on the images through his window to the world below, drawn down as if he were only able to move in slow motion.

He raised his head to take a breath, closing his eyes to the brilliance on the surface. *When did the wind get so noisy?* He lowered his head again. The salty water reminded him of when his mother had made him gargle for the sore throat he had had last winter.

It's quiet down here, so soft and peaceful. He saw the fleeting movement of a school of purple and yellow fish. They seemed not to notice him. *This is like being invisible inside a giant aquarium.*

To his left was Iris, swimming in slow, easy loops. Then he saw Dear One shoot by like a rocket, right through the circle Iris was forming. *She's here! She's here! And look how big and fast she is.*

He raised his head, his heart beating hard and fast as a surge of excitement washed over him. He wanted to be down there with the dolphin. Letting go of the tube, he furiously waved his arms up and down, attempting to push himself underwater. Though fighting against his vest, he kept bobbing back to the surface.

Looking down again, he saw Dear One circling Iris as the two of them pirouetted through the water. Entranced, Skylar floated motionless as he watched the dance. This was a new Aunt Iris, someone he hadn't seen before. She seemed to be part dolphin. He couldn't keep from smiling, letting bubbles of air escape through his teeth.

His stomach fluttered as the two of them swam closer and closer. After his next breath, he saw only Aunt Iris. She was looking in his direction, but where was Dear One? He felt the water swirl and tickle his legs. He looked down to see a huge white belly glide by below his flippered feet. Dear One rolled on her side, one big dark eye looking into his.

You're looking at me! You can see me with only one eye at a time, like a pirate with a patch. Do I look different with your other eye? Skylar closed one eye, then the other, to gain a different perspective.

He was mesmerized. Time stood still and his only awareness was of the dolphin. She was looking at him. *This feels so strange… It's like meeting someone, and wanting to say hello, but they're from another planet.* His body tingled all over, as though he had swallowed a sparkler.

Skylar reached out to the dolphin who drifted upward toward his outstretched cupped hand. *What about her teeth? Will they hurt me?* Simultaneously with his thoughts, Dear One opened her mouth and wagged her head slowly back and forth. Skylar kept very still, then to his wonder this huge animal gently nuzzled his upper arm and shoulder. Abruptly, Dear One darted away.

She's playing with me. Tag. I must be "it" now. How did she know I wanted to see her teeth? Wonder what she wants to see of mine.

The dolphin had been watching Skylar. She swam close enough for him to reach out and tentatively touch her side. *Firm, just like the inner tube, except silky and cool.* As he reached out to touch her again, she nuzzled his hand. *You must like me. I know you like me. I don't know how, but I know.*

Dear One floated next to him on the surface as though she wanted to be close. Utterly captivated, Skylar gently stroked the dolphin's side. *How can you stay this still?*

As he reached for her dorsal fin, she streaked away. The silver-gray form made one elegant loop and circled back to nudge his legs. Skylar drew both legs together in imitation and fluttered only his feet. He brought his arms down to his side and rotated his cupped hands. *You make it look so easy.*

He imagined slipping off his life vest and following Dear One…*the water surging over him…the cooler water of the depths…schools of small fish darting out of his path…barrel rolls and loop-the-loops…clouds of sand swirling in his wake…leaping into the sunlight, then a grand belly-flop…racing in unison with Dear One.*

As he bobbed back up, he kicked his feet furiously— as though he could continue his flight all the way to the sky. He whooped in excitement at this dream come true. This was the most fun thing he had ever done. He lowered his head to see Dear One again. *Thank you.* He blew bubbles of gratitude toward her. He thought his chest would burst. *I never want to leave you.*

Skylar lingered in the water long after Iris signaled him back to the boat. He reluctantly climbed back onto the dive platform, pulling the inner tube in behind him.

"We'll come back again soon Skylar," Iris assured him as she hauled in the anchor.

Dear One swam up to the platform, next to Skylar's leg. He reached out to touch her beak and bit his lip to fight back a tear as she slid back into the water. As he climbed into the boat she stayed near the surface, watching him intently. He saw that one eye again, as she seemed to smile at him. Playing with him still, she tracked his every move. Skylar hung over the gunwale, not willing to lose sight of Dear One for even an instant.

As Iris headed the boat back to Bryson Beach, Dear

One followed at a distance. When she stopped, she held her head out of the water until Skylar could see her no more.

Alexander adjusted his sun visor, then pushed his sunglasses back up on the bridge of his nose.

Skylar had noticed that he never did get the sunglasses fixed right, even though he constantly bent and stretched the ear pieces. The creamy white sunscreen obviously complicated matters, causing the sunglasses to glide slowly right back to the point just above where his nostrils flared. Skylar continued telling the story of his swim to Alexander, who reclined comfortably in the chaise lounge next to him.

"She lives way out there, past that island with all the trees. She's the biggest animal I've ever seen. When she came up next to me, it was like I was some kind of toy or something—she's so much bigger than me!"

"That was brave of you, Skylar."

Skylar continued. "Aunt Iris went in the water with her first. They've been together a bunch of times, so they know each other. But Dear One was really friendly to me! She came by, looking and swimming backwards and clicking. I think she was saying something to us. And sometimes it sounded like she was laughing."

He lowered his voice and leaned toward Alexander. "I was a little scared at first. Do you know how many teeth a dolphin has?"

Alexander shook his head.

"Me neither, but it's a lot. She showed me her teeth,

but she didn't hurt me." He buried his toes under the hot sand, leaving only half his foot exposed to the sunshine.

Alexander adjusted his sunglasses again before he responded. "I'm not sure I would have gone in the water, myself. I'm not a very good swimmer. You must have really wanted to find out about that dolphin."

"Yeah, I did, and then it seemed like Dear One invited me, you know? And Aunt Iris was there." He paused.

"Did you know that Dear One can stop completely still in the water? Even the waves don't push her around. I don't know how she does that. How does she keep the waves from making her bump into stuff?"

"I don't know," Alexander said.

Skylar rose and stood in the sand.

"Then she came by extra slow—I mean she was barely moving at all, and she came right under where my hands were, so I touched her!" His hands rose up in the air, floating magically as if supported by water. The left hand moved up, bent at the wrist, then waved gracefully forward and backward.

"Then she zoomed off and disappeared. She's so big, but she just disappeared right into the water. And you know what else? Her skin is really neat. It's tight, and smooth, and cool as the water." Skylar paused again, obviously formulating another question for Alexander.

"I wonder what we feel like to her?"

Skylar became quiet, savoring his adventure.

Finally Alexander broke the silence, "That island you mentioned, the one you saw? Well, Tom and I—you remember Tom, don't you?"

"Yeah, he was with you at Aunt Iris's restaurant."

"We were great pals in high school. I used to come down here with him and his family during summer vacations. That island was one of our favorite places to go. It's called Biermann Island."

"How did you get there? I never saw a bridge, or anything."

"Tom's father had an old row boat. We'd take it and row like crazy trying to get there. It wasn't easy."

"What's over there?" asked Skylar.

"Just the foundation of an old house, plus part of the chimney, a few outbuildings that were part of the old Biermann estate and some storage sheds and shacks. Nobody has lived there in many, many years."

"Did lots of people go over there back when you did?"

"No, it was really deserted. We pretended we were the owners of that continent—Tom always insisted on being the king," he chuckled. "We felt like natives on a secret island. We explored and searched for treasures."

"Why did you stop going there?"

"Tom's mother found out and said it was too dangerous. She told us we were not to go there again."

"Let's go one day," Skylar said, eager for another new experience.

"We don't have many days left, since you'll be going back to Texas soon. Maybe next summer we can come back and that will be one of our adventures."

"That's a long time to wait," Skylar muttered glumly.

CHAPTER FOURTEEN

Skylar stood on the front porch, his nose pressed against the screen door, listening to Iris's voice speaking into the telephone.

"That's Delta flight 1250. How long is the layover in Dallas?"

The faint odor of the rusty screen met his nostrils as he brushed the burnt orange dust from his face. He pushed the door open and let it slam behind him as he headed toward the dune. Reaching the top, he sat down and dug his heels into sand scorched by afternoon sun. A lump began to harden in his throat as he looked over the water behind the house. He thought of Jack and his mom, but mostly of Jack, and made up his mind to carry out the plan he'd been forming.

He heard the car door slam. Iris's Jeep turned around and headed down the road. When it was silent again he returned to the house. On the table he found a note from Iris saying she'd gone to the Sand Dollar and would be back later.

Skylar knew he would have to hurry. He ran to his room and retrieved his green tackle box from under the bed. He found a large black plastic garbage bag and packed Sandy, a towel, clean shorts and a shirt. Then he changed into his swim suit and went into the kitchen to find some food. Raisins and peanuts, a peanut butter and jelly sandwich and some candy went into a plastic container and then into the bag. He filled his Star Trek thermos with juice and added it to his supplies.

"I'm not going back to Texas," he muttered defiantly. He dragged the black plastic bag out of the house and clunked down the steps. He rummaged through the storage area under the deck looking for useful items and settled on an old rope, a paddle, and a casting net.

He glanced at the house and went back inside to scribble a note to Iris. Taking one last look around, he headed out the door.

With effort, he loaded up his stores, throwing the net over one shoulder, the black plastic bag over the other, clutching his precious tackle box with his free hand. Dragging the paddle behind him it was slow going through the sand. He tried to stay away from the beach until he was well away from the area where he was likely to encounter anyone. When he came to a break in the dunes he threw down his burdens and inched out to the beach to see if the way was clear.

No one was visible to the right, but as he turned the other way he saw Elmore standing a little way down the beach smoking a cigarette. He froze and closed his eyes. When he looked again Elmore was leisurely walking away. He let out a whoosh of breath and set his mind to the task ahead.

He had decided to embark on his journey from the dunes at the edge of the bay across from Biermann Island. When he reached the point past Iris's house, he climbed a dune and gazed across the bay which formed the mouth of the Pachacola River. He could see Biermann Island. From where he stood, the trees on the island looked like miniature spikes, rising up green out of the snowy sand. The island abruptly narrowed into a point on the end. The bay was deserted.

Skylar quickly set to work building his raft. From behind a dune he dragged out the two foam blocks he and Iris had found washed up on the beach the week before, and placed them side by side on the sand. Iris had said they were probably from an old floating dock. He took the round casting net, which had small lead weights attached around the edges, draped it over the blocks of foam and tucked it under the sides.

He looped a piece of nylon cord back and forth through the net under the foam block and pulled the net tight over the foam like a fitted sheet. The finished raft was about four feet by six, and a foot high.

He stuffed his tackle box into the black plastic bag and wrapped rope over the bag and through loops in the net to secure it to the raft. Once everything was ready, he jammed the end of the paddle under the bag and pushed the raft out into the water.

A light breeze was at his back and the incoming waves gently raised and tugged at the raft as they washed past. When he was waist deep he tried to climb onto the raft, but it pitched up on end. He got his weight on the edge and fell back into the water. Swimming back to the raft, he gently pulled his chest up onto it. Again the raft heaved to one side, but he was able to swing a foot up, catch the net with his toes and pull himself all the way up.

"Hold still," he shouted as the raft suddenly pitched forward with the next rolling wave. He grabbed his paddle and furiously tried to propel the raft out beyond the breaking waves, where he thought he'd have an easier time of it. It was a lot harder to maneuver than he had expected, but he kept on.

The deeper water of the bay was calmer, but the swells still caused the raft to heave uncontrollably. It was slow going, and Skylar began to feel very alone. He had not counted on the current of the river and the receding tide, which made it harder and harder to maintain his course toward the island. He grew tired and quit paddling. Suddenly the water seemed dark and threatening. The Gulf loomed much larger than it had before.

The wind began to pick up and the swells grew larger. The raft turned and pitched, out of control, like a cork. Several times the force of the waves lifted the raft on its side and nearly tipped it over, despite the weight of Skylar and his belongings. To stabilize the raft he lay prone, anchoring himself by holding onto the net with his hands and toes. The island seemed close, until he realized the tide was pulling him out into the open Gulf. It was too late to turn around and head back.

He thought of Iris and his mom, with whom he had been so angry just a few hours ago, and he started to cry. His tears were washed away by a swell which unexpectedly broke over the side of the raft. His fear pushed him toward action. He ignored the queasiness in his stomach, slid to the back of the raft, held onto the net, and began to kick wildly, trying to move the raft toward the shore.

It was no use. The open water of the Gulf stretched before him. Skylar slowly pulled himself back up on the raft and inched his way toward the front. The raft heaved violently as he tried to stabilize himself in the center. He couldn't find the paddle.

"Help!" he shouted. "Help! Help! Please, somebody, help me!" His screams were lost in the vastness of the sea.

Suddenly a new fear gripped Skylar. The constant action of the swells had begun to pull apart his raft. The foam slabs were bumping against each other. This added motion was causing his ropes to pull loose. Abruptly, his plastic bag slid out from its mooring, and before he could grab it, the raft pitched up. His tackle box and Sandy were washed overboard. He could see his box of treasures floating upside down in the water.

"Oh no, my tackle box. Help! Help!" he wailed. He quickly abandoned the idea of going in after them and began to cry again. Gritting his teeth, he grabbed his plastic bag of food and clothes to keep it from washing away too.

The swells gradually carried his tackle box and Sandy farther and farther away. He caught a glimpse of the distant beach as the raft rose on a swell, but there was no one in sight. He was soaking wet and exhausted as he clutched the remnants of the raft.

Iris's movements became calm and deliberate as she again told herself not to panic. She checked Skylar's room once more, stopping to pick up the note this time, then making a slow and careful survey of the house, searching the deck and yard, calling, "Skylar!" Convinced by now that he was not around the house, she wrapped herself in her beach sweater and made her way to the dunes.

The sun had set, and night was falling. The wind was blowing steadily, and she could feel tiny pellets of sand around her ankles and legs. Iris surveyed the beach as best she could in the hazy twilight, then switched on the powerful flashlight she carried, and headed closer to the shore.

For twenty minutes she searched up and down the

expanse, calling his name. Her heart pounded as she moved faster and faster. The wind lowered. The air was humid. She shrugged off the chill as the damp air seemed to hover and cling in little beads to her skin.

Making her way back to the house, she switched on the lights in the living room, glanced down at the crumpled scrap of paper in her hand, and read the note again.

Dear Aunt Iris,
I love you very much and I don't want you to worry, because I am all right, but I had to go away for awhile. Please don't worry because I am taking food and I will be in a safe place. Please don't try to find me because you won't be able to.

Skylar

The thought came to her that Alexander might know where Skylar was. Reaching for the phone to call him, her grip on the receiver tightened. She remembered that Alexander wouldn't be home. Skylar had told her yesterday that he was going to be in Atlanta for a couple of days. She dropped the receiver back in its cradle, and wondered if she should call the police. A wave of fear washed over her. The mental pictures which she had been willing away now crowded in.

Where have you gone? she thought. *And why?* Anger was welling up. She stood up, strode across the room, and pulled open the sliding door leading out to the beach. *I've got to get help.* She moved back into the warmth of her lamp-lit room, and picked up the phone.

"Jaid, it's Iris. Is Skylar over there?"

"No, dear. I haven't seen him since around noon. Is something wrong?"

"He's gone. Run away. I've searched the house and beach but there's no sign of him. I'm worried."

"Listen, Iris, I'll round up a search party and have a look around the grounds, then come to your place. Don't worry, we'll find him."

Iris hung up, feeling heartened by the warmth and love that came through her friend's voice.

She dialed the Sand Dollar, pacing the small room and stretching the cord as she walked and listened to the ringing. Finally, Elmore answered, with voices of the evening crowd in the background. "Elmore, I'm looking for Skylar. Is he there?"

"Gosh, Iris, I haven't seen him."

Quickly she explained the situation.

"Damn, Iris, I'll grab some of the crew and be right over." She thanked him and hung up.

After a few moments of hesitation, she called the local police station. Arthur, a regular at the Sand Dollar, answered.

"Arthur, this is Iris. Skylar's run away."

Arthur responded quickly. "I'll get the four-wheel and search lights and be right over."

She walked back over to the sliding glass door, and slid it open. The moisture of the air wrapped itself around her. It was a moonless night, still and cloudy.

You are OK! She shut her eyes tightly and began talking fiercely to him, picturing his animated eyes and thin face, and feeling the brush of his silk-soft hair against her cheek. *Nothing bad has happened to you. Nothing bad is going to happen to you. I love you too much.*

Underneath the fear, she felt anger and hurt. She thought she had earned his trust, and felt she deserved it. The feeling of betrayal was uncomfortable, and she pushed it away. She wondered if he was under some kind of pressure. Maybe too many new things, too fast? She thought of Rose and Jack in Texas, and her heart went out to the young boy, wherever he was. He would never fit in there, and he knew it. At his age, he could have no concept of growing up and moving away, and making the best of things until then. Why hadn't he talked to her?

She wrapped her sweater tightly around her, and returned to the beach to see if she could find him.

As Jaid sat alone in her studio the next morning, she began to feel the anxiety she had previously hidden. She had received the news of Skylar's disappearance with deep concern and fear for his safety, but through the long, terrifying night, she had maintained a pretense at calmness in her effort to comfort Iris.

She paced back and forth in her studio. "No," she exclaimed aloud to the walls. "No! No! No!"

Pictures were flashing through her head like a slide show gone mad. Skylar and his drawing of a castle. Skylar's eyes widening as he heard of the "Land That Was," and the dreamers. Deciding he was a dreamer. Skylar with so much potential—a famous artist—her star student.

As she continued to pace, the panic lessened and she scanned her mind for any ideas that might have eluded the search party.

She reached for one of her big straw hats and Miss Natty's harness. "We'll go talk to the children," she explained as they left the studio grounds.

Miss Natasha only understood that something big was bothering Jaid and walked briskly beside her, uttering a companionable grunt from time to time.

"He'll be okay. We'll find him," Jaid said emphatically as she resumed her countenance of assurance and calm.

Turning toward Iris's house, Jaid saw two students from the class walking at the water's edge. "Have you seen Skylar?" she called anxiously, only to hear the same negative reply she had heard from all the others. It was Jenny Cooper and her best friend, Barbara. Jaid remembered with stinging clarity a recent conversation she had overheard between them.

"It makes me so mad the way Jaid treats Skylar."

"Giving him all the attention? He's teacher's pet and nothing we do is ever as good."

"Yeah, and the way she keeps telling him he's going to be a famous artist. He just sits and stares."

"He told me he wants to build things, but he didn't tell her."

"I think he's afraid to."

That conversation continued to haunt Jaid. Now it added poignancy as she remembered the assignment of sketching his dreams, the one Skylar never turned in. Didn't Iris say she caught a glimpse of thick, heavy strokes filling the paper? "Anger and frustration with me," she spoke aloud. "Surely that's not why he ran away."

"Miss Natty, how could I have been so blind and stupid? Pushing him to be what I wanted, rather than letting him be himself." Her walk was slower. Her feet felt heavy as she pondered other areas of her life.

Before she could get totally lost in her self-absorption, she was abruptly pulled to the present by a tug of Miss Natasha's leash. "What's that you've found?" she asked, as she bent over to pick up the soggy brown lump that had washed in with the last wave at Miss Natty's feet. As she turned it over, Jaid recognized the floppy-eared face of

Sandy.

"Not a good sign," she said. "Where *is* our boy?" She squinted and looked out to the horizon. "I think I'd better go see Iris."

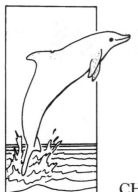

CHAPTER FIFTEEN

Birds called and circled lazily as the sun dropped red into the horizon. Quiet water lapped peacefully at the shore. The island had been little changed by centuries of powerful storms; more or less sand, irate sea creatures that flopped and burrowed back to their proper locations, folded sea grass left stranded past the tide mark. Within days, the evidence faded entirely. Fine mist rolled in, hurrying the night.

A child's tennis shoe lay half-submerged in foam. Chunks of Styrofoam and a tattered plastic bag were within feet of it. A rainbow of colored pencils danced as the waves washed in and out.

Everything kept moving around. Whatever he reached for kept moving past his small hands. Something was wrong...the colors were all off... Nothing had edges... where was this place anyway?... Things were flashing... There was an awful roaring in his ears...inside, his chest was on fire...

"D...Drr... Dreamer, are you there? Anyone home?"

He stumbled forward. He was shivering and burning up at the same time. Tears burned down his cheeks now, and his lip cracked when he went to catch one with his tongue.

"Dreamer, I need you. You there? You there?"

"WHOOOO... CAAAALLLSSS... MY...

NAAME???"

"Me. Skylar." Now his ears were whistling. Or was it the wind?

"YESSS...

"I wish Grandpa were here..." Vicious coughing consumed him. When he looked up, the colors had changed all over again. He didn't remember being here at all....

Irritable, familiar grumbling and thrashing startled him. In walked— Grandpa!!— carrying twigs and small limbs.

"Well, mercy! I was wondering if you'd ever get here! How are you doing there—warmed up yet? Got quite a chill. Here, have a little of this." He handed Skylar a thermos cup of hot chocolate.

Skylar was confounded.

"Grandpa??"

"Yep, sure is. Who did you think I was, Santy Claus?" Grandpa broke into his characteristic guffaw, making fun of his own white hair, new white beard and ample belly.

"Here, let's get this fire going so we can warm you up...."

Grandpa motioned Skylar over to him and they snuggled a very long time. Then, together they laid out rocks, twigs and small limbs. Grandpa pulled his pipe lighter out of his pocket and soon the fire was crackling and warming them both. The night settled around them unnoticed.

Hours escaped them. Skylar now wore a cuddly flannel shirt as he and Grandpa roasted marshmallows. Around them were the remnants of dinner, crusts of peanut butter sandwiches, orange peels and an empty Oreo bag, some of the food Skylar had packed in the bag lost at sea. A compass and two drafting tools, items also lost in the water, were drying next to the fire. Grandpa listened as Skylar described his journey.

"...Yeah, it took hours to put it together! It was hard to get the right stuff—you know, not everything floats in water, Grandpa! I didn't know that."

Grandpa puffed his acknowledgment through a swirl of pipe smoke, temporarily disguising them both.

"And the rope was supposed to work a lot better, too. How come it all came undone?"

"Knots, my boy. Didn't use the right knots, Skylar! You've got to have the kind of knots that pull tighter from the strain. Otherwise, all the lines slither loose. I was wondering what happened when I saw all that stuff come washing onto shore.

"Here, let me show you a few you can use...."

Grandpa withdrew from his pocket, as if by magic, two pieces of line exactly the right length. He sat right next to Skylar so the boy could match his every move. Together they started looping, unlooping, pulling under, over, through the center. Soon the grandfather and boy were moving in absolute unison, ballet-like, amidst whispery pipe smoke, the flicker of a friendly fire and the ever darkening shadows of the night.

In the half-light of a crescent moon, hundreds of knots made from cords and lines and threads of every description hung off tree limbs, around tree trunks, in Skylar's shoe laces, even around marshmallows dangling at the end of green branches. The two of them were settled back, looking at a glorious display of stars.

Skylar spoke with difficulty. "Grandpa, I...I don't want to... go back."

"Back?" Grandpa asked tenderly.

"To Texas....to Jack's house."

Grandpa remained silent, patient.

"Except for Mom. I'd like to be with her. But... but she's

with Jack, now, and Jack Jr., and the new baby, and, I...I... don't want to go back...to... their house."

Grandpa drew deeply on his briar pipe, covering them in cherry aroma.

"Will you miss her?"

Skylar followed a shooting star that sizzled across the horizon and faded away. "I do now," he said quietly. "She's not like she used to be, you know, before Jack, and everything."

Grandpa waited for him to continue.

"She's, she's always busy taking care of what Jack wants, or the baby, or Jack Jr... she doesn't have time anymore."

"Time for you?" Grandpa asked. Skylar nodded yes, tears welling.

"Since you moved to Texas?" Grandpa continued. This time Skylar nodded no.

"Since Jack." Skylar pulled his knees under his chin and looked into the crackling fire.

"I see." Grandpa reached a hand over and gently placed it on Skylar's knee, patting him.

"Since Jack, she's always busy. Or tired. Or sometimes she cries. But then Jack gets mad when she cries, so she doesn't do that much anymore. At least not in front of him." He threw sticks into the fire. "Since Jack, she's always working or something. Besides, she has Jack's kids now. She has to be with them instead."

"Not much to go back to," Grandpa affirmed.

Skylar agreed. "Grandpa, I don't know what to do...."

"Do?" Grandpa questioned softly.

"I don't want to go back. But, what about Mom?"

"What about her?" Grandpa followed.

"What'll happen to Mom? What'll happen if I don't go back to Texas, to her?"

Grandpa pulled himself up to a sitting position and looked directly at him. "Skylar, one thing's for sure. Your mother is a grown woman. She can look out for herself."

"You sure? Even with Jack?" Skylar knew how mean Jack could be.

"Positive. Even with Jack. Jack isn't as tough as he thinks. Your mother knows that. Rose can look out for herself." Skylar was proud his Grandpa knew so much about people.

"What would you like to do?" Grandpa asked.

"I'd like to stay here, with you, or Iris…or even have Mom come here." His voice grew more firm. "But not Texas, and not Jack."

"Skylar, you can be with me any time you want. You know how to find me. Besides, something could work out… it's happened before, you know, something working out…."

Skylar hoped against hope. "You think so?"

"Why of course, child. Look at us, we worked out, didn't we?"

"Well, yeah, but…."

"So you must decide how you want things to turn out, Skylar. That's all. You have to decide how you want things to be. And then you dream them that way."

"Grandpa, do you know the Dreamer?"

Grandpa chuckled lovingly and tousled Skylar's hair. He looked at Skylar for a long moment, and continued in a hushed voice.

"You know how to dream, boy, don't ever forget it. Most important thing in this world, knowing how to dream. Lots of folks forget that once they grow up…. Doesn't make a bit a sense, does it? You grow up, learn how to do everything, get a job, raise up a wonderful family, and all of a sudden you realize—where'd it go? Seems like the best time of all to dream would be when you grow up."

"Grandpa, you never forgot."

Grandpa's eyes sparkled back. "Got to keep your dreams, Skylar. Got to keep all your dreams to make up for those folk *that gave theirs away!"*

"Like Jack. He doesn't dream. He's too mean. Do mean people have dreams, Grandpa?"

"Seems to me the reason they're mean is they gave all their dreams away... but you can dream one for them, Skylar. That's one thing you can do for sure. Kinda evens things out...."

"I, uh, don't think I want to just now, Grandpa, not for Jack. But for Mom, I could do one for Mom..." Skylar poked at the fire and released a million sparks to the sky.

"Sure. You can dream something that makes her happy. You know what that is. She never has to know it was you, unless you want her to. That's the best part—you get to keep your dreams and give 'em away! Better'n Christmas!"

Grandpa laughed. Skylar, catching on to the joke that he and Grandpa alone would know, began to laugh as well, the full, free laugh that only nine-year-old boys and their grandfathers share. The two of them caught their breath again.

Skylar looked at Grandpa expectantly. "Can we make a dream now, Grandpa, the two of us? A dream for me?"

"Why, of course, we can, son. Whatever you'd like," he answered. Grandpa reached an arm around Skylar and pulled him in, close and warm. With eyes closed, Skylar soon saw the entire family on an island of glistening, shimmering sand, with cool, clear water lapping at the edges. Within a climate-controlled geodesic dome, all were dressed in their formal silver and gold space suits, appropriate for the occasion on Colony Seven.

Rose, sleek helmet to her right, sat on one side of a perfectly clear conference table. Jack, Jack Jr., baby Jennifer, and a dozen attendants stood behind Rose, looking across the room and whispering among themselves in excitement. Crystal light sources from each point in the frame of the dome glowed light and dark as the energy of the room increased and waned.

Those gathered grew hushed. Rose stood and came to attention, hand at heart. Triangles swished open, making a portal. There, leading a squadron of officers, stood Skylar, perfectly fitted in a uniform of golden hue with a platinum star centered above his heart. He stepped forward. As one, the entire gathering bowed their heads. The lights dimmed, then twinkled their delight.

"Ambassador," Jack acknowledged.

"Representatives of Planet Three, be at ease. Please, be seated." Jack lifted his head, as did the others. Skylar moved to his position standing across from Rose, and placed his fingertips on the surface of the table. His officers flanked into formation behind him.

"State your purpose, Representative." Rose unfurled a document and placed it face down on the table. A small screen came into view in front of Skylar, projecting the contents for his review.

"I see. An offering of peace. And who makes this resolution?"

At this point, Jack stepped forward, Jack Jr. and Jennifer in tow. "Ambassador, we do, the children and I."

Rose gave Skylar her special look, filled with the joy mothers feel for their children's happiness. Skylar basked in it, breathing it in so he could remember it long afterwards.

Jack spoke. "If I may, Ambassador." He cleared his throat. "Ambassador, we, uh, I regret the many years of bad blood between us. I, too, pray you will accept our offer. On this matter, the four of us are one." The sands below them, which had continually changed color depending on whether those present needed to be energized or calmed, glowed a soothing sea green. Rose and the family were encircled in rich purple.

"Your hearts are true," Skylar announced. "The request of this woman and her family is granted. Between us shall be peace. The past is dismissed."

With a sweep of his hand, Skylar activated a transporter beam that carried the resolution of peace to the Hall of Eternal Records. The ceremony was completed. The crystal lights jingled harmoniously. The attendants burst into applause, and everyone hugged.

Rose captured his attention. She mouthed the words "I love you," and waved a private good-bye. Jack came to attention again, honoring Skylar with his best salute. Skylar acknowledged them both with a touch to his platinum star, turned, and departed with the officers closing ranks behind him.

The green and purple sands faded to gray, and the crystal light sources phased into a single sun. Behind him trailed Iris, Alexander, Jaid and Elmore, splashing through surf at high noon.

He opened his eyes again to find Grandpa watching over him. Grandpa spoke again.

"So, are you ready to go now?"

"Yes, but I'll miss you so much, Grandpa," he whispered.

"You can find me in a dream, son, any dream you want."

The sun was just beginning to set as Alexander pulled into the driveway. The trip to Atlanta had been necessary but distracting. And now that he had checked on his house and picked up a few supplies, he was happy to be back at the beach.

As he grabbed his bags out of the back of his old Volvo, Alexander gazed at the purple-pink sky and breathed a sigh of contentment. It surprised him how relaxed he felt, how renewed his spirits were. He must remember to thank Tom again, and tell him how right he had been to suggest coming here.

As Alexander set down his bags and reached in his pocket for the house key, Muon came up to greet him.

"Hello, boy. Good to see you. Are you hungry?" he asked, as the cat rubbed his head against Alexander and walked in and out between his legs. It was then Alexander saw the paper folded up and wedged between the storm door and the jamb. He stepped into the foyer and switched on the lights. It was a note from Iris asking him to come to the Sand Dollar as soon as possible.

It was dark when Alexander arrived. The parking lot was crowded. Alexander swallowed hard as he hurried past an ambulance and several police cars ominously parked near the entrance.

Once inside the restaurant, Alexander scanned the small clusters of weary people sipping coffee until at last he saw her. He hurried over. "Iris, what happened? I got here as fast as I could."

Her hollow eyes seemed to take a second to register who he was before she could speak. "Alexander, Skylar's gone. He ran away and we can't find him." She bit her lip and with the back of her hand wiped away a tear from her cheek. Alexander sank slowly into the empty chair next to her. Gently, he reached out and touched her arm.

She looked up with bewilderment. "How did I ever think I could take care of a nine-year-old boy?"

Alexander took her hand. "We'll find him."

A few moments later he found Elmore in the kitchen and barraged him with questions.

"Last time anybody remembers seeing him was yesterday morning," Elmore answered. "Everyone's been searching since last night. We've covered the beach, the marshes and the tidal pools. Fishermen have been searching in the Gulf, and the Coast Guard helicopter is still out there."

Alexander pulled out his pipe and began to chew on the stem. "Now where would he have headed? Where would a nine-year-old boy go to run away and hide?" he wondered aloud. Alexander stopped talking abruptly.

"Anybody using your boat right now, Elmore?"

"No."

"Come on, then. Let's go."

Minutes later they slid to a stop in a cloud of dust in the parking lot.

"You know there's a cold front moving in. It's going to be fogged up out there. Likely to be a storm, too," Elmore said as he cranked the engine of his small runabout. A plume of blue smoke rose from the stern.

"Well, no time to waste then," said Alexander. Gunning the engine, Elmore veered dangerously close to the other boats moored in the marina, speeding past the marker buoys and on into the nighttime Gulf.

When the storm hit, Alexander lay flat on his belly on the slippery wet foredeck of the small boat. The rain pelted his face. His hair was plastered to his head.

"You see anything up there?" Elmore called out.

Alexander slithered backwards and climbed into the cockpit of the boat. "Can't see a thing out there. Nothing."

"The wind's picking up. The swells are rising. I've been watching the compass, but I don't know how much to allow for the current. If we miss the island, we could go all the way to Mexico before we hit anything. I won't feel good about this until we see a channel buoy."

"Any good news?" Alexander asked.

"Yeah. There's been no lightning," responded Elmore, who had taken the question seriously. "I hate being on the water when it's lightning."

Then, as if on cue, a bolt of lightning shot through the fog and struck a marker buoy just yards off their port bow.

Elmore let go of the wheel and ducked, regaining his grip barely in time to keep them from crashing into the looming iron buoy.

By the time they beached the boat on the island, the rain had stopped. The fog was patchy, settling in the low spots, entwining the brush and pine trees. As Alexander and Elmore began to hike carefully down the overgrown path, protected from the wind by the undergrowth and trees, an eerie silence settled upon them. The fog swirled around them, at times swallowing the beam of their search-light, at other times parting to reveal the harsh terrain.

Intermittently they called out Skylar's name. Nothing stirred in the darkness except the wind, which was beginning to rise again. At the end of the path they came to a clearing. This was the highest point of the island. It was covered with tall grass, bent now in the quickening winds which threatened more rain. In the middle of the clearing lay a pile of bricks that once had formed a chimney. Had it been seventy-five years earlier, they would have been standing beneath the crystal chandelier in the dining room of the old Biermann mansion.

"Sort of gives me the creeps. I always feel like some of them are still around," whispered Elmore.

"Well, if they are, I wish they'd tell us if Skylar is here."

Elmore cupped his hands to his ears and turned full circle, like a radar dish. Alexander shined the flashlight in ever-widening circles, scouring the clearing like a light-house.

"I don't like this, Alexander. We haven't seen any-thing."

"You don't think he's out here, do you, Elmore?"

"I don't see how he could be."

Alexander stood at the edge of the clearing. With the powerful searchlight he pierced the remaining pockets of mist, searching the shadows behind them. He focused the light on a pile of brush, then circled it around the clearing again. Standing dejectedly in the unyielding dark, Alexander realized there was no more they could do.

"We might as well head on back, Elmore," he said softly, turning toward the path. Suddenly, he stopped in his tracks and cocked his head. "Did you hear something?" Elmore froze beside him.

"Shhhh. It sounds like it's coming from over there." Alexander started toward the clump of scrub oak at the edge of the clearing. He stopped and motioned for Elmore to stand back as he slowly lifted one of the branches. There was a sudden rush of sound as a startled bird flew out of the brush. Both men jumped. Alexander dropped the light, which went out.

"It was just a bird," Alexander said. "Where's the light?"

Elmore found the light and shook it. "Damn, it's dead."

Alexander shrugged. "I guess that's that. Let's find our way back to the boat."

As he spoke he heard the unmistakable sound of whimpering, like a wounded animal crying. Carefully, slowly, Alexander again lifted the limb and started to crawl into the bushes.

"There's something else in here," he whispered to Elmore.

"What is it?" Elmore ducked down to follow Alexander.

Alexander whispered, "Got any matches?" Elmore held out a disposable lighter. The flickering light illuminated the dark cave created by the thick growth. Gnarled trunks and roots cast their tortured shadows on the golden floor of pine needles and sand. In the soft yellow light Alexander saw the faded blue denim of a dirty pair of jeans, and the huddled shape of a small, blond-haired boy crying softly in his sleep, unaware of his imminent rescue. Gently, Alexander called Skylar's name, reaching out to touch the boy's shivering back. Skylar jumped at the touch and recoiled from Alexander.

"Skylar, it's all right. It's me, Alexander, and Elmore. You're safe now. We're here to take you back."

Alexander felt two small arms encircle his neck as he swept Skylar fully into his arms. He felt the warm wet tears as Skylar sobbed, burying his head in the crook of Alexander's neck.

"It's all right, Skylar. It's going to be okay. We're here now and it's all okay," Alexander kept repeating as he stroked Skylar's head and back.

Elmore reached out to ruffle Skylar's hair, unashamed of the tears flowing unchecked down his weathered cheeks. Skylar lifted his head briefly and reached out a shaky hand to touch Elmore's shoulder.

"Let's get you home now," said Elmore gently.

Above them, the now-thinning clouds skittered and wisped across the glow of the emerging crescent moon.

CHAPTER SIXTEEN

"**C**an I get you some more coffee?" Charlene asked softly.

Iris looked up, glancing away from the Gulf long enough to give her a grateful look. "Thanks, that would be nice." Her eyes returned to her vigil, squinting, as she tried to see the details of the channel in the pre-dawn light. Iris was tired, weary. She'd set her mouth in a thin smile, holding herself together with grim determination. She felt she might cry but was trying not to.

If something has happened to him.... Her mind could go no further with that train of thought.

Iris surveyed the room which, hours before, had been bustling with people involved in the search for Skylar. Now only Charlene, Elmore's eldest daughter, remained. The restaurant was eerily quiet. The clatter of the coffee pot as Charlene set it down was the only sound that disturbed the stillness.

Then Iris heard someone come in. She turned to see Elmore walk through the door. In the commotion, earlier in the evening, Iris had noticed Elmore disappear along with Alexander. She hadn't thought about it then, but later, she had wondered where they were and what they were doing.

"Where were you?" Iris demanded. As she asked the question she noticed something out of place about him. His complexion was flushed, his shoes and pant cuffs were wet and he was wearing the hat he always wore on his boat. Then she realized he was smiling. Elmore was smiling!

"What happened, Elmore? Did you find him?"

Before Elmore could answer the question, Alexander and Skylar walked in. The expression on her face changed from weariness to relief to joy.

"Skylar!" Iris was on her feet and beside him in the next instant. Tears began to well in his eyes, streaking the dirt smudged on his cheeks.

"I'm sorry, Aunt Iris." He looked afraid.

She knelt and hugged him, and his look changed to one of relief. He held her tightly.

"Skylar," she whispered in his ear. "I was so scared. I didn't know what happened." Holding him at arm's length and examining him carefully, she asked, "Are you all right?" She was crying softly. Skylar let out an audible sigh, his shoulders loosening. He nodded his head vigorously in reply.

"Let's all go and sit down," Elmore suggested. Charlene brought coffee and hot chocolate to their table. Elmore patted Skylar's shoulder. "So, tell everyone where you've been."

"Aunt Iris, I heard you making the plane reservations on the phone," he said in a small voice. "I didn't, I don't want to go back to Texas. I decided to go to the island across the channel. Alexander told me he went there when he was a kid."

"That's how you knew," said Iris, looking at Alexander, her eyes searching his. Alexander nodded quietly. "But how did you get there?" Iris asked.

As he described his adventure, Skylar's audience

seemed to stop breathing. They exchanged looks, realizing the danger that Skylar had been in.

"But you made it," said Elmore, "and this old Navy man is pretty impressed."

"Elmore, would you let the police and everyone know Skylar's back?" Iris asked. "I'm going to take him home. He can barely keep his eyes open, and I could use some sleep, too."

They all hugged, smiling through tears, then Iris led the weary boy back home.

Skylar slept well past the morning. Iris helped him with breakfast, and then seated him on a kitchen chair to salve and bandage everything that needed it. She reported his condition.

"You're mostly sunburned, Skylar, just a few scrapes. You'll be sore, but you will recover. Baggy clothes for the next few days, okay?"

"Hm-mm" he mumbled as she rubbed thick white sunburn cream on his lips.

"I want to talk with you about something, now," she continued. Skylar was chastened as he sat opposite Iris in the sunny kitchen.

"Skylar," Iris began, focusing her gaze directly on him. "It wasn't okay to run away like that. You understand that, don't you?"

"Hm-mm," he mumbled again, lowering his eyes.

"I was scared, Skylar, really scared. Lots of people were. Anything could have happened to you, and we wouldn't have known. I was afraid… that… something awful... had happened to you." Her voice grew soft, intense. She leaned forward to meet his eyes, and placed a hand on his knee. "I don't want you ever to do that again. Understand?"

"I understand, Aunt Iris," Skylar said softly.

"If you're mad about something, come and talk to me, okay?"

"Okay, Aunt Iris. Promise. I didn't want to go. I like it here, not Texas. Besides, I...uh...can't go back there." Skylar's voice cracked.

"Why not?"

Hesitantly Skylar began telling the story of Spock's death. Iris's eyes widened in horror as the boy spoke, reluctantly at first, then with a rush of pent-up emotion.

"I'm sorry, Skylar. I didn't know. Something awful already *has* happened to you," Iris said. The two sat silently for a few moments.

"I talked with your mom this morning and we've decided you can stay for a while." Iris reached to hug Skylar, then caught herself. Finding a spot on his upper arm that was not burned, she touched him softly.

Skylar jumped up and hugged her tightly, then, feeling the effects of the sunburn, released her with a big smile.

"I won't...run off again, Aunt Iris," he said seriously. "I promise."

"I'm glad," she answered, equally serious. She was as pleased as he was with the new agreement with Rose.

Jaid watched the boy from a distance. He was lying at the edge of the surf, letting it rush in and cover him. He lay perfectly still as the foaming sea washed up around his chin, as if he were being covered with an overflowing glass of seltzer.

She walked closer and softly called his name. Skylar opened his eyes and, seeing her, scrambled to his feet.

"Skylar, it's wonderful to see you," Jaid said, beaming at him. "You gave us quite a scare."

"I know," he replied, "I'm sorry I scared you, Jaid."

"Let's sit over here," she said, indicating a drier area of beach, "and you can tell me where you went and what happened to you."

Skylar recounted his perilous adventure to her, kneeling in the sand and paddling furiously, then rolling over as though he had been pitched off his raft by a wave. Jaid hid her amusement when she noticed how Skylar's wet body was becoming coated with sand, like a sugar doughnut.

"Skylar, I thought you might have run away because of the way I've been treating you at camp," she said.

Skylar looked at her, wide-eyed.

"When I was a young girl," she continued, "I felt like running away many times. I didn't seem to fit in very well with my family. They always were telling me to talk more quietly, to not laugh so loud, to move slower, eat less, pay attention, care about different things than I did. I guess I felt that they didn't like me very much, not the way I was anyway. So I promised myself that as soon as I could, I would leave and never go back."

"Did you?" Skylar asked.

"In a way I did. I went off to college when I was sixteen and I never have gone back. I didn't really run away, but I understand how you must have been feeling, Skylar."

They sat in silence for a few minutes, watching the hypnotic surf rushing in and listening to the music of it, as a lone black skimmer flew just above the boiling edges of incoming waves. Jaid reached out and tousled Skylar's hair, shaking the sand loose. She put her arm around his shoulder and gave him a squeeze. He leaned into her hug.

Finally, Jaid stood up and said, "Well, I've got to be getting back to the gallery. I just wanted to see for myself how you were doing, and let you know how much I care about you. I'm so glad to hear you'll be staying."

Skylar smiled and blushed a little.

"Oh, yes, I almost forgot… I think this belongs to you," Jaid said, reaching into her bag and pulling out a worn stuffed toy, its fur stiff and matted from the salt water, its eyes clouded with moisture and scratched by the abrasive sand.

"Sandy!" Skylar yelled, seizing his treasure and holding it tightly, oblivious to its flaws. Then he threw his arms around Jaid. "Oh, thank you for finding Sandy."

Jaid smiled as Skylar turned and ran toward home. "I've got to show Aunt Iris right away," he called back to her.

CHAPTER SEVENTEEN

Alexander sat staring at the page of calculations he had been working on for the last hour. His consciousness was totally focused on the intricate atomic arrangement of the surface of the palladium rods in his cold fusion cells. If only he could figure out a way to fabricate the rods so as to increase their surface area. He wished he had the equipment in the metallurgical laboratory at the university. Then he could cast the palladium rods in different shapes and experiment with alloys.

With a sigh he shifted his focus to his makeshift lab. He was conscious of the hum of the fluorescent lights that hung low over his equipment-laden tables.

At a cleared space on a table near the door, Skylar was working quietly on a picture of an imaginary underground city. Muon sat on the corner of the table, tail twitching, watching Skylar's pen move across the paper. Skylar's city was actually more like an engineer's drawing, complete with plan views of each level and cross sections which showed how the different levels connected.

Alexander greatly enjoyed their afternoons together. In the two weeks since his adventure on Biermann Island, Skylar had come to visit Alexander almost every day, and Alexander had taken a deep interest in the boy.

"Hey, kid, it's time for a break. Let's head down to the beach for a while," said Alexander.

Alexander and Skylar had a game they played on their beach walks. They would make up stories to explain the things they found. They called it the "What's this?" game.

"What's this?" asked Alexander, pulling a once brightly-painted piece of wood out of the sand. It was covered with barnacles.

"That's a deck board from an oyster boat that capsized in a storm last spring and was washed out to sea," replied Skylar.

"What's this?" asked Skylar, as he retrieved a light bulb from the seaweed that marked the previous night's high tide.

Alexander examined the markings on the bulb's base and announced "It's from the captain's cabin on a Russian coal carrier that left Mobile Bay last week bound for South America. Here, look at the writing on it. That's the Cyrillic alphabet, the one the Russians use."

Skylar looked at the stamped letters for a long time. It was the first object he had ever seen that came from so far away.

"What's this?" asked Alexander, holding a bright orange plastic cylinder that was once a marker float for a crab trap.

"That's used by spies to send secret messages," answered Skylar. "They probably sealed microfilm in it and then released it from a submarine. It has a radio transmitter so they can find it when it gets to the beach."

They grinned at each other, then walked in silence, watching the sea birds chasing the receding waves, looking for lunch. As they rounded a curve they spotted the great blue heron who claimed this section of beach. The bird stood impassively at the edge of the dunes and watched them approach.

"Wait," said Skylar quietly. "Let's see how close we can get."

"Okay," replied Alexander in a whisper. "Hold your arms at your sides so we won't scare him, and take little steps."

Like penguins in slow motion they moved down the beach toward the watchful heron. When they got about fifty feet away the large bird lazily took a few steps and, with strong flaps of her wings, glided gracefully out of sight over the dunes.

"I drew a picture of a heron in my art class yesterday," said Skylar.

"How's your class going?" asked Alexander.

"It's more fun than it used to be," replied Skylar. "We're learning about perspective. You know, drawing a picture so it looks like it has depth. It's fun."

Iris was sitting in a chair on the deck waiting for them when they got back to Alexander's house. "I figured you two were playing in the sand again," she smiled.

They both laughed. "We have been," they said in unison.

"Can we show Aunt Iris the lab?" suggested Skylar.

"Good idea. Come on in," said Alexander, "and I'll show you where I've been hiding most of this summer."

"I'd like that," she responded.

As they walked down the stairs to the laboratory Skylar said to Iris, "You aren't going to believe this."

They entered the makeshift laboratory where Alexander had his calorimeter and computer, with their attendant accumulation of cells and wires.

"So this is cold fusion," said Iris. "Somehow I expected something a lot bigger, like a miniature reactor. How does it work?"

Alexander walked over to a table which had on it a row of four heavy glass boxes, each about eighteen inches on a side. Within each box was a tall glass cylinder half filled with a clear liquid. Several wires and rods extended into the cylinders, and some of the rods were surrounded with tiny bubbles. A maze of wires ran to another table laden with computers, electrical converters, and terminal boxes.

"These are my cold fusion cells," explained Alexander. "Each one of these has a slightly different mix of chemicals. But they're really quite simple. Did you ever take chemistry in high school or college?"

"Yes, but it's been a long time," replied Iris.

"Well, these are almost exactly like the cells you probably used if you ever did an electrolysis experiment. You know, when you run an electric current through electrodes in water, and the water molecules separate into hydrogen and oxygen."

"Yes, but we didn't do cold fusion in high school," smiled Iris. "How does fusion work?"

"Okay, let's start with a little physics lesson. Our present nuclear power plants make electricity from the energy which is released when we split apart atoms of uranium. That is called nuclear fission. When the atoms come apart tremendous heat is released, and that heat converts water to steam. The steam turns a turbine, which turns a generator, which makes electricity. But splitting uranium atoms creates a tremendous amount of highly radioactive material. And we'll have to isolate and manage this waste for two hundred and fifty thousand years. How and where, nobody knows.

"Fusion, on the other hand, creates energy by combining two hydrogen nuclei to form helium," said Alexander, and he pointed to the shiny metal rod in one of the cylinders. "The nucleus is the inner part of the hydrogen molecules we see bubbling out of the cells here as hydrogen gas. The trouble is, these hydrogen nuclei don't want to collide on their own. You see, they have what is called a positive electrical charge, so they repel each other the same way two magnets do when pushed together.

"There are basically two approaches to fusing hydrogen nuclei into helium. Scientists at Princeton and other research facilities are working on hot fusion. They use extreme heat and pressure to force hydrogen nuclei to fuse.

"Imagine how much energy it takes to heat something to the temperature of the sun and compress it to the density of the center of the sun. You see, fusion is the reaction that powers the sun. A successful fusion reaction will produce enough excess heat to run a power plant like the one I was telling you about earlier. So far the hot fusion physicists have been able to get a fusion reaction to yield only six percent of the energy that they put into it. They've got maybe thirty years of work ahead before they make it commercially feasible."

"So where is all the heat here?" asked Iris.

"This approach is much different from hot fusion," answered Alexander. "It doesn't require that type of heat. Cold fusion is what we call a room temperature process."

"What do you mean?" asked Iris.

"In cold fusion we don't add very much energy to the process. I guess you could say we hope the hydrogen nuclei will fuse on their own initiative without the heat, but with a little help from us, of course.

"Let me explain," he continued, with excitement in his voice. "In quantum physics, we've recognized that if two nuclei remain close enough, for a long enough period of time, there's a chance that they will collide and fuse together on their own. Of course, we theorize that if a collision does take place there will be enough heat produced to cause surrounding nuclei to collide in a chain reaction, causing the release of more energy.

"The way we help this to happen is by using materials and chemicals which will bring a lot of hydrogen nuclei very close together. The rod you see in this container is made of a material called palladium, which acts like a sponge to absorb a large amount of hydrogen. The water is actually deuterium, which is different from regular water in that the hydrogen atoms contain an extra neutron in their nuclei. This gives them more mass, and that's why we call it 'heavy water.' I've also added chemicals that encourage the hydrogen nuclei to move closer together.

"So at this point in my research, I'm waiting for the hydrogen to collide within the palladium. And when that happens, heat will be produced." He pointed to a set of thin tubes in the cell. "These are the sensors for my calorimeter, which measures the heat in the cell. A sudden increase in temperature indicates that fusion has occurred."

Iris nodded and looked at the cells, not quite sure of the importance of this whole set-up.

Alexander noticed that Skylar had returned to his drawing. Looking up from his paper, Skylar asked, "Alexander, where do you get heavy water?"

"A little bit of it is found in lakes, rivers and sea water, all over the earth. And only a little bit is needed. Just one gallon of sea water would provide enough energy for your Aunt Iris to drive you in her Jeep from Bryson Beach to Seattle and back."

"Wow!" he replied.

Skylar returned to his drawing. Alexander looked down to see that Skylar had begun to sketch Iris's Jeep. On the gas tank lid was printed HEAVY WATER in block letters.

Smiling, Alexander turned to Iris. "Why don't we adjourn to the deck?"

Iris turned to Skylar, who was already absorbed in his work. She smiled and followed Alexander to the deck.

"I can offer you a glass of wine," Alexander said when they were seated. "White or rosé."

"White would be nice."

She was gazing at the sea when he returned. "Thanks," she smiled. She was quiet as she continued to stare at the water and sip her wine. He watched the way she held the wine glass by its stem. *Her simplest movements have an elegance about them,* he thought. *And she actually seems interested in my work. I wonder what she's thinking?*

CHAPTER EIGHTEEN

The boat rocked gently as waves rolled underneath. Iris and Jaid lounged on board, lulled by the warmth of the sun and the motion of the boat. Jaid had a sketch pad laid out on her lap to record the moment. Iris had decided not to bring her scuba equipment today. They sat together in comfortable silence.

Iris was lost in thought, remembering her evening with Alexander. There was something about him that had stayed with her, that imposed itself between her and her enjoyment of the day. She mused over their conversation, remembering his passionate stories about his research, about his dreams. It had seemed that they would never run out of things to talk about.

She recalled the moment when she had quit listening and had watched him as if from a doorway, looking into a warm and inviting room. She had observed his child-like excitement and joy as he described his work. And she had sensed the depth of his frustration.

His passion appealed to her most, the spark in his eyes that conveyed both love and steel. Within the core of his enthusiasm was a strength that could carry him through great adversity. She saw in him both a gentle child and a strong and loving man.

And she had become aware of a forgotten feeling, a longing. He had stirred in her an intense awareness she had not felt around a man in years. She had wanted him to hold her in his arms, without words.

And his work! Iris's mind raced, thrilled and fascinated by the changes that could occur as a result of cheap, clean and abundant energy. Travel would be inexpensive because fuel costs would go down. Everyone's standard of living would rise. Reduced shipping costs would make goods less expensive. The costs of heating a home would be minuscule. And the world could stop producing energy that resulted in hazardous wastes and pollution.

Something pulled Iris out of her reverie. She turned toward Jaid. "I can feel you looking at me. What is it?"

Jaid peered at Iris over her outrageous sun glasses. "You're right. If that line between your eyes is any indication, you mind is going a mile a minute."

Iris smiled at her friend. "Alexander and Skylar took me on a tour of the lab."

Jaid raised an inquiring eyebrow. "Oh? I never thought of the Hawkins house as a place for the pursuit of science."

Amused, Iris nodded. "It's impressive. He told me what he's attempting to do with his cold fusion project."

"Which is?"

"You'll have to ask him for the details. But basically it's a room temperature nuclear process which will produce very cheap, very abundant energy. It can be used for everything from making electricity to heating your home. The fuel for the process comes from sea water. Alexander told me that the world's energy needs could be met for the next thirty million years by just the top few feet of water in our oceans. Can you imagine?" She shook her head.

"What intrigues me are the implications," Iris continued. "Cold fusion could change so many things in so many ways. Eventually we could substantially cut back on burning fossil fuels. That means that if he perfects cold fusion, it will stop a lot of the pollution. Cold fusion doesn't produce the kinds of radioactive wastes we get in all the nuclear power plants we have now, and it isn't dangerous."

"That's mind-boggling," said Jaid. "It sounds like we'd have a cleaner environment."

Iris focused on Jaid. "Just what I was thinking."

Jaid smiled. "Well, he must find the answer. How close is he?"

"He says he's this close," Iris indicated with her thumb and index finger. "But the results are not consistent."

"Must be frustrating."

Iris nodded.

Silence fell, broken occasionally by the shriek of a seagull.

Jaid opened the cooler and extracted a bottle of sparkling water. Breaking off a piece of cheese, she offered it to Iris.

Iris shook her head, "Think I'll go for a swim first."

Jaid nodded and closed the cooler. "There *may* be some left when you get back," she said with a wink.

"Thanks," Iris smiled as she collected her equipment. Moving onto the dive platform, she pulled on the fins and adjusted the mask and snorkel. With a graceful step she entered the inviting water.

The surface closed behind her. She cut through the water to lower depths, feeling her body reacting to the added pressure, not threatening, but reassuring, much like a gentle hug.

She surfaced near the bow of the boat and lifted an arm in greeting to Jaid, then began swimming in a wide circle.

She once again dived and swam underwater, all the

time moving her head back and forth, searching the area for her friend. Her body began an undulating motion, up and down, much the same as the movement of the dolphin. She became the dolphin for whom she searched.

She surfaced, allowing herself to be rocked by the mild swell of the water. She felt the presence of Dear One moments before she saw the gray shape with the familiar nick in the dorsal fin. This time, though, Dear One approached with an uncharacteristic hesitancy. Puzzled, Iris edged her way closer. Close enough to reach out and touch Dear One, she kept her hands at her sides, head face down in the water.

Instead of Dear One's usual playfulness, there was something different this morning. She was very quiet, her usual clicks and whistles replaced by a rasping noise from her blowhole. The large gray eyes were glazed. Iris reached out to stroke the firm cool side of Dear One, but her hand stopped midway as she saw several menacing skin lesions, mostly on her melon-shaped forehead. Iris forced herself to remain calm, but her heart was racing. For an instant, Dear One seemed to lose the glazed look and focus more directly on her, and Iris responded by stroking her very gently while murmuring softly. Iris held the moment like an embrace.

Without warning, Dear One turned and headed out to sea. Iris felt pulled to follow, to comfort and care for her friend, but resigned herself to watching as Dear One slowly moved out of sight.

As Iris returned to the boat, she found the distance very difficult to swim. She pulled herself onto the boat.

"What happened, Iris? Iris, what is it?"

"She's sick, Jaid. She's very sick."

"Iris is a gourmet cook. Damn, how could I have invited her and Skylar to dinner?" Alexander mumbled to himself. What madness had possessed him, he wondered, as he wrestled with the big stock pot he planned to use for the spaghetti sauce.

At least he had a good recipe, which he had gotten from an Italian friend. Now he was having second thoughts. Everybody had their own special recipe for spaghetti sauce, and they all thought theirs was the best.

It was too late now. He started chopping the fresh parsley and garlic.

He'd use the linen napkins tonight. And he'd found some pretty daisies at a shop in town. He had the Chianti, and the pungent, crusty garlic bread he liked. Ice cream and cookies for dessert. *Couldn't go wrong with that*, he thought.

He realized he was out of practice with entertaining, but why was he so nervous about this? He wanted it to be just right. *Why didn't I make the sauce yesterday? It's always better the second day.*

He heard them as they approached the house, and opened the door to greet them. Iris looked stunning in a blue dress made of wispy cotton. The full skirt was blowing in the breeze. Her eyes were the color of the dress. The healthy, tanned athletic woman looked soft and feminine. *Another facet of Iris. As soon as I think I know her, I see another...."*

Skylar entered enthusiastically. "Hi, Alexander, I brought a special shell to show you. I can't wait to tell you the story that goes with it."

As they ate Alexander could tell by their intense concentration that they were enjoying the meal.

Iris put down her fork and smiled. "I think that's the best spaghetti sauce I've ever tasted."

Alexander beamed. "Let's take our cognac and sit on the deck."

As they settled into the deck chairs, Skylar pulled out his shell.

"That's a delicate little thing," observed Alexander. "Where did you find it?"

"I was sitting on the beach near Aunt Iris's house, feeling so happy that I was going to get to stay here longer. I told my guardian angel, 'Thank you,' and that's when I found it." He paused, waiting for Alexander's reaction.

Skylar sat upright, his voice lowering to a conspiratorial whisper, "It floated right up to me. Then I looked it up in Aunt Iris's book and found out it's an 'Angel Wing.' It means she heard me."

"Oh," said Alexander, "like 'You're welcome.' Right?"

"Right!" Skylar said. "This shell looks weak, but the book said it can bore right into the sand."

"That's very interesting. I don't think I've seen one like that since I've been here."

"This is one of my really important treasures," Skylar beamed. He held up his shell in the moonlight.

Alexander turned his attention to Iris. "Skylar told me he swam with your dolphin. She sounds amazing."

"She's not my dolphin," Iris said quietly, "but she is a dear friend, a very intelligent animal. I care very deeply for her."

"How did you get to be friends with a dolphin?"

"She saved my life."

She recounted the story of Dear One's rescue of her and Ray, as Alexander listened intently. "After that I had the feeling I had to find her again. I had no idea how. Finally, through what seemed like a miracle, we found each other."

"Then she continued to come back?"

"Yes, we swam together, got to know each other. She'd bring me gifts, like shells. We built a respect and trust between us."

"Did you see her on your dive today?"

Iris didn't answer, but looked away, out over the water.

Abruptly she stood and said, "It's getting late. Skylar needs to be in bed."

His eyes followed them as they walked away down the beach.

Iris was busy catching up on some paperwork while Elmore wiped down the bar. She had gone out on her boat several days in succession searching for Dear One.

Hearing the door open, both turned. Ralph McBain walked in and sat down at the bar.

"Iris," he nodded. Turning back to Elmore he patted his stomach. "How 'bout a burger, fries and a beer?"

Elmore nodded. "What're you doing here this hour, Ralph?"

Ralph shook his head. "Group canceled on me. I took these four guys out yesterday, and they were supposed to go out again this afternoon. Didn't show."

Elmore shook his head. "Damn shame." He turned and headed toward the kitchen.

Ralph cleared his throat. "Figured you'd be out in your boat, Iris."

"Work." She indicated the piles of paper in front of her.

"Probably rather be out swimming with that dolphin."

Iris smiled. "Right."

"Figured. You know, I've gotten where I can even spot it. It's got this big nick on its fin." He pointed to his back, indicating where the dorsal fin was located.

Iris looked at him expectantly. "Have you seen her recently?"

He shook his head. "Nope."

Silence settled over them. Ralph sat staring out of the window at the ocean. "Times sure are different."

Iris looked up. "What do you mean, Ralph?"

"I'm fifty-five years old and I've been fishing these waters since I was old enough to haul the nets. I used to go out with my daddy and my granddad. It was his boat, then. I'd catch fish 'til my little arms were ready to fall off. Years later, when it was my daddy's boat, I was his first mate. Same thing. We pulled 'em in. 'Bout twenty years ago, the Henrietta became mine. My boys would go out with me and we'd catch a load in no time. We made real good money."

He paused as Elmore placed his platter of food in front of him. He ate a couple of fries. "Whew. They're hot, Elmore."

"Guess so," Elmore said. "Just fried 'em."

Ralph drained his beer and tapped the bar with the empty bottle. Elmore replaced it with a full one.

"Well, you know, Iris. Nowadays my boys are all gone. Found work elsewhere." He tested another french fry, and took a big bite out of the burger.

"But, I can't say I blame 'em. There ain't no damn fish out there worth catching. Nowadays, we catch more trigger fish than any other kind. I sell 'em. But hell, we used to either throw trigger fish back or use 'em for bait. Nobody ate 'em." He shook his head. "You should see some of those fish. Why, me and some of the boys—Hank, Slim, Ed—

well, we were talking just the other day. Some of the fish are deformed. Honest to God, they got bumps where there ain't supposed to be any. Some got missing fins or funny-colored spots. I won't eat 'em. I throw 'em back. I'd rather eat beef." He gestured with the remains of his burger. "My daddy'd roll over in his grave if he could see this." He looked down at the now-empty bottle. Grimacing, he banged it on the bar with so much force that Iris was surprised it didn't shatter. He pushed away the rest of the burger and stared at it.

Softening at last, he looked up at Iris. "Well, Iris you've only been here a short time, maybe ten years, but you're family. We care about family here." His face showed his discomfort.

"I appreciate that."

"If you ever need us, you know we're here."

Elmore came out of the back and placed another cold beer in front of Ralph. As Iris picked up her paperwork and headed toward the kitchen, she stopped and looked at him. "Thank you, Ralph."

Ralph grunted as Iris walked out.

CHAPTER NINETEEN

I ris woke early that morning, her limbs heavy, with a disquieting feeling that something was wrong. Unaccustomed to waking in the dark, she searched her mind for the remnants of her dreams, thinking they could be the source of her unease. But nothing surfaced to help explain her feelings.

Her physical lethargy was countered by an itchy, restless need to be doing something, to be moving. *Why am I feeling this way?* she thought, wondering again if it could have been a dream. *Maybe it was a noise that woke me.* Slipping into her kimono, she left her room, looking in on Skylar on her way down the hall. She was relieved to see that he was peacefully asleep, arms and legs wrapped around the spare pillow in a fierce-looking hug, Sandy nestled in the small of his back.

Careful not to wake him, she moved out to the deck. The predawn morning struck her as unnaturally still. *The world is waiting for something,* she thought.

Knowing it would be some time before Skylar was up, Iris decided to walk, hoping to work off some of her restlessness and shake the tension that was dogging her. She set off across the dunes, her feet relishing the familiar feel of sand yielding to her step, cool now, soft and silent.

Even the waves were subdued in this hour before the tide began to come in, their rhythm more of a background hum than the energetic pulse she was used to.

Iris stood at the edge of the water, ankle deep in the gently lapping surf, and gazed out to sea, seeking the peace she normally found here. As always, her thoughts turned to Dear One. *Are you up, my Dear One, or are you resting somewhere?* she called softly in her mind. She knew dolphins breathed consciously, rather than automatically, so they didn't sleep in the way humans did. But she could picture Dear One at rest after a day of energetic exploration and play. She would bob quietly at the surface, rocked softly by the gentle swells and perhaps bathed in moonlight, resting and recharging for the day to come.

Have you needed rest, Dear One? The question reverberated in her mind, echoing off her concerns about Dear One's recent lengthy absences and the mysterious sores on her silky skin. Iris was afraid for her, but unable to help beyond directing love and energy to her beloved friend. In her heart she was unwilling to accept the fact that Dear One could be seriously ill. *You'll be all right,* she affirmed. *I know you'll be all right. Rest and be well.*

Sending her thoughts outward, Iris had the sense that the thoughts were swallowed by the sea, the sense that things were different. She hugged her arms to her chest to ward off the sudden chill that ran through her, then turned and walked back up the dune to sit and wait for dawn.

Before long she could feel the sun beginning to warm her back, and see the long shadows cast by the dune like an irregular gray-blue carpet over the white sand before her. She kept her eyes fixed on the sea for what seemed like a long time, silently waiting, her thoughts stilled. Finally she rose, shaking herself out of her reverie, knowing that Skylar would be up and wanting his breakfast.

Arms overhead in a languorous stretch, Iris took a moment to gaze up the beach in the direction she had been heading when she stopped. Several hundred feet further on, the peak of a dune cast an arrow-like shadow that seemed to point to a darker spot on the beach just above the surf's edge—oval and featureless, the spot could itself have been a shadow, except for the fact that there was nothing to cause it. Curious, Iris decided to investigate this variation in her familiar world.

Descending onto the hard-packed sand below the high-tide line, it was immediately obvious to Iris that what she saw was not a shadow at all, but something three-dimensional. And from this angle, each step closer revealed details that, bit by bit, became icy shards of pain driven into Iris's heart. It was a dolphin.

Not Dear One, please, don't let it be Dear One, she prayed to whatever God would listen, now running toward the still form. *Oh, God, please!* Her breath caught in her throat as she knelt at the dolphin's side, willing Dear One's telling characteristics not to be there. The dolphin's skin was obscured by a dusting of sand, which for a moment let her believe that it was some other dolphin. But when Iris forced herself to look at the dorsal fin, she saw the triangular nick that had been the first way she had come to identify Dear One. Now, it would be the last.

Unable to move, to think, Iris felt she had turned to stone. Her eyes were the only things that seemed to work, and all they could do was fill her mind and heart with the fact of Dear One's death. It wasn't until she saw tiny tracks forming in the sand on the dolphin's back that she realized she was crying, her tears spilling out of their own accord, without any accompanying sound.

The sight of her tears broke the final barriers to her grief. Iris stretched her arms around Dear One's still, cold body, pressing against the now-rough skin, oblivious to the stinging grit cutting into her face. "Oh, Dear One, Dear One," she cried. "What will I do without you?" Her tears turned to sobs, and her body shook as though she would shatter.

Slowly the sobs quieted, and Iris sat up again, brushing the sand from her face. As she gazed down at the dull eyes of Dear One, memories leaped unbidden to her mind, memories so alive it was hard for Iris to believe that her beloved dolphin was actually dead. Iris pushed them back, fighting for control, knowing she had to think, before she could give herself permission to remember, to grieve. The thought of what came next terrified her. What was she going to do? How could she take care of Dear One's body? She barely had the strength and will to move, and yet the thought of Dear One lying here, exposed and vulnerable, was more than she could bear.

The sun, now well above the dunes, pierced Iris's swollen eyes as she searched the beach for an answer. It was still deserted at this hour, except for some tiny figures moving far down the beach. *Stay away, leave us alone*, she thought, wanting no one to intrude on her private grief. But as they came closer, she realized it was the one person she knew would immediately understand. It was Jaid, on her morning walk with Miss Natasha.

Jaid approached, running the last stretch of distance as she realized what she was seeing. She stopped short, dropping the lead attached to Miss Natasha's halter and motioning to the pig to stay. Obedient, Natasha tucked her legs under her and sat down, floppy ears perked in interest at this change in their routine.

"Is it... ?" Jaid started to ask, but stopped, the look on Iris's face giving her the answer.

"Oh, Jaid!" Iris said, voice choked, tears beginning to

well up again. Jaid kneeled down and gathered Iris into her capacious embrace, and Iris felt herself enclosed in more than arms. Wrapped in her friend's enormous strength and warmth, Iris was soothed for the moment by wordless compassion and understanding.

The two women sat there for a while, together enduring the waves of grief that periodically engulfed Iris, until Iris's tears began to ebb. Finally, she spoke.

"I have to take care of her," she said. "I'm not sure how, but I have to take care of her."

"What do you want to do?" asked Jaid, gently.

"I have to get her out of the sun." Iris answered. "I have to bury her."

Jaid nodded wordlessly, thinking through the implications, knowing immediately that the best service she could offer Iris now was to handle the practical details.

"Will you be all right if I leave you for a little while? I'll need to get some people organized," she said.

Iris nodded, then Jaid asked, "What about Skylar?"

"Skylar," Iris breathed, putting her hand to her flushed face, knowing he would feel the loss almost as keenly as she did. "Jaid, I have to be the one to tell him—but I don't want to leave Dear One alone. Would you wait here with her while I go and get him?"

"Of course, my dear," Jaid answered quietly. "Take as long as you need. I'll be here."

Iris set off down the beach toward home, running now, anxious to get back to Dear One as soon as she could. Her mind reached fruitlessly for words she could use to tell her nephew that his wonderful new friend was gone. She was still groping when she brushed the sand off her feet and entered the house.

Skylar was awake, sleepily rubbing his eyes as Iris entered his room. "Been for a walk?" he asked. Iris didn't answer immediately, watching Skylar's eyes widen in fear as he took in her red and swollen eyes. "Aunt Iris, what's happened?" the boy asked in a small voice.

Iris sat down quickly next to Skylar and put her arm around his shoulders, trying to communicate some of the warmth and strength given her by Jaid. "Skylar," she said, "it's Dear One. I found her on the beach this morning."

"On the beach? How could she be on the beach?" Skylar demanded, confused and frightened. "Dolphins can't come out on land."

"Remember I told you I was afraid she was getting sick?" Iris said. "I guess I was right. Skylar, she has been sick, and now she's dead."

"Dead." Skylar repeated the word so softly Iris could barely hear him. Then he shuddered slightly, and clutched Sandy to his chest. He looked up at Iris with eyes that knew too much about death and loss. As they held each other's gaze, Skylar's eyes began to brim over with tears.

Iris held him, slowly rocking him, knowing that to Skylar this must bring up memories of his grandfather, and his beloved Spock that Jack had destroyed. Heartbroken to be the one bringing news of another loss, her own grief set aside for the moment, Iris searched for ways to make it easier for him. She held him, saying more without speaking than words could convey. As he slowly quieted down, she spoke.

"Skylar, I need to go back to her," she said. "Do you want to come and say good-bye?"

"Yes, Aunt Iris," Skylar replied, his face very serious.

"I need to warn you that she doesn't look the same as she did in her world," Iris said gently, trying to prepare him for the sight of death. "It made me very sad, and I'm sure it will make you sad, too."

Skylar nodded, his eyes large and moist.

"Let's go, then," she said.

Iris left him to get dressed, and went into her own room to change into shorts and shirt. Waiting for Skylar in the living room, she ran her hands over the shells on the special shelf. Nubby and smooth, from tiny to fist-sized, each one she touched flooded her mind with a scene that brought back the familiar sensation of Dear One's silky skin in the cool water, the magical world they had shared for so long. On impulse, she slipped two of the shells into the pocket of her rumpled khaki shorts.

Skylar joined her, slipping his hand trustingly into hers. With her free hand, Iris picked up a yellow plastic bucket from the bench on the deck as they left. Iris and Skylar continued to hold hands during the walk back to where Dear One lay, Skylar only letting go to accept Jaid's warm hug. He clung to her for a moment, then took Iris's hand again.

"I'll be back soon," said Jaid, and started off down the beach, Miss Natasha by her side.

"Jaid—Alexander," Iris called after her.

Jaid nodded. "I'll call him," she said, and walked on.

In the bright light of morning, Dear One's skin was visibly drying, beginning to peel as if from a two-day-old sunburn. Iris could see that the blow-hole had begun to pucker; her body, effortlessly and magically weightless in the sea, was beginning to flatten now from the crushing weight of gravity.

Heart aching, Iris disengaged her hand from Skylar's and went to the edge of the advancing surf. She filled the bucket with sea water and gently began rinsing the defiling sand from the dolphin's body, knowing her act was as futile as dressing a dead woman's hair but wanting to do something, anything, to ease the pain of her loss. Skylar helped her, cupping his hands to carry water, tenderly smoothing the skin around Dear One's eyes and on her dorsal fin. Then they sat down next to her, Skylar nestled into the shelter of Iris's arms, and waited, each lost in private memories of Dear One and their time together.

The sun was well above the horizon when they heard the sound of voices, and looked up to see Jaid returning, a small group of people at her heels. Iris could see Elmore, Charlene, Hank, Alexander, Ralph, and several other fishermen who used Bryson Beach as their home base. *Jaid must have caught them just before they headed out,* Iris thought. Two of the men juggled a rolled-up tarp, and several carried shovels.

Iris and Skylar rose to greet them, dusting the sand off their legs. As the others approached, Iris braced herself, feeling an unreasoning resentment against the intrusion, yet grateful to Jaid for gathering the help she so desperately needed.

The group was respectfully silent as they neared the dolphin. Most everyone in the small community knew of Iris's special relationship with Dear One. Elmore was the first to reach them, his rugged face twisted with compassion and sadness. He grasped Iris's shoulders in a gruff hug, then stepped back while the others took turns, touching Iris on the arm, clasping her hand, silently communicating their understanding and feeling. Skylar also received these attentions, brief touches on the cheek, a quick hug.

"Have you thought where?" Jaid asked gently.

"Behind the big dune, on the point," Iris answered. Jaid nodded, and motioned to Elmore, who began spreading the tarp with the help of the others who had come. They carefully rolled Dear One's body onto the tarp and, at a nod from Elmore, lifted it. There were five people on each side to bear the five-hundred-pound weight, awkward now where it once had been eloquently graceful. Iris and Skylar walked at the back edge, steadying the load, maintaining a contact with their friend.

As they walked with their burden down the half-mile of beach to the point, Iris was aware of a silent gallery of watchers looking down on them from the dunes. *Word must have spread quickly*, she thought, and sent silent thanks to her family of friends for not crowding around.

At the point, Iris and Skylar sat quietly with Dear One while the others began to dig, far enough back from the dune to be in firm ground, in a spot shaded by a small clutch of oleander bushes. Then, unable to stand on the sidelines, Iris walked up and took a shovel from someone's hands. Grim and determined, she forced her muscles to obey, scooping out the resisting earth in measured strokes.

Iris was composed as they lowered the body into the hole. Her eyes were dry. She was unwilling to grieve in public. Skylar left her for a few minutes as she stood there, saying a silent good-bye to Dear One. When he returned, it was with the yellow bucket, filled again with sea water. He asked her permission with his eyes, and when she nodded, anointed Dear One with the sea to send her forth with memories of that world. Skylar's tender act brought the tears to Iris's eyes, and they flowed unchecked down her immobile face.

Those who had come to help moved away now, giving Iris and Skylar privacy for their final good-byes. Only Jaid and Alexander stayed close, ready to help if they were needed.

Reaching into her pocket, Iris drew out the shells she had brought. Oblivious to her surroundings, she held them tightly for a moment, once again letting the scenes and the memories engulf her in wonder and gratitude. Then she knew it was time. She tenderly placed the shells next to Dear One's body and, kneeling by the grave, lifted a double handful of the sandy earth and sprinkled it over the dolphin's skin. She stopped and looked at Skylar, who also gathered a handful of dirt and dropped it in. Then Iris took up the shovel again, methodically filling the grave until the job was done. On the edges of her awareness, she knew Jaid and Alexander were helping. When they finished, Alexander gathered the tools and prepared to take them away, but he paused for a moment, reluctant to leave while Iris and Skylar were still there.

Iris walked over to him to acknowledge his help. "Thank you," she said softly, touching his hand briefly, then turned away.

Jaid walked with Iris and Skylar back to the beach house, an arm around each. When they got there, Iris slumped into a chair on the deck, her eyes drawn to the sea. Skylar gave her a hug and went inside, and Jaid followed. They were back in a moment, Jaid saying: "Iris, Skylar's going to come home with me for a while so you can have some time to yourself. I'll check with you later."

Overcome with sudden weariness, Iris looked at Jaid with gratitude. "I'll call you," Iris said. Jaid and Skylar left, Skylar carrying his small duffel bag in one hand, his stuffed dog under his arm. Iris was alone with her grief.

The sunset that night was spectacular, streaking the sky with vivid gold and orange, shading to a velvety indigo that coaxed the stars out, one by one. It was a time of day Iris usually welcomed. She could savor the cool evening air after the warmth of the afternoon, and the special peace that seemed to fall over the beach at dusk.

But on this day, the sunset's beauty was stained in Iris's mind with an ominous tinge of finality. As the sun sank into the sea, far down the curve of beach to her right, it seemed to be taking with it much of what had made her life so joyful, so special. The day was ending, and it seemed her life was ending, too—at least a part of it she dearly treasured.

All afternoon Iris had watched the sea, dry-eyed and detached. She knew the tears would come again, but for these hours her feelings were numb while her mind drifted from one thought to another, fixing on none, avoiding many. The avoidance was automatic, whenever a memory of Dear One threatened to surface. She wasn't ready for those memories, not yet.

It was full dark when at last she rose from her chair and turned to go into the house. The weakness in her legs puzzled her at first. Then she remembered she had not eaten since the previous day. She walked through the dark living room, down the hallway to the kitchen, and flipped on the overhead light. It was too much trouble to cook anything, so she opened the refrigerator door and looked to see what she could find that would take no preparation.

For minutes she stood, indecisive, the cool air a balm to her flushed face. Then she gave up, unable to bear the thought of food, and simply poured herself a glass of orange juice. But her throat resisted even that, seeming to constrict further with every swallow, until it seemed she simply couldn't drink any more. She set the glass down, and went back to the living room.

Like a magnet, her display of treasured shells drew her gaze as soon as the light was on. She turned away, but then, bracing herself for the storm of feelings she was sure would come, she moved deliberately closer until she could see every detail of every shell, smooth and textured, pale and brightly colored.

How can I say good-by, Dear One? she thought. *You're here, in every shell.* Tenderly, she lifted the shells, one by one, and grouped them on the worn rug in front of the picture window. She stood looking down at them for a moment, then went to the hall closet and pulled a small cardboard box off the shelf, returning with it to the living room.

Sitting down, cross-legged, in front of the shells, she deliberately faced the memories, now allowing the pain of farewell. Lifting a smooth-textured cowry shell, she cradled it in her palm and closed her eyes, as if to memorize the shell by touch. With the touch came the memory, of course, a memory she had avoided earlier but faced now without flinching.

As the cool surface of the shell slowly absorbed the warmth of her hand, it seemed to turn softer, as if its glassy exterior had become liquid, silky. *Like Dear One's skin,* Iris thought, remembering through the medium of her fingers the misty cool water, the dappled sunlight near the wreck, on the day she and Dear One had found this treasure. The shell took her back there, with scenes so vivid she talked to Dear One in her mind, just as she had when they had been together.

Dear One, she thought, her furrowed brow relaxing into a gentle smile, *how I loved to go treasure-hunting with you.* In her mind's eye, Iris saw Dear One dancing through the water, playing a joyful game of hide-and-go-seek with Iris, or swimming in rapid circles around her until she was dizzy with trying to follow. When Iris swam up to the old bell on the bow of the wreck, her signal to Dear One that the dive was almost over, Dear One often would lead her to a spot she had overlooked, and that particular dive was no exception. That was when she found the cowry shell, smooth and silky, almost sensuous, and reminiscent of the feeling of Dear One's skin.

Iris smiled again, and opened her eyes. She wrapped the shell carefully in a piece of tissue paper and placed it in the box. *That's one,* she thought, and picked up the next one, a slender, banana-shaped razor clam shell the color of dark chocolate, with ridges so subtle they couldn't be detected by sight, only by feel. With this, as with the cowry, she lingered over the memory it evoked, wishing to spare herself nothing.

And so it went, each treasure sending its final message to Iris's mind, each being tenderly wrapped and stored in the slowly-filling box. The tears didn't start until she lifted the final shell, the one she left until the last, knowing it would be the hardest. It was a clam shell with a star, that to Iris symbolized all that Dear One's love and friendship had meant to her. The ability to trust, both herself and others… the sense of being loved…when Iris had begun to perceive the world differently, as if colors were somehow brighter, waves more caressing, stars more brilliant. She would never forget. Iris let the tears flow, holding the shell close to her heart as she had on that incredible night.

Closing the box, Iris taped it shut and stowed it in the back of the closet. She knew she would want the shells around her again, but for now, she needed some distance. Otherwise, she was afraid she would never stop crying, would never be able to accept that Dear One was really gone.

Suddenly very tired, Iris stumbled into the bedroom, stripped off her clothes and fell onto the bed, not bothering to turn down the bedspread. Drained, both emotionally and physically, she fell quickly into a leaden sleep, mercifully dreamless.

Iris didn't stir, even when the sun had touched her

eyes with its warmth and the gulls had begun their raucous morning ballet outside her window. She was awake, but felt too heavy to move, and sore. It was Thursday, a day she usually spent at the bar preparing for the night's special, but somehow there seemed no reason to make the effort to get up.

The morning was well advanced when she heard footsteps on the deck approaching her door. She closed her eyes, willing the visitor to depart, not knowing if she could summon the energy to speak, much less entertain. But the visitor didn't knock, didn't call out, merely let herself in with the ease of familiar custom.

When Jaid walked into the bedroom, she made certain that Iris was awake, then sat down next to her on the bed. She tenderly smoothed the disheveled hair from Iris's forehead, her eyes filled with concern. Iris gave her a wan smile in return, feeling the need to let Jaid know she was going to survive.

"How are you?" Jaid asked, the tone in her voice giving the question dimensions far beyond those it carried in day-to-day normalities.

"I think I'm all cried out," Iris said in a hoarse whisper, her voice unexpectedly dry. "And I think I just passed out, I was so tired."

"Have you eaten?"

The grimace that crossed Iris's face was all the answer Jaid needed. Without saying anything, she rose and went to the kitchen, where she pulled out milk, vanilla ice cream, chocolate sauce, and, lastly, an egg. She mixed up a thick, frothy milkshake and carried it in to Iris.

In spite of herself, Iris had to smile. "This reminds me of my mom, and the time when I was nine and stuck home for days with the mumps. She made me a milkshake every day until I was better."

"Well, I'm willing to do that for you, too, if that's what it takes," Jaid said, smiling warmly in return.

"Is Skylar okay?" Iris asked. "I felt a little selfish, letting him go off with you so I could be alone."

"We talked for a long time last night, and he cried some," Jaid said. "It seems to hit him in waves. "

"I feel that, too," Iris said. "I'm never sure just when the grief will hit, so I'm constantly braced for it. And I feel so heavy, too heavy to move out of the way."

"I know," Jaid said, softly.

She took the now-empty tumbler from Iris's hand and carried it back to the kitchen. When she returned, she was carrying a dampened face cloth, which she used to gently stroke Iris's face and neck, sticky now with the midday heat. Iris closed her eyes and allowed herself to be taken care of, grateful for the love of her dear friend.

Jaid left soon after, by which time Iris had risen and dressed. That seemed to be enough of an effort, and Iris merely sat on her deck, gazing out to sea, until the afternoon wore away into sunset and she could reasonably return to her bed.

That became the pattern of the next few days. Jaid came over each morning to make sure Iris had eaten, and to visit for a little while. Iris was unwilling to leave the house, content to sit and sleep and be still. On the third morning, Iris was aware, in the space between sleep and wakefulness, that she wasn't going to be able to sleep any more. She resisted getting up, because she longed for the numbing sleep to ease her pain. But she finally rose from the bed, untangling herself from the sheet that had wrapped itself around her legs. She felt almost ill, her stomach twisting and her head throbbing.

She pulled on her kimono, and walked slowly into the living room, arms folded protectively, eyes almost closed.

The deep and gnawing feeling of anxiety grew stronger, and she felt confined by the house. She went outside and sat down on the peak of the dune overlooking the sea.

The sense of terror she had been pushing down all night seemed to charge up through her now, and dissipate. Tears rolled down her cheeks. She squeezed her eyes shut to hold them back, clenching and unclenching her hands. A sense of fury—at herself, at God, then Dear One and the very water that had been Dear One's home—raged through her. She stood there, feeling the sand gritty between her bare toes. She thought of the soft silky sweetness of Dear One's skin against her legs, and a sob escaped her throat, deep and guttural.

Head in hands, Iris's vision turned inward now, black with grief. Sinking deeper into the raw gaping hole of pain, she sobbed, "I thought you loved me. Why did you leave?" Over and over, she cried, "Why? Why?"

Finally the fury passed, like a summer storm, and she sat quiet, spent. The waves of aching loneliness rolled back a little and she closed her eyes, letting the clenched jaws and fists slowly relax.

Back at the house, Iris dressed and drove slowly to the Sand Dollar. When she walked in the back door, Elmore's face showed his surprise at seeing her. He stood up awkwardly. "Want some coffee?" he asked, his voice uncharacteristically gentle.

Iris took the mug he offered and walked into the bar, moving immediately to stand in front of the hand-hewn sculpture of the dolphin that she had loved for so long. She reached out to touch the dorsal fin, then drew her hand back as if she had been shocked.

"Elmore," she said, turning to look at him. "Please put this away somewhere."

Elmore silently nodded his assent and Iris walked to

the front door. Reaching it, she stopped and turned to look at him. "And Elmore—thanks for everything."

CHAPTER TWENTY

I ris sat on the deck, recognizing the lone figure walking up the beach. She rose to greet her approaching friend. They smiled at each other, as Jaid stepped onto the deck and lowered herself into the nearest chair.

"Guess I'm not accustomed to the noon sun," she panted.

She sat and they both gazed out at the horizon. Iris had almost forgotten she wasn't alone when Jaid reached out and squeezed her hand. "You know you're in my thoughts a lot these days."

It was a statement, not a question that required an answer, so Iris just nodded. "Thanks for being so good to Skylar...."

Jaid lowered her head and said softly, as if to herself, "That boy has had more losses already than some folks have in a lifetime." Silence settled over them again. Jaid finally asked, turning toward Iris, "And what about you, my dear?"

"It's been hard, Jaid. I've cried, I've sat and stared into space, I've gotten angry. Then I seem to repeat the same cycle. If I just knew what happened...." She turned away. "Then there are times I don't want to think about it. I don't ever want to see a dolphin again, but ..." she paused. "I went to the bar yesterday and I had Elmore store your sculpture." She slowly turned to look at Jaid.

"I know. I was there last night. I pried it out of him."

"I just couldn't look at it, not yet. I hope that doesn't hurt your feelings."

Jaid shook her head. "I just wish there were something I could say or do."

"Thanks for being my friend and understanding," she said softly.

Jaid opened her purse and pulled out a folded piece of paper. "I came across this in one of my papers. It's a few months old but... well, I thought you might like to see it." She handed it to Iris.

Iris took the scrap of paper and unfolded it. It was a single column of type that had been clipped from the paper. The title leaped out at her. "Dolphin Death Toll Mounts." "What? Where did ..." her voice trailed off as she began to read. Her mouth tightened and she looked up at Jaid, "Three hundred and twenty deaths in the Gulf." She looked back at the article. The paper crackled as her hands clenched. "They've yet to analyze the tissue samples?" She finished the article in silence then looked up at Jaid, her eyes full of fire. "I can't believe this." She shook her head and looked out at the water. "If they had analyzed those tissues, maybe, just maybe, Dear One might still be alive." She quickly got out of the chair.

"Have they done anything," she glanced at the clipping, "since the end of May? Have they found any answers?" She looked at Jaid. "This is outrageous. It makes me sick."

Jaid stood and came to her. "Agreed. Absurd, isn't it?"

Iris reached out and took her hand. "Thanks. I know this must have been hard for you, bringing this to me."

Iris held the receiver to her ear as the phone rang. "National Fisheries Service. How may I direct your call?"

"I'd like to speak to Dr. Ernest Fullerton, please." Iris waited, motionless, her reflective blue eyes staring out at the Gulf.

"Dr. Fullerton's office. May I help you?"

"I'd like to speak to Dr. Fullerton please."

"Who may I say is calling?"

"My name is Iris Sanders. Dr. Elaine Potts at the Smithsonian referred me to Dr. Fullerton."

"One moment please." Iris waited. "Dr. Fullerton is leaving for a meeting," she said, when she came back on the line.

"Wait," Iris said with conviction. "This is a very urgent matter and I will only take a few moments of Dr. Fullerton's time. I must speak to him. Please tell him it's about the dolphin deaths in the Gulf."

Iris was holding the phone tightly, determined to speak with him today, when he came on the line. "Yes, this is Dr. Fullerton."

"Dr. Fullerton, my name is Iris Sanders. I'm a resident of Bryson Beach, Florida, a small town on the Panhandle. I am personally concerned with the dolphin deaths in the Gulf. I had a continuing interaction with a particular dolphin that died suddenly last month. Dr. Elaine Potts said you might be able to answer my questions."

"I don't know if I can," he said tentatively.

"What's killing them? Do you know what it is?"

"The cause of the deaths is difficult to pin down. It may be a variety of things. They seem to be suffering from a diminished immune response as a result of the pollution that is building up in the waters, especially around urban areas that have heavy industry. It's not unlike the die-offs in the Northeast in '87 and the one last year in the Mediterranean. We've found high levels of chemical pollutants in their bodies, including heavy metals and PCBs, though these toxins do not seem to be the immediate cause of death. The toxins build up in their body fat and then, when food is not plentiful, when algae blooms occur for instance, and their fat tissue is used, the substances are released into their systems."

Dr. Fullerton had stopped talking but Iris was unable to speak, as her mind considered the implications of what he had just told her.

"Is it possible to do a biopsy on this dolphin?" he asked.

"No, she died several weeks ago. In any case, I was under the impression that there is already a backlog of tissue samples that haven't been analyzed."

"I see you're very well informed, Ms. Sanders. We are working on our funding, though, and hope to have that handled soon."

Iris thanked him for his time and as she hung up the phone, turned the question, "What can I do?" over and over in her mind.

Iris was washing the dinner dishes and Skylar was sprawled across his bed, drawing, when the storm came blowing in from the Southwest. Usually the summer thunderstorms announced themselves with escalating winds and distant thunder. But this one came on suddenly, with a boom and flash of lightning which blew out the power transformer on the pole beside the house.

Iris was drying her hands in the dark when the second lightning bolt struck nearby. The wind picked up rapidly and the house began to shake. Suddenly, Iris was afraid. She had been melancholy, remembering Dear One, once again feeling lonely for her friend. The storm moved her to anger, because in its power she felt her own powerlessness to save Dear One.

"Aunt Iris?" called Skylar from his room.

The fear she heard in his voice released her, and she replied, "I'm coming, Skylar. Let me close the windows." The rain was blowing fiercely against the house, and she ran from room to room slamming down the windows.

She found Skylar on his bed under the covers, with a pillow pulled over his head. Sitting next to him, she said, "It's okay, Skylar." She put her hand on his chest and could feel him shaking. "Skylar, it's all right. Come here and let me hold you." She gently pulled him onto her lap and slipped the pillow out of his arms.

She cupped his head to her shoulder and repeated, "It's all right." Skylar started to cry softly as Iris stroked his hair. Gradually, he began to sob, holding onto her. "Skylar, you're safe with me. It's okay."

She knew he was crying for Spock, Grandpa, his mother—all his losses, including Dear One. Iris held him close for a long time without words, rocking him slowly as the storm raged around them.

Iris cried, too, quietly, for her losses. But soon a feeling of calm came over her, and in that moment she knew what it would feel like to love a child of her own. She squeezed Skylar tightly to her.

"Aunt Iris, I love you," said Skylar.

Iris smiled in the darkness and said, "I love you, too,

very much."

Another blinding flash of lightning was followed by rolling thunder, and the moment was broken. "I'm not scared any more," said Skylar. "Can we light your oil lamp?"

The rain stopped as suddenly as it had begun, but the wind continued to blow. "I have an idea," said Iris. "Let's go outside and watch the lightning."

The storm had moved off to the north and the lightning flashes were distant now. Iris and Skylar climbed the dune behind Iris's house and sat on the wet sand to watch the storm. The air was rich with salt tang and that special thunderstorm smell, fresh and pungent. Iris felt exhilarated by nature's display.

"Do you know how to tell how far away the storm is?" she asked Skylar.

"No, but I can see it's pretty far away now," he replied.

"You count the seconds between the lightning flash and the thunder." They waited until a jagged lightning bolt crossed the distant sky. "One one-thousand, two one-thousands," counted Iris. "Seven one-thousands." And she was stopped by a distant rumble.

"How far was that?" Skylar asked.

"Well, the sound travels a little less than a thousand feet every second. That's just over three football fields long. And we see the lightning almost immediately. So, if the thunder comes seven seconds after the lightning flash, it's about seven thousand feet away, or almost a mile and a half."

"Wow," said Skylar. "That's great."

"If the time between the lightning and the thunder is getting longer, you know the storm is moving away from you," Iris added.

For a while they continued to calculate the distance of

the receding storm. But when they no longer could distinguish the thunder, they lay back on the sand and watched the thinning clouds silhouetted against the star-filled sky. Iris closed her eyes and listened to the waves, totally at peace for the first time since Dear One's death.

CHAPTER TWENTY-ONE

Alexander found himself fighting a rising sense of frustration and hopelessness. The lab felt smothering today. He thrust his hands through his hair, and stood up to stretch, rotating his head, then his arms, to relieve the tension. His eyes rested on Skylar. Alexander walked over to see what commanded his young friend's attention.

Skylar had sketched a meticulously detailed stretch of beach, and was looking at some photos in a glossy book. He smiled up at Alexander.

"I'm getting ready to draw a sand dollar. Elmore told me there used to be a really big one up over the bar, but it got knocked down, and broke. Aunt Iris has been wanting one ever since, but hasn't found the right one." He looked down at his drawing. "I sure would like to give her one, especially since Dear One…" His voice trailed off.

"I think she'd like that a lot."

"Elmore says they're mighty scarce. But I have a plan." He picked up several well-sharpened colored pencils.

"What is it? Can you tell me?"

"You know how I've been learning about dreaming my dreams, like Jaid taught me?"

"Maybe you'd better tell me again."

Skylar's mouth curved into a smile. "Things you want, really want, you think about. You think about the way it looks and feels, and then you imagine already having it. You have to believe in it. I draw it so I can see it. Then I dream. When I get done with this sand dollar, I'll put my special dreaming crystal on it, because crystals help the dreaming." He took a long breath.

"I used to make crystal radios when I was a kid, and I know that the chips they use in computers are crystal, but I never thought of using them the way you do," Alexander said. He removed his glasses and polished the lenses with the bottom of his knit shirt, then turned back to his thoughts.

He heard the whisper of Skylar's pencil strokes on the sketch-pad, and fervently hoped Skylar would actually run across a good-sized sand dollar, so he wouldn't be disappointed.

The day after the storm, Iris arrived early at the Sand Dollar, coming in right after she took Skylar to Jaid's. Elmore arrived to find her standing at the window.

Iris turned and looked at him, "I've decided to change the menu, Elmore. I'd like to know what you think." They walked over to the bar where the restaurant's menus were stacked. Iris handed him a handwritten sheet of paper.

Elmore stared at the page for some time, reading intently, before saying, "Iris, there's no seafood on this menu."

"I've decided to stop serving it. I believe Ralph's right. I can't serve it any more."

"But Iris, we're a seaside restaurant. People expect us to serve seafood here. It's going to ruffle some feathers."

"I know. They'll have to adjust. I don't want to use any more polystyrene either, or paper, unless we can recycle it. We can go to cloth napkins."

Elmore stood there, nodding in agreement, not surprised at the quiet determination in the gentle and willowy woman.

Iris saw them milling around their cars that afternoon. The men who filed in regularly every day were assembling in the parking lot. Red was at the center of things. They stood in the entry at the foot of the bar, awkwardly, not sure of what to do next. Iris put down what she was doing and looked toward them expectantly.

"We hear you're taking fish off your menu here, Iris. We want to know, what good is that going to do anybody? You're just takin' money out of our pockets and food out of our children's mouths." Red colored visibly as he spoke.

"I'm sorry, Red, fellas... I believe there's something wrong with the fish, with the water. You've seen it, I know you all have. Ralph won't eat seafood any more because he's seen too many diseased fish."

Ralph shifted nervously, "That's a fact, Iris."

"Dear One's death has affected me deeply. I don't want to hear of one more dolphin washing up on the beach. Until we know what's going on, I'm not willing to serve seafood to ..."

"Well, that don't do shit for me," Red interrupted her angrily. "I'm just not going to do my drinking here anymore. Come on, guys."

Red stormed out of the bar, alone. The others looked at each other, embarrassed and uncertain. Then Ralph climbed onto the stool and said, "Well, I guess I'll have a burger an' a beer."

Iris smiled at him. "Thanks, Ralph."

"Well, Iris, you've bought a lot of fish from me and the others over the years. You've stood by us, an' I'm not going to walk away from you now," he said, then added, with a glimmer in his eye, "especially since I kind of agree with you."

The rest of the men just stood in the entry not knowing what to do next, until Ralph yelled out authoritatively, "Y'all just gonna stand in the doorway? Come on and sit down."

Fishing and fish was the topic for the rest of the afternoon and into the evening. Finally, Ralph announced, "Well, if I'm not going to eat the damn things, I guess I better think about finding something else to do."

Silence fell over the bar that only a moment before had roared with conversation. Each person there understood that something important had changed.

Iris sat cross-legged on the floor, sorting through the magazines that had accumulated over the past several months. As she was setting aside the well-illustrated ones for Skylar to use in his collages, a story caught her eye.

The photograph was ethereally beautiful, taken underwater, showing a dolphin ascending a stream of sunlight toward the water's surface. *What a magnificent crea-*

ture, Iris thought, the surface of her skin feeling the coolness of the water, the palms of her hands remembering how it felt to caress Dear One's skin. She closed her eyes for a moment, the image of the dolphin lingering in her mind, and once again she was playing in the water with her magical friend, a memory she knew would never leave her.

When she came back to herself, she relaxed against the end of the sofa and began to read, interested in how someone else might describe an encounter with a dolphin. To her surprise, the article accompanying the photograph was scholarly in tone, setting forth a scientific basis for concern about dolphin health—the fact that dolphins hold a place in the food chain similar to humans, so that sickness in dolphins caused by environmental factors should be thought of as an early warning signal of trouble ahead for the human population.

That's another gift they're giving us, Iris thought, *a truly priceless gift*. She read on, moved by the meaning behind the measured, rational words of the article's author. As she neared the end of the article, she wondered if the author felt anything like she felt. In the closing sentences, she had her answer.

"In times to come," the article concluded, "we will have ample reason to be grateful for the lessons taught us by our dolphin friends. Our job now is to apply ourselves as students, so our learning ceases to cost the lives of our teachers. Their lives, and the beauty and grace they bring to our world, are too precious to sacrifice."

Yes! Iris thought. *Yes!* She wanted the whole world to read this article, and more like it—to get the message that dolphins were more than just lovely sea creatures, that they were important to our world's survival and health. With a wrench, she realized that the magazine was two months old, and she herself had overlooked it until now.

I'm so attuned to dolphins, she thought, shaking her head. *How could I have missed this?* Then she stood up, feeling as if she had wasted too much time, needing urgently to act.

Pulling paper and a pen out of a drawer, Iris sat down at the kitchen table and began writing a letter to the author of the article. She was hesitant at first, wanting to tell her story, and yet afraid. It was one thing to share her experiences with Dear One with friends who loved her— quite another to send them out into the world, where she didn't know how they would be received. She visualized her story, printed in a magazine like this one, and felt vulnerable and exposed.

Iris suddenly realized what she was doing. Dear One had been willing to take a risk in rescuing her and Ray. In honor of her friend, she also would take a risk. *I can't bear to watch even one more dolphin die,* she thought.

Squaring her shoulders, she let the words begin to flow.

CHAPTER TWENTY-TWO

T he front door slammed, distracting Alexander for what seemed like the tenth time that day. He bristled and ground his teeth on the pipestem. This day had become a procession of jangling telephones, computer program screw-ups, and now visitors, all united in a common effort to prevent him from attending to the adjustments he needed to calculate.

The quickness and lightness of the approaching steps told him that his visitor was Skylar, rather than Tom. He was in a hurry, too.

Skylar flew through the open door to Alexander's lab. He grabbed Alexander by the hand, and burst out, "Guess what! Guess what! It's there. You have to come see it. I haven't moved it, 'cause I wanted you to see it just like I found it. Come on!" He tugged on Alexander's hand. "You can leave that for a minute. Come quick."

"Skylar, what? What is it you're so excited about?" Alexander heard the sharp edge in his voice and tried to soften it.

"The sand dollar! My treasure. Come on."

Alexander could hardly keep up with Skylar, who seemed to be defying the laws of gravity. They reached the beach, and Skylar pointed. "There, that way. Not far."

Away he raced.

When Alexander caught up with him, he was standing next to a slightly indented stretch of sand. Skylar pointed down at an unbroken, beautifully formed sand dollar. It was the largest Alexander had ever seen, at least six inches across. The delicately filigreed, bleached surface, like unglazed bisque ware, lay in a bed of seaweed.

Alexander put his hand on Skylar's shoulder. He was speechless. Skylar, too, stood mute, eyes shining, drinking in the sight of the treasure.

"Wow," said Alexander, finally. "That really is something, Skylar."

"It sure is. It's in a different place than I drew it. I had it up in the low dunes, so it would be safe for me until I found it. But I guess it was safe out here on the beach, after all."

Alexander looked at him. "I'm glad you brought me out to show it to me."

"I wanted you to be the first one to know. Besides me, of course," said Skylar. "I only told Jaid the other time."

"The other time?"

"Yeah. The other time when my dreaming worked. That one came out a little different, too, but Jaid said that's sometimes the way it works. I thought it was just practice, but it was even better than I expected. I was at the studio, after class. I made a treasure map of Aunt Iris taking me to the Malt Shoppe for ice cream. I could really taste the cold chocolate on my tongue as I drew it, and I showed my hand holding the cone, with little drips of strawberry and chocolate melting from the top of the gigantic scoops. But when I got home, guess what! Aunt Iris had out an ice cream maker. Did you know people could actually make ice cream, in their own house? We *made* ice cream, right then and there. Lots of it. The best I *ever* tasted."

The unmistakable resonant voice rang out from down the beach, "Yoo-hoo!" They turned to wave at Jaid and her faithful walking companion, framed against the blue water. Skylar took off in her direction. Moments later, Alexander saw him tugging and gesturing at Jaid, who threw back her head and shouted, "Hooray!" to the brilliant sky. They quickly reached Alexander, who felt like the guardian of a priceless treasure.

Jaid reached down and stroked the sand dollar, then turned and clasped Skylar's hands.

"And so, dreamer, this is where you found it."

"Yes, Jaid. Isn't it wonderful?"

She enfolded Skylar in her arms briefly, agreeing that it was, indeed, most extraordinarily wonderful. They both began to laugh, then Skylar kneeled down, gingerly touching the delicate sand dollar. He picked it up, holding it firmly and carefully.

"I've got to go take this to Aunt Iris. I can hardly wait to see the look on her face!"

Not running this time, he set out for the familiar path between the high dunes that led toward town.

Jaid winked at Alexander, and, addressing Miss Natasha, said, "This calls for a celebration." She pulled out a wedge of potato and gave it to her appreciative companion.

They began to walk, slowly, and Alexander fell in step with them.

The silence was broken by Jaid. "Alexander. Your hands are jammed deep in your pockets and your face is set in what can only be described as a scowl. Now, as one carefully trained in observation, I would venture to say you have something on your mind."

Alexander debated with himself for a few moments. His eyes scanned the hazy horizon, then he turned to look at Jaid. Her warm and steady eyes met his.

"Jaid, I feel uncomfortable saying this, but I'm concerned about what you're teaching Skylar. He seems to think he has some mystical powers as a result of a lucky find."

"My friend." Jaid spoke in a measured tone. "I guess I don't believe that you really think we're talking about luck."

"What is it then that we *are* talking about?"

"Well, from what I understand, we could be talking about your own arena—quantum physics."

"What does quantum physics have to do with luck?"

"Doesn't quantum physics say, 'the observer determines the outcome'?"

"Yes, in a manner of speaking."

Jaid shifted Miss Natasha's leash from one hand to the other and lifted her head. Alexander listened to the sounds of the beach—the small waves lapping, the seagulls calling, and the cadence of the surf.

"Alexander, I'm no physicist, but I believe that we *do* determine the outcome. Not as observers, but as active participants."

"But that would mean that there is no objective reality." As he spoke, Heisenberg's Principle of Uncertainty suddenly flashed through his mind. *The observer is a participant in the experiment.* After all, he had always agreed in theory with Heisenberg. *Could he have meant…? Have I been blinded by my own shortsightedness? Impossible! Heisenberg's theories were hypothetical—not meant for real life.*

Jaid continued. "I have been a student of these ideas, and related ones, for some time. And I've learned much about myself, and how and why I have certain things in my life and in my world. It's quite fascinating. I'm beginning to share some of the things I've learned with Skylar. His experiences are not luck, believe me."

Alexander scowled as he paced toward a retreating flock of terns.

Jaid asked, "Can you remember any time recently you wanted something really intensely? To where you could just about taste it?"

"Yeah. This cold fusion project I'm working on. I got forced out of it at my university, but now I've got this great set-up with my friend Tom as my business partner. Except I'm not doing any better with the research right now. I'm kind of stuck."

Jaid nodded vigorously. "What have you been expecting out of your research?"

"Well, ultimately, I want to be able to consistently replicate the cold fusion phenomenon, to the point where it can be used as a cheap, abundant energy source. There are several aspects to it, but right now I need to demonstrate measurable amounts of heat."

"Do you expect this?"

"It would be nice." He smiled wryly.

"I know. But do you honestly expect it? In your heart? On any level?"

"Well, eventually. Of course."

"I guess then you'll have it. Eventually."

The sound of the surf seemed suddenly to be inside his head. He realized he had been holding his breath. He blew his breath out between slightly parted lips, then inhaled deeply. "Jaid, that's ridiculous. Science doesn't work like that. Just because we expect something, doesn't mean it happens." *The observer is a participant—dammit! If I don't stop listening to her, I'm going to lose my objectivity.* "Jaid, come on. You can't be saying that if I expected it now, it would happen now."

She nodded, and leaned over to scratch Miss Natasha behind the ears. "But that's a little over-simplified. If it's not happening, then either you're getting something else out of it's not happening that you want more, or you have reservations about being able to handle the consequences of your success. Or both."

"What do you mean, want more? Like what?"

"Well, some people just like to feel sorry for themselves and pretend they are victims of the world they live in. Others like to struggle."

"*Like* to struggle?" he asked.

With dramatic flair and a twinkle in her eyes, Jaid said, "Against impossible odds the lone scientist slaved selflessly, night and day, barely pausing to eat or sleep, to find the secret that would save a world that had never understood or appreciated him."

Alexander reached to his chest and grasped the handle of the imaginary dagger, and forcefully withdrew it with a gasp. Jaid chuckled appreciatively.

"So that's what Tom was getting at," Alexander muttered.

"What's that?"

"Tom accused me of working so hard on this project because I wanted to prove that my teaching colleagues, my dean, and even my father, were wrong. He said I was driven by revenge."

"Well, if that's so, you may be justifying your current hard work with the thought that someday you will show them the magnificent error of their ways. The problem is that, in my experience, someday never comes. If you decide to give up that motivation and climb down off your cross, then you will have removed an obstacle to your success."

"You make it sound like all I have to do is expect cold

fusion to work now, and it will happen. I don't believe it."

"Like I said earlier, this is over-simplified. I'm talking mainly about attitude and honesty about your real intention. It's like my painting. I still have to pick up my paint brush and put paint onto a canvas. And it's a good thing. What else could I do all day long that would be more fun for me? But the attitude I bring to that process governs the results of my work and the pleasure I get out of doing it. So, you can't give up working on your experiments any more than I can paint without my palette.

"Also, think about some of the very valid reasons for *not* expecting it now—or for not wanting to be the observer/creator. No, really," she held up her hand at his unbelieving look. "Have you thought, for instance, about the notoriety? Or the other ways your life might change? Of course, you can also decide how you would like to 'observe' these things, too. That helps a lot. But it's very good to think about it. It's amazing how you can actually keep something from happening if you fear or resist it for various reasons. Or, of course, don't really believe it. I mention this because I'm thinking of myself, and some resistances I had to achieving success as an artist. For me, there were several intertwining issues that I got sorted out—and I continue to find more ideas to examine. As you may know, I was recently hell-bent on trying to *make* something happen—Skylar, my budding protégé, you know—just for the satisfaction of my ego. But I digress."

"So according to what you're saying, I'm in charge of this," Alexander mused. "My thoughts will determine the outcome of my experiment. My thoughts and my true intention." *I'm glad Blankenship and his damn committee aren't hearing this conversation. They'd really think I've lost it.*

Jaid nodded. "I certainly believe it, and isn't that the whole idea behind double-blind experiments, which you scientists are so insistent upon?"

Suddenly Alexander's brain began to spin like a kaleidoscope. Bits and pieces of information he had known for years suddenly fell into place.

Double-blind experiments. Of course! The participants in an experiment can't know the anticipated outcome lest they influence it. God! Has Heisenberg's theory passed down from the hypothetical realm to physical science, and bypassed me along the way? Could Jaid be right? Is it my expectation of "someday" and my—what was it she had said?—"getting something else out of it's not happening"—that are interfering with my results?

"I believe you can make cold fusion work, Alexander."

"Speaking of cold fusion, I've got to get back."

Jaid took his outstretched hand. "Yes, I think I'll get on back and do some work, too."

Alexander swiftly made his way back to the house. It came down to a choice. Did he want to make a point, or find the key to cold fusion? He entered the cool entrance way, and spoke out loud to the shuttered silence. "Dammit, I'm going to do it! I want results!"

When Skylar went to the studio that afternoon to visit with Jaid, she beckoned him upstairs.

"How did Iris like her sand dollar?"

"Wow, she loved it! She said she'd never seen anything like it. I told her I dreamed it. We talked about dreams. She told me about some dreams she has for what the world can be like."

"Yes, Skylar. I'm glad you're here. I wanted to talk to

you about dreaming, too. I have an idea for a fun project. How would you like to help me dream a dream for Alexander?"

"Sounds like fun. What dream?"

"Of course, he's dreaming it for himself. But we can sure help. The dream of his work — cold fusion. Do you know anything about it?"

"Yes. He's taught me a lot about it. Wait, I'll draw us a treasure map, and then I can show you."

When Jaid looked at his drawing, she saw a cartoon of two hydrogen nuclei. They had round, fat bellies with long arms and legs. Each wore a yellow tee-shirt with a large red H printed in the center. They were hugging each other tightly, sparks flying from their bellies.

Looking on was a dancing and clapping calorimeter, with a broad, toothy grin. Across its teeth was written, "YOU DID IT!!"

Alexander glanced up from the computer printouts he was studying. He was surprised at his own calmness. Jaid and Skylar had just come in, summoned by Alexander's phone call.

"Let me show you what's happening." Alexander tapped a lean forefinger excitedly on the places he had marked on the printout with a yellow highlighter.

"Do you want to wait for Iris?" Jaid asked. "She'll be here any minute."

"Absolutely. But I thought she couldn't get away from the restaurant."

Jaid sat down. "She got too excited, and decided to

steal away. She called just as we were leaving to say she'd be here as soon as possible."

Skylar watched as the printer methodically pushed the paper through, then moved over to Alexander and stood close.

They heard the knock on the door. Skylar leaped out of the room, calling out, "I'll get it!" as he sped towards the door.

Skylar and Iris entered the lab together a few moments later. Alexander noticed that Iris was still wearing her white apron, which she always folded up short. She had her hair tied back, so that it flared out unexpectedly around her shoulders.

"Okay, great. We're all here now, so look at what I've got to show you. Some observed phenomena!" He laughed and pointed once again to the yellow highlights.

"See this line—goes up here, and continues to stay there. That's a very measurable increase in temperature. Things are happening. Yes!"

Skylar looked again to the new pages tumbling crisply out of the back of the printer. "Look, Alexander, it's still doing it!"

Alexander walked over and looked at the page where Skylar was pointing. His vision blurred for an instant.

He removed his glasses, rubbed his eyes, and set the glasses back on the bridge of his nose. His hands trembled and he began to pace excitedly back and forth in the small lab. "Whew. That's even a higher temperature, and more consistent, than any research has shown to date!"

Iris and Jaid were smiling. Skylar grinned. Alexander opened his eyes, shaking his head, looking from one to the other. Jaid caught his eye, and nodded.

Iris quietly reached into her large brocade shoulder-bag, and popped the cork on the bottle of Moet & Chandon she just happened to find there.

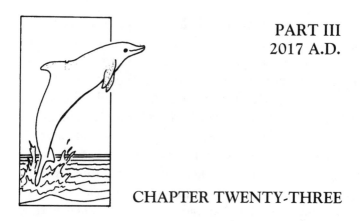

CHAPTER TWENTY-THREE

She sat back on her heels and reviewed the work in progress. The large entry hall was complete except for the south window. From the hole just behind her, she took watery sand and carefully dribbled it through her cupped hands to form the last of the two towers of the parapet.

The wind which scanned the beach surface blew a fine mist against her skin. A dark shadow moved across the sand structure and stood still. The builder turned to see her architect place a bucket of sea water next to the adjacent pit, and then he too knelt in the cool moist sand.

Bent over their work, the two shared remarkable similarities. One appeared to be a miniature version of the other. Both had a shock of blond hair which refused to behave, one highlighted by sunlit gold, the other by strands of silver. Almost at equal intervals, they reached up to push the hair back out of their eyes with identical motions, leaving identical residues of sand on their foreheads. Liquid brown eyes squinted below blond eyebrows and looked over freckled noses, one suntanned, the other sunburned. Lean and gangly, the two were totally absorbed in the task at hand.

Two meters away, a red silk tie marked the end of a

trail of clothing which included a pinpoint oxford shirt and a pair of dress shoes with socks stuffed in them. The suit jacket at one time had been carefully folded on top of the shoes, but by now the wind had unraveled it and opened the sleeves, lightly dusting them with sand. The jacket reached to embrace a scruffy pair of formerly neon green tennis shoes, now well-bleached by sun and saltwater.

Close by lay a scrap of plywood which served as the plane that smoothed the sides of the structure. A large serving spoon, several cups, a piece of screen, a spade with the handle broken, and an old retractable pen lay within arm's reach.

The ambitious construction stretched four meters to their right. The walls along that axis were completed. Last night's sea mist had left them in perfect condition for building. The finished tops of the structure had turned lighter as the sun dried them out.

The two had been working for almost two and a half hours now, with bursts of excited conversation interrupted only by the disrespectful cries of gulls. Just inside the seaward wall a ghost crab had been discovered, the city's first official inhabitant.

The two stopped their work as a tall, attractive woman dressed in turquoise approached them, her full easy strides across the sand belying her maturity. More striking than beautiful, her arms and legs had the long, powerful muscles of one at home in the sea. The wind toyed with her bushy, shoulder-length blonde hair, glistening with silver and tied back with a sheer coral scarf. Loose tendrils framed her tanned, lined face, illuminated by deep-set eyes which borrowed their color from the cerulean blue of the ocean depths.

The architect rose to his feet. The builder shyly returned to her work.

The woman surveyed the complex sand structure, fully taking in its detail. As she raised her gaze from the sand to him, he was enveloped in the powerful affection she radiated.

"Of course, Skylar. Dream cities," Iris said softly.

With a smile, Skylar shrugged his assent, once more caught red-handed doing what he loved. He reached over and wrapped his aunt in a gentle bear hug.

The seven year-old girl looked up and smiled.

"She's you, thirty years ago." She looked at them both with fondness. "I'm so glad you're with us for the celebration. What's all this?" she asked, gesturing toward the structure.

"Carla, why don't you explain it to Iris? After all, you started it—I just pitched in."

The child looked over the entire structure, stepped inside and walked to the finished wall. She stopped to assess the ghost crab's burrow, then looked at each of them with a mischievous smile.

"He's the mayor. He's busy. He's on the videophone." Carla laughed at her own joke. Skylar and Iris joined in. Becoming serious, she continued.

"We haven't finished this yet, but the levitrain will go along the tops of all the walls. This smooth part is for the heliport. Over here is the Transport Center. And this is the little building where people store and recharge their Personal Power Packs—that's for short trips, like taking the kids to school and stuff. Most families have anti-gravity cars so when you get done, you just hook them down on these pylons." She pointed to several upright sticks arranged in angled lines.

Carefully, she stepped over to the opposite wall. "Over here is the Recycling and Fusion Plant, like the one Dad finished last month in South Carolina. All the energy the city needs comes out of it, except for the gardens; they have their own solar energy, even on the cloudy days. The food everyone needs is grown right here, in the Plant Plant. That helps the fresh air come in too. We don't need any garbage dumps or anything like that. See where the water comes in and out? That's sea water over there, and the fresh water flows out of the desalination plant and into its own canal. This is my favorite part—the Animal Garden. The whole garden is open to them, to walk around wherever they like. The people walk behind a fence so they don't disturb the animals." At this point Iris and Skylar looked at each other, then burst into delighted laughter.

"Were you cloned, Carla?" Iris asked, winking at Skylar.

"No, I'm a biological, but I have a friend who was," Carla replied with all the naive sincerity of a seven-year-old.

Iris's voice softened. "That means you're unique, as is your father," she said tenderly, her glance embracing them both.

"People will be getting to the gallery around two, and Jaid can't wait to see you. Can you leave this for a while?"

"Give us a few more minutes and we'll get cleaned up and meet you there," Skylar replied. Iris nodded and walked back through the dunes toward the restaurant.

"Will this be here when we get back, Dad?" Carla asked, as she smoothed another portion of the wall.

"Well, maybe," said Skylar. "I've got an idea. Let's ask the mayor to help. He can keep an eye on things overnight so we don't have to start from scratch in the morning."

"Right!" Carla agreed. While Skylar gathered the scattered clothing, the child squatted down beside the crab's burrow. Skylar waited patiently as Carla gave earnest instructions to the caretaker of their domain. They left, walking side by side up the beach toward the party held in honor of Jaid's ninetieth birthday.

The next morning, Iris arose at dawn, and slipped onto the deck outside her bedroom. The sunrise bathed her in its brilliant hues. The first crimson crease of light interrupted the lavender, mauve, and blue, graduating into rose, fuchsia, orange, yellow, white. She watched the colors move quickly across the horizon, releasing the night, burning off the morning mist, offering the day. She closed her eyes to its bright light and allowed the sun to warm her, becoming relaxed as she absorbed its energy. The warmth caused her to stretch and move, gently tugging at muscles that welcomed the motion. Pulling at the sky with one arm, then the other, she yawned luxuriously, deeply inhaling the still-damp air and releasing it fully. It felt so good she continued until she was quite awake, her blood rich with oxygen, her mind alert.

She loved this time of the morning. Dawn seemed to her the only time the world truly ceased its activity, became dormant, settled into itself. It was as if the world left its agendas behind. This was a time to cherish, a time of rest, refreshment, nourishment, a time to appreciate the details.

She loved how the ocean awakened. The soft, heaving water appeared to take on energy, increasing its tempo until the surface broke and splashed and slapped the shoreline. Leaving its nighttime silence, it articulated daytime laughter in frothy waves, sometimes even whitecaps. The water birds followed its lead, rousing themselves in a raucous cacophony of shrieks and screams and jealous pursuit of food. Upon closer inspection, she detected scurrying, burrowing crabs or an occasional fish that flopped itself back into the water.

She reached for her coffee, enjoying its warmth as she wrapped her hands around the irregular ceramic cup. This was the mug Alexander had given her to keep beside her, filled with her energizing brew, as she finalized the manuscript to her first novel. Since then, he had given her several more, to celebrate the birth of a new book idea or the signing of a publishing contract, or just to give her inspiration when she wasn't sure of her next step.

That was one of the things about him she adored—he never seemed to tire of doing little things out of love. Three weeks ago it had been a coffee cup. Yesterday it was getting her car completely washed and waxed. Each time he simply handed her his gift, or offhandedly reported what he'd done, not to diminish its importance but to communicate his complete willingness to do it. She realized that Alexander demonstrated his love for her by the things she didn't ask him to do. The coffee cup, releasing the delicious aroma of the fresh-brewed Mocha Java, was indeed a special gift.

Alexander lay asleep in their bedroom just behind her. Another of their jokes was the difference in their sleeping habits. Iris was clearly at her best between five in the morning and nine in the evening. She often began her day with a quiet interlude overlooking the water. Alexander, on the other hand, could barely ambulate until nine a.m. He would signal his ability to speak by greeting her, well after he got up, frequently after he'd finished his breakfast. She loved him by respecting the quietness and order he needed in the morning. She would brew the coffee, leave freshly-squeezed orange juice in the refrigerator, and a choice of cereal, breakfast rolls or toast for him to prepare. She could tell his day's agenda by when he spoke: before breakfast meant an early commitment, after breakfast a leisurely morning. He would repay the kindness by bringing her a cup of chamomile tea at bedtime each evening, always fresh, and exactly the right temperature.

It was his consistent consideration that she had grown to love so intensely, and to miss when he was away. It felt good to realize that their marriage of nineteen years had grown comfortable to them both. They were certainly not free of disagreement and outright yelling on occasion, but even in their anger they took care to be straightforward and honest. After a fight was over, they forgave each other, and themselves, and got on with their lives. They had realized that their relationship had a life of its own, and each of them worked to respect and honor it. She felt safe, secure, enriched by the love she shared with Alexander.

She restrained herself from stepping into the bedroom to give him a quick kiss, deciding instead to let him sleep undisturbed after the revelries of the night before. She finished the last sip of coffee, placed the cup next to the insulated carafe, and stepped off the deck toward the water.

Iris enjoyed knowing that, had Jaid planned it herself, her birthday party would not have been more festive. The Indigo Moon Gallery had been transformed into a magical underwater seascape by strategically-placed gauze sunfish, parrot fish, barracuda, and redfin suspended between floor and ceiling. The gossamer creatures and plant life had been air-brushed in their true colors, and moved hypnotically in response to the circulating air from the ceiling fan. Atop a mound of sand lay an old wood locker, the bow of a row boat, and a barnacle-encrusted anchor. Painted fish, suspended magically by invisible plastic threads, swam

about the "treasures" revealed in the open locker. Someone had created papier-mache brain coral and fan coral
reefs and attached sea horses to them. People moved about
the party marveling at its beauty, their conversation and
laughter rising in the air, like bubbles, from their imaginary
underwater setting.

Seeing the treasures reminded Iris of the difference
between her dive locations now and then. Years ago when
she dived, certain of the populated areas had been stripped
of their natural plant life, coral broken or crushed, creating
an underwater desert devoid of color, interest, the ability
to renew itself. Those places were now healing, the result
of the massive cleanup effort at the turn of the century.
Alexander's cold fusion had taken off, along with newfound
respect for many other alternative sources of energy. For
whatever reasons, and there had been many, the human
population had joined in partnership with their earth.

Iris took a course toward the point, walking just inside
the water's edge. Jaid had gloried in her party. Near the
front of the gallery was a banner which asked the question
"IS 90 MIDDLE-AGED?" Practically every person in
Bryson Beach knew that Jaid had asked that question each
decade for the last fifty years. Almost every one of them
had signed the banner, leaving personal messages to her.
Her gallery had been a mainstay in this community for as
long as most residents could remember. Iris pondered the
fact that Jaid had enjoyed enormous success as an artist, yet
remained here in Bryson Beach, among those who loved
her. It was clear to Iris that Jaid understood the value of
remaining close to her true family, these who loved her,
and grew only more focused and enlivened as she explored
the depths and success of her creativity.

When their frequent morning walks were interrupted
by travel, the two of them were able to resume exactly

where they'd left off. Their distance was only in time or space, never between their absolute, unconditional commitment to each another. In the forty-odd years of their friendship, how many times had they talked together? Through these decades never once could she remember Jaid trying to change who she, Iris, was. Jaid and Iris had high expectations of each other. But the expectation was for authenticity, to act from a genuine feeling or idea, never to squeeze themselves into a form that didn't fit. Jaid could take all the power of her extroverted personality and direct it toward Iris with exquisite tenderness, a word, a lift of eyebrow, a touch of fingertips. Iris stopped a moment and let the sandy water scour her feet and ankles. *There are some who never know this kind of love*, she thought. *And my life overflows with it.*

She had reached the point. Behind her, fifty yards away or so, was a clump of sea oats standing tall, wafting elegantly in the early morning air. Not one of the townsfolk had taken credit for this remembrance, but it had been here for almost twenty-five years, continually cared for, replanted when storms uprooted it, thriving. To those who knew, it marked the place where Dear One had been buried.

Dear One. Another unexplained miracle in her life. Their brief time together had changed forever the way she looked at the world and her place in it. Dear One's death had marshaled in her unpredictable changes. She remembered with wry humor the uproar when she took seafood off the Sand Dollar's menu. Elmore's ability to work through that with the locals had propelled him into becoming mayor. Dear One's death had initiated her first novel. Her story of that special relationship had became woven into the fabric of public awareness of dying oceans, oceans which now were respected and protected, on their way to recovery.

She turned back and looked at the little cluster of buildings which surrounded the Sand Dollar. Alexander's company, with Skylar as architect, had reworked most of them with cold fusion systems. Several others had solar panels on the roofs.

She recalled when her skinny nephew from Texas had arrived for his summer visit, a summer that stretched into forever. She had grown as close to him as if he had been her own child. She had discovered, inside the package of that nine-year old boy, a delightfully spontaneous and inventive spirit, a kid who had the courage to dream. He had grown up, he had married and was now a father himself. And still he dreamed.

So much had changed since that summer. What had remained constant was the most beautiful of all, the rich connectedness she felt to this place, these treasured friends. She began the return route. Far down the way two figures approached, one tall and billowy, the other short, white. She continued toward them.

What a remarkable story these people would make, she thought. *There's another book here, somewhere, a book about love, vision, magic...*

THE END

S T A R S T R E A M
P R E S S

City of the Dreamers

City of the Dreamers, Jordon Avery's visionary novel, is a story about dreams that come true in a summer that never ends.

City of the Dreamers weaves love, dreams and imagination into a rich and multi-dimensional tapestry which you will never forget.

Please send me additional copies of City of the Dreamers.

Name _____

Address _____

City _____ State _____ Zip _____

Quantity _____ x $9.95 $_____
Postage & Handling*   _____
Sales tax (where applicable)   _____
Total amount enclosed   _____

*Add $2 for the first book and 50¢ for each additional book.

Send check or money order (U.S. funds) to:
StarStream Press
P.O. Box 11668
Atlanta, GA 30355
(800) 673-0240